Million

Ang

TJ L

DEDICATION

To anyone who knows this – life sucks. It's up to us to make the best of what we can to fix it or survive it. If you have figured out how, then this book is for you.

Now... will you email me and let me know how you did it?

Chapter 1

Elizabeth

"Come on, Liz. Suck it up, you can do this." I mumbled to myself as I pulled down the rim of my two sizes too small little white dress.

I took a step closer to the club entrance and jumped as a motorcycle came roaring around the corner, like this was a NASCAR racetrack and not an industrial area. Not used to my three-inch stilettos, I nearly twisted an ankle.

I let out a self-deprecating groan as I straightened my body awkwardly and pulled the low neckline back up, trying to keep it over my ample chest. With the way my luck typically went, I was either going to fall and flash my Southern Lady bits to everyone in the area, or trip just enough to pop out the top.

I told the girl at the store this dress was too small. She insisted it was just right. She knew a sucker when she saw one. I was so wrapped up in my goal for tonight that I let her convince me.

Today was supposed to be a special day for me. This was supposed to be how I celebrated my 21st birthday. Happy birthday to me!

I hope you heard the sarcasm, that line was slathered in it.

Never in my life had I been in a club, let alone a bar.

Never in my life had I ever worn something so revealing.

Never in my life had I ever even drunk alcohol.

Maybe it would be different if I had actual friends to do this with. But I didn't. I probably could have asked one of the other ladies from work to come with me, they seemed to like to do this kind of stuff. Not that I spoke, or even saw, them all that often.

If I had done that though, then I would have had to go through with it. Besides, if I flaked out or embarrassed myself tonight, who would know? That thought was one of the few things pushing me up the stairs and closer to the large man at the door.

Maybe I would get lucky, and they wouldn't let me in. I mean, technically I was cutting the very long line.

1

A big part of me was hoping he would give me an excuse to turn tail and go home.

See, my whole life, I had been an extreme introvert. It wasn't that I didn't like people, it was just, I didn't know how to talk to them. Some had said that I was shy, but I didn't really think that was it either. I think I was more a product of my upbringing.

You have to understand, when I was little, both my parents were killed. As far as I knew, neither of them had families. They were both only children and their parents weren't in the picture. From what I could remember of them anyway.

Nor did I exactly have family coming out of the word work to claim me at the time. Or... ever.

Once my parents were gone, I bounced from one foster home to the next, until I was 18 and able to move out on my own. Most of the places I lived at were awful. It was better to keep my head down and my mouth shut.

So, I did.

Now that I was officially 21, I decided it was time to straighten that spine and live a little. Time to break out of my protective box and enter the real world of actual human beings.

It couldn't be all that bad... could it?

I watched every shaky step, making sure I didn't fall on the few stairs leading up to the door. I held tight to the metal rail like it was my lifeline. When I glanced up, I noticed that the very large man was watching my progress with an amused expression.

Please let him turn me away. Please let him turn me away.

"Evening, sweetheart. Going in?" His voice wasn't quite as deep, nor as scary as I had been imagining.

"Uh. Yeah." I turned quickly and looked at the line full of over eager men and women who were wearing fewer clothes than I was.

"Can I see your ID? Have to be 21 or over to get in here."

"Oh, uh, yeah." I opened the small matching clutch I was carrying and pulled out my ID to show him. He was nice enough not to mention my shaky hands.

He looked me up and down again and grinned. He leaned back and pulled the door open with one hand.

"Happy Birthday, sweetheart. Good luck in there."

I gave him a shaky smile in return, silently cursing because now I really had no choice but to go in. At least he didn't make me pay, that was a good thing. Right?

"Th... thank you."

As I stepped through the door, I was immediately bombarded with the sounds of the music. The bass was so loud, I could feel it in my chest. It was like my rib cage had just turned into a set of bongo drums.

I gave a small yelp when the door closed behind me, the ghost of a deep laugh disappearing behind it.

I took a steading breath, straightened my spine, and stepped forward.

Bad idea.

I had to grab the wall to keep me from falling when my foot twisted to the side, again. I quickly straightened back up, grateful no one saw me, pulled my skirt back down (for the hundredth time), and continued my way further in.

I looked around the dark, foggy room, filled with flashing lights that were dancing to the beat of the music. The dance floor was filled with bodies that swayed to the tempo.

It all reminded me of a snake pit, with all the snakes writhing on their tales. Not that I had ever seen one in person. But I had watched them on the discovery channel.

Yeah, no way I was going inside that mess. I was nowhere near ready for that.

I looked around the room and saw tables and booths outlining the walls, all filled with people laughing and drinking with their friends and hopeful hook ups. A few held couples that had apparently forgotten, or were too drunk to remember, that they were not invisible or in a private room.

In the very last booth, I saw a man with his head back like he was looking at the ceiling. I looked up, seeing if there was something interesting up there. I didn't see anything, and when I looked back at him, I saw a woman sliding out from under the table, wiping her mouth.

At the same moment, the man's eyes met mine.

No, that couldn't be right. I was just in his line of sight.

Then he winked at me. I blushed, I was sure scarlet red, and quickly averted my eyes.

Maybe this wasn't such a good idea. I was so far out of my comfort zone right now. It was like I had somehow left planet Earth and ended up on some strange erotic planet.

What was I thinking coming here? This wasn't me. This would never be me.

I was doomed to forever be the weird cat lady, even though I hated cats. I should just go home, and wallow in my solitude just like I did every other day. Maybe even pick up a small cake on the way home and sing happy birthday to me... again.

Before I could turn back to the door, I stopped. One drink, just at least make it through one drink, Liz. You could at least do that much. What was the harm in having one drink?

I was not going to let myself fall back into the pity pit. I took another deep breath and walked towards the bar. I let out a relieved exhale as two stools became empty. I greedily sat down, taking the weight off my feet. No more falling for me!

"What can I get you?" The bartender hollered over the noise.

He wore a tight black shirt, with a towel thrown over his shoulder, just as I had pictured. The man's skin looked pale, not what I had pictured, as though he never saw the sun. Most of his hair was still black, but the gray was encroaching and trying to take over.

Riiight, I had to actually choose something. I had forgotten about that part. The older bartender must have noticed my apprehension. His face softened and he leaned in.

"This your first time in a bar, darling?"

I nodded mutely, embarrassed that it was so obvious.

"Don't worry. We'll start you off with something light." He winked and stepped away, pulling ingredients out from under the counter. A few minutes later, he set down a reddish drink in front of me.

I looked at it warily. "What is it?"

He smiled. "This is called a Dirty Shirley Temple. It's not too strong. Drink that up and we will try you with something else next." He immediately walked over to more customers and started refilling their pitchers. I slowly picked up my drink and took a sip.

Huh. Not bad. It tasted like cherries.

I smiled as I took a bigger sip.

I was doing it! I was in a bar, drinking alcohol, and I kind of liked it. One, maybe two, of these and then I could run away and call tonight a success.

Go, me!

I climbed out of my car and threw my keys to the valet standing nearby. I smiled, closed my eyes, and took a deep breath of ocean-fresh air.

Man, it was good to be home again.

Back in my own territory.

I spent the last three months traveling the country, going to every bar and club worth its dime. My version of hunting in the wild. I found many new treasures for my collection. But, unfortunately, the real prize still eluded me. The crown jewel. My million-dollar angel.

One of the rarest of its kind these days.

A few months ago, I was approached by a client, and occasional partner. He had a special request. His son was getting married, and they had a tradition to uphold. Now, it was time for me to prove why I was the best at what I did.

I needed to prove I earned the illustrious reputation I had.

I needed to maintain it.

I never backed down from a challenge, I thrived off them.

I started walking up the steps to my own personal jungle and smiled at Raul, one of the bouncers. I didn't usually hunt on my own home turf, but desperate times called for desperate measures.

"Welcome back, sir." Raul greeted me with a congenial smile.

I smiled in return. "Thank you, Raul. How's business tonight?" I stopped next to him and looked out towards the line of people waiting to enter. So many people ready to get down and dirty, on a weekday!

Man, I loved New Orleans.

He smirked. "Busy as usual, sir."

"Good!" I barked. "Glad to hear it." I wiggled my eyebrows at him. "Any I might be interested in?"

He thought carefully for a moment then a wicked grin crossed his face. Oh, that looked promising. He opened the door a touch and did a quick glance around.

My interest spiked higher. Maybe coming home was the best call after all.

He turned back to face me with a triumphant grin. "Angel at the bar. Still has her wings."

I copied his movements and peeked inside.

At the end of the bar, talking to Carlos the bartender, sat a woman in a tight white dress. Her black hair was braided down her back, her skin copper. And from this angle, she had the curves to match.

"How pure are those wings?"

"Today's her 21st birthday, she came in alone. Probably her first time in bar," Raul smirked sardonically, "or even in heels."

I raised an eyebrow. Promising indeed. Tonight, might just be my lucky night. Good, because I was down to the wire. My reputation was on the line here. And my reputation was all that I cared about. It was all that mattered.

One failure and I could kiss all my hard work goodbye. It wouldn't take long for the competition to knock me out completely. This was a cutthroat world I lived, and thrived, in. I should know. It was how I took over my predecessor. One failure was all it took. Its been years, but he was still trying to find footing again. Well, among the heads anyway. He mostly worked the streets, barely scraping a living by.

I fist-bumped Raul. "Good looking out, man. Call in a special chariot. You know, in case she can't hold her liquor."

"Yes, Sir." He gave me a knowing grin, pulled out his phone, and sent off a message as I walked through the door.

Raul knew he was about to get a decent sized finders fee. What he didn't know, was that it would be higher than normal. He probably thought she was just for stock. Meaning a thousand-dollar bonus. If she was what I needed, I would triple that. I always took care of my employees.

I carefully made my rounds around the room, greeting my regular customers. I talked to my security, checking in as they watched my girls. There was only certain clientele allowed to touch any of my girls or to take them into one of the rooms in the back.

The entire time, I kept an eye on the angel at the bar. I studied and observed as she sipped her fruity little drink. I caught the slight movement of her pulling the bottom hem of her dress a little lower and then the top a little higher, shaking up those delicious talents she was obviously born with.

This angel was all natural.

7

I must have not been paying good enough attention to right next to me, as I soon felt a small pair of hands wrap around my waist and a chest move along my back. I sighed in disappointment as I turned around to face her. No sooner did I turn, than she pressed herself flush against me.

"Candice. We talked about this." I scolded the store-bought bottle blonde still rubbing herself against me.

She pouted while tracing a fingernail along her ample chest.

"Andre," she whined. "I just wanted to welcome you home properly and show you how much you were missed." Her tone lowered and purred seductively.

"You are not here for me. You are here for the clients." I grabbed her waist carefully and pushed her off of me. "Get back to work."

Candice scoffed and stomped off.

I sighed as I watched her go. How many girls over the years thought they could climb the ladder by climbing me? I chuckled quietly. They could climb me all I wanted, but they would never climb out of my pit. That sucker was much deeper than six feet.

I turned back to my prize and started walking towards the bar finally. I had watched my prize for nearly an hour, I was almost certain she was what I was looking for.

Not once had I ever failed to meet the "unique" needs of my clients, and I wasn't about to start now.

I leaned onto the bar, cutting her off from the guy next to her. He may have been trying to talk to her, who knows. I didn't care. She leaned back, startled, and looked at me confused. She looked utterly shocked that she was getting this kind of attention.

I did a slow checkout of what she was working with.

Hmmm. Perfect.

She was like a cool summer day at the beach, the waves moving up and down. Her long black, thick, braid was now over her shoulder, blocking the view of some of her talents. Her brown eyes practically screamed innocence at me. My blood warmed at the sound of it. I loved me a good screamer.

I knew my women. I could estimate their measurements and worth with nearly perfect accuracy. Candice, and others like her, were always willing to spend time in the back room. Or even perform their jobs in the open.

They were my paid employees. They were overly eager.

My hidden stock was a special kind. They were the rare breeds. I've learned to read women well over the years. And this angel right here, well now, she was the rarest of them all.

I leaned into whisper in her ear. "I hear today is your birthday." She blushed and turned away. Oh yes, she would do nicely. "Mind if I buy you a drink to help celebrate?"

"Who are you?"

I laughed as she realized how rude that probably sounded and covered her mouth. I leaned in again, making sure only she could hear me.

"My name is Andre. I own the club." I watched as the confusion warred with something else - disbelief? "Let me buy you a drink." I waved Carlos over. "Two gin and tonics." Carlos nodded and got right to work. I smiled as she still looked hopelessly lost. "What's your name?"

"Um...Liz...short for Elizabeth."

She was nervous at just saying her name. I could just see the delight in my client's face when I delivered this beautiful jewel to the party.

I gently tucked a hair behind her ear. "Beautiful name for a beautiful woman."

She blushed again and ducked her head. I chuckled to myself. I was feeling quite giddy now. I could already hear the sound of the million dollars being wired to my account. It was nearly as satisfying as a good scream.

"So, Liz. Why are you here celebrating your birthday all on your own?"

She shrugged her shoulders and sipped what looked like Carlos's version of a Dirty Shirley Temple. The new drinks came, and she picked hers up carefully, slyly sniffing it before taking a sip.

Don't worry little angel, there was nothing in your drink.

Yet.

Not that you would smell it if there were. Ryan, my supplier in New York was the best there was when it came to things like this. His concoctions even blended seamlessly in water.

I spent the next thirty minutes getting her to relax and start talking. I pieced little things together from what I saw and what I heard.

She mainly worked from home, only going into the office once or twice a month.

She didn't seem to have any family or real friends to speak of. Tonight, was her trying to break free of that.

I was so glad I decided to come home before heading out to a new area.

She.

Was.

Perfect.

After the Gin, I had her try a beer. I laughed as Liz obviously did not care for that one but drank it anyway.

By her fourth drink, she was increasingly giggly. I signaled to Carlos and ordered my *special* Rum and Coke. With his fast hands, he put in the special ingredient while mixing, then slid the drink over.

"Here, you have to try this one." I encouraged her as I put the drink into her hand.

She made a little scowl. "I don't know if I should. I think I drank too much already. I should probably go home and lie down." Her words were slurring, and she wasn't sitting as straight as she had been when I first walked in.

I leaned into her ear again, leaving whisper soft kisses on her cheek. "One more drink and I will personally escort you to a VIP room to lay down for a bit."

"Fine, one more drink. But I lay down alone." Liz tried to hold a stern face, but she didn't have that much control.

I watched as she drank down the new drink, not as carefully as she had with the others. Not that it mattered. I took the glass and set it back on the counter before taking her hand and leading her away from the bar.

Oh, how easy this was. The naive and innocent always were.

I led her towards a back room, not the ones the clients used, but one I kept for my own personal use. She came to a sudden stop when she walked through the door as I held it open. It wasn't a large room, just big enough for a bed, a small table and two chairs.

Standing behind her, looking down, I had a great view of what was underneath that dress.

Oh, the temptation.

It would be very easy to just reach around her waist and slowly pull that dress up. I frequently took a taste of the goods before releasing them to clients.

A taste test, of sorts.

Sadly, not with this one.

No. The client specifically requested that she be untouched. Pure as the day she was born.

"Why am I in here?" Liz's slur was thicker now, and her balance nearly gone. I caught her as she tipped to the side and held onto her.

"You wanted to lie down for a few minutes, remember? Go. Lay on the bed. I will help you take these shoes off."

"Oh, right. Yeah. Good idea."

She dropped down on the bed, landing on her butt, and then fell to her back. The best parts of this girl were practically falling out of that dress now.

I would have to make sure we picked her out something sweeter to wear when I delivered her.

The proper gift-wrapping could go a long way.

I carefully took off her shoes, rubbing her legs to help her relax. A couple of minutes later I had to stop my hands as they traveled up her thighs. The small moans she was making were not helping any.

Soon enough, she was completely unconscious. Another way I liked them. While I didn't mind a little fight in my women once in a while, free play was my favorite time. I could do what I wanted, however I wanted.

I put her shoes on the table, she wouldn't be needing those anymore, and walked to a hidden back door. I opened the door and whistled.

Less than a minute later, two men came into the room.

"Take her to the holding facility and get her and the others ready for transport. She's the last one. Keep her separated from the rest."

"Yes, sir." They both said.

One bent over and picked her up in his arms with excitement in his eyes.

"This one is a special delivery. Client says no touching. Make sure the word is spread. Anyone touches her and they owe me the million it will cost to replace her."

The excitement faded fast as they replied "yes, sir," again. I laughed at their disgruntled faces.

One of the benefits of working for me, they got to help with orientation. I also let them choose a girl for stress relief when they needed it.

Gotta have my men relaxed and happy. Fewer mistakes. Fewer chances of betrayal. I paid them well, and the benefits were not of the kind they would find anywhere else.

I watched as they loaded her into the van and took off. I looked down at my pants. Dang. There was nothing like completing a deal to get the blood flowing. Now, what do I do?

I could go find Candice. But no, that would be too easy. I needed another prey. It was a good thing I had a club full of them. I may not find another angel to corrupt, but there had to be one close enough that I could take advantage of.

Chapter 2
Elizabeth

Oh, my. I groaned, holding my eyes closed tight.

Ow. Why did I feel so awful? I couldn't even remember what happened last night.

I went to a local club to celebrate my birthday. The bartender was nice and gave me weak drinks. Well, I guess for normal people they were weak. For me they were plenty strong.

That guy came up. Was he really the owner? I didn't know. He seemed nice enough though. Really interested in me too. We talked more about me than we did about him.

All in all, it was a good start to meeting people and branching out.

I rolled to my side and tried to sit up.

It was then that I heard the clanging sound and felt the cold pull on my ankle.

What was that?

Why was it so cold in here?

Did the pilot light go out on my heater again? The super really needed to replace my heater already. He swore it was fine, mostly because he knew I was too chicken to say anything.

I rubbed my eyes and slowly opened them. The room was dim, barely any sunlight coming through. I looked around, becoming completely confused with where I was.

I shifted and heard that weird clanging sound clearer this time and felt that coldness on my ankle again. I looked down to where I was sure my feet were - my head was still a bit foggy - and saw a thick silver chain wrapped around my right ankle and attached to a wall. I reached down to see if it was the sheet wrapped around my ankle. My eyes were pretty blurry still, I could be seeing things.

Nope. Too hard for a sheet.

In the spasms of a complete panic attack, I sat up fast and then regretted it. That really hurt my head, but I needed to think beyond the pain for the moment.

I rubbed my eyes and blinked a few more times. When my vision cleared a bit more, I studied my surroundings again. I was in a small, cold, empty room. The floor was concrete, the walls were... I didn't know what, but they looked creepy. If I had to guess, which was really my only option, I was in an abandoned warehouse somewhere.

New Orleans was full of those.

I was sitting on what looked like a really old dingy cot and mattress. I almost jumped off it with a grossed-out squeal when the thought of what all could be hiding inside it came to me.

At least until I heard the small squeaking of a rat.

I ended up jumping further onto the bed instead.

The minutes ticked by like hours before I could hear noises coming from outside the room. The door looked thick, with a small hole at the top. Kind of like what you saw in movies with high security prisons, or high security crazy hospitals.

I listened carefully, trying to decipher the sound and whether I should scream for help or not.

It sounded like someone was walking down a very echoey hall. The footsteps stopped outside my door, and a floating head of black hair showed through the hole.

As the door opened, I pushed myself into the corner of the wall, where the bed met it. Light followed the new person in, casting their face in shadow.

"Well, well, look who is finally awake. It's the little princess." A rough, scratchy voice taunted me.

I did not like the sound of that voice. It gave me the same shivers as nails on a chalkboard. I watched him carefully as he closed the door behind him and stalked into the room.

"Wh... who are you?" My voice quivered with the fear of the unknown.

"I'm your host for this tour. The name is Paul. Remember it well, so you know what to scream by the time I am done with you."

"What do... do... do... you want with me?" I'd like to say the stutter came from the cold, but let's be honest here, I was scared half to death. This guy had a major dark alley scary vibe-thing going for him.

He sat down on the foot of the bed and reached a cold rough hand onto my ankle.

"Hmmm, now that is a tricky question. One I am so glad you asked. I am going to teach you what I want from you, and what many will want from you. By the time I am done, you will be able to meet any needs. If you behave, maybe I will be nice and do something for you. But first," he yanked my leg over to him, hard and fast.

I screamed in surprise.

"Hmmm..." Paul closed his eyes and rolled his neck in satisfaction. "Yeah, that's a good scream." He was practically purring.

Did men purr?

He held my ankle to the foot of the bed with one hand and began unzipping his pants with the other.

"Let's see what else you got in you, shall we?"

"Please, no. Please. Don't." The tears ran down my face freely as I begged and pleaded for him to stop.

Unfortunately, that seemed to be exactly what he wanted. His wicked smile grew ear to ear, as he hummed with approval.

He moved to his knees, his parts hanging out of his clothes. He pushed my legs apart, my dress having already slid up to my waist when he pulled me down to him.

I continued begging and pleading with him as he lowered himself onto me, pinning me with his weight. Which freed his hands to begin ripping the top of my dress, a hungry look in his eyes.

I screamed and wiggled some more, trying to throw him off. He laughed and grabbed my hand, bringing it to him.

"Now, pay attention and do just what I say." He demanded.

He held my hand to him tight and moaned with pleasure while I cried harder. Before he could go any further the door opened again. He paused but did not let go.

"Come to watch or join, boss?" He chuckled at the newcomer.

"Come to collect what you will owe me if you do not get off her right now. Did you or did you not get the instructions for this one?"

Paul grumbled a response but let go of me. "Come on, boss! This is the best part of the job!"

His boss laughed. "I got ten more girls out there for you, Paul. You can play all you want. But this one is a special order. You nearly cost me a million bucks. I catch you, or anyone else, anywhere near her again and you will no longer get to play... ever. Lo entiendes?"

Paul stood back up, tucking himself back into his pants, but did not zip them up. I quickly pulled myself into a ball in the corner again, tucking my ankles in as tight as I could, ignoring the pull of the chain.

"Yeah, I got it." Paul grouched on his way out, passing the boss.

The new man closed the door behind him.

"So, how did my million-dollar angel sleep?"

"Who are you and what do you want with me?" I demanded through my fear.

"Tsk, tsk, tsk. You are going to need to work on that attitude before we get you to your new home. They won't take that very kindly."

He pulled over a chair I hadn't noticed before and set it in front of the door. He sat down, facing me, and placed a plastic bag on the floor next to him.

"I must say, I am a little offended. I didn't think I would be so easy to forget." He chuckled to himself. "Then again, we never made it to the more unforgettable part of the evening, and you did drink quite a bit."

There was only one person I remembered from last night, besides the bartender.

"Andre?" I was going to blame the darkened bar, and the hangover for not recognizing him. And the panic. And the room we were in wasn't all that bright either.

"At your service, senorita." He did a mock bow without getting up.

"Why did you do this? Why am I here? What are you?"

"I am nothing more than a businessman. A collector of sorts. I have a very wealthy client who made a request, you meet every detail within that request. You, my dear Elizabeth, are my million-dollar angel. My crown jewel, so to speak." He reached for the bag and sat up. He pulled white material out and held it in his lap. "Now, it is time for you to look like one. Take off that dress and change into this one."

I stayed in my little ball and stared at him incredulously. He had to be kidding. He continued to just sit there, staring at me.

Andre gave a frustrated sigh. His relaxed tone tightened into a more demanding, and scary, one.

"Stand up and take the dress off, Elizabeth. Do not make me tell you again. I can always allow Paul to come and take it off of you. If you prefer."

I studied him for a moment before slowly standing up. I reached my hands behind me and unzipped my dress. I kept one arm across my chest, holding it up.

"It is my duty, and pleasure, to inspect every inch of the merchandise before delivering it to my clients. I would be remiss if I didn't do that now. Drop it." He ordered, snapping his fingers, and pointing at the ground.

With new tears running down my face, I pulled the dress over my head, and then dropped it on the bed. If it weren't for the stupid chain on my leg, I would have just let it fall to the floor.

I may have been innocent in many ways, but I was not naive, nor was I stupid. I was going to have to choose my battles carefully.

Andre carefully walked around me, studying every inch of me as the sun began shining through the high windows. When he made his way back to my front, he held a new dress over my head and then slowly slid it over my arms and down my waist.

He grazed his knuckles down my back, back and forth under my strapless bra, then slowly zipped the dress up.

It was a simple white sundress; the top was in a tight bodice style that accentuated my naturally amplified chest. The skirt flowed out over my hips, accenting those curves as well, ending just above my knees. It was a very pretty dress. Too bad it came with the worst intentions.

"Much better," Andre murmured to himself.

He sat back down in his chair and continued studying me. He mumbled something else but all I caught was something to do with his million-dollar angel again. He seemed to pull himself out of his little trance and pulled a small packet out of the bag.

"Clean yourself up. All of you."

I looked at the packet he handed me and realized they were wipes. At least I was fully dressed, and I was doing it by myself. I focused on wiping my arms and face-off, then my legs. I was about to call "done" when he insisted I clean other areas as well. I refused to look at him while I did this.

It was quiet enough in the room that it was impossible to miss the small sound of his zipper opening or the sounds that he made as he watched me.

My hands shook aggressively. I was terrified, wondering what kind of hell I landed myself in. I knew I never should have gone into that club. My life was just fine. I should have been happy with what I had.

Who needed friends or the world?

From somewhere down the hall I heard a scream, much like mine earlier, and the ghost of a dark chuckle. I shivered and felt grateful that I at least did not have that fate.

Not yet anyway.

As I went to straighten up and set the wipe down, I was pushed roughly against the wall. Andre had a dark and terrifying look in his eyes as he looked down on me. He spun me around, putting my back to him, took the wipe from my hand, and lifted my skirt.

"You missed a spot." He growled into my ear.

He lifted one of my legs onto the bed and moved the wipe in between my thighs. His other hand went around my mouth and smothered any screams before I could make them.

"You're lucky you are worth so much more to me untouched right now. If not for that, I might just keep you for myself." He maneuvered the wipe roughly as he growled into my ear. "Now, bite your tongue and don't make a sound, or I may change my mind on how much you are worth."

I did as he said while he removed his hand from my mouth. I couldn't see what he was doing, but I had a pretty decent idea. He left one hand on each of us and moved them in tandem until I felt him shaking behind me.

By the time he was done, my tongue was bleeding.

Before letting me go, I felt him rub himself against me one more time and moan with approval. I stayed facing the wall as I heard him pull another wipe from the bag, I assumed to clean himself up with this time.

"Lunch will be brought to you shortly." He threw two small bands on the bed. "Put your hair in two braids. I will be dropping you off at your new home this evening."

He picked the bag of dirty wipes up off the bed and walked out of the door. I waited until the count of ten before letting myself sink into the germ-infested cot again, sobbing.

I was grateful that for some reason I was worth more money to him than the others, but at the same time, terrified at why that was. I took a deep steadying breath and separated my hair into two sides.

I would play their game for now, but not for long. One way or another, I was finding my way out of this. Let them think I was docile and obedient. They had no idea what I was really capable of.

Chapter 3

Antonio

I studied the room carefully, always on guard, never relaxed. Especially with these men.

The room held nearly two dozen men: including my padre and myself. Some were from the Valdez cartel, some were from the Ortiz cartel, my cartel.

All were top men in their own respective fields of expertise. All were egotistical, arrogant, and ambitious. And out of all of them, I only trusted two.

Sadly, my padre was not one of them.

This was a cutthroat business. Loyalty and trust were earned, not freely given. Padre has not earned my trust, maybe if it weren't for this latest stunt, he would have.

Maybe.

Don't get me wrong, I loved my padre. I just didn't trust him. He was a man after his own desires.

Then again, weren't we all?

Normally, we would not all meet like this. It was an FBI agent's wet dream to find us all together. Which was why we were doing this here, in Queretaro, located in the heart of Mexico.

The FBI had no jurisdiction down here.

If any of these men were going to make a move, this would be a prime time to do it. Most of them were already drunk. Easy pickings.

"Atencion!" My padre stood up in the front of the room, banging a spoon against his shot glass. He cleared his throat and called again "Atencion!"

Once it was quiet and he had everyone's attention he continued.

"Caballeros. Thank you all for joining us this evening, as we celebrate the joining of the Valdez familia and the Ortiz familia. This union will spread the reach of both our families and make us all a lot more *money*!" The men in the room raised their glasses and cheered. "Now that dinner is finished, the real celebration will begin. Before we get to what we all are really here for, I would like to propose a toast to mi hijo, Antonio. Everyone raise your glasses. To Antonio, may your new wife be strong enough to handle your endowment. May she bear you many healthy sons. And may you always have a mistress to fulfill your desires!"

Following that really touching toast, all the men echoed "To Antonio!" I pointed my glass at my padre and downed the last of my scotch.

"Alright, now time for what you have all been waiting for! If you will follow me to the other room, Andre has brought some of his best pieces to share with you." He then turned and led the way down the hall.

The room filled with more cheers and grunting as they followed him out of the dining room and towards the largest room in the house.

Our home was once a Spaniard Plantation. The room we were headed to was once used to hold fancy balls. Well, I assumed it did at any rate.

As this was technically my bachelor party, I was hustled to the front of the crowd, right behind my padre.

The larger room held the six couches like normal, as well as the four matching chairs, in the shape of a square for sitting and conversing. Another dozen chairs had been added to the room, spread throughout.

Each chair had one girl chained to it, and each couch had two. Altogether, there were 32 women chained up inside the room.

All were dressed in what could only be considered as cloth bikinis and skirts. They were all skinny, the razor-thin kind of skinny. Some had larger butts and breasts than the others. Their hair and skin colors all varied, as did their heights.

A veritable buffet of women. Something for everyone.

Except me.

I took one look around the room and then aimed for the small bar in the corner. I never cared for this type of entertainment. I preferred to keep my women to myself.

Before I could get very far, padre stopped me.

"Antonio."

"Si, padre?"

"Give me a few minutes, then I need to talk to you privately."

"Si, padre."

I watched as he walked off towards one of the girls sitting on a couch. By the time he plopped down, he was already hanging out of his pants. Something no son should ever have to see.

He grabbed the girl's red hair and yanked her down to her knees. I shook my head and continued to the bar.

I ordered a shot of whiskey and watched as the other men trailed in. Not one of them cared about any of the other men in the room. They each had at least one woman servicing their needs. Some had two. I seemed to be the only one not participating in this.

I shook my head again as two of the men traded girls after.

Seriously, it was disgusting.

How did they not care that they literally just saw someone else inside that girl? To me, they might as well be eating from the same bowl of cereal and using the same spoon. Or worse, passing around the same piece of chewed up gum.

I turned my back on them all, not wanting to watch the debauchery. Padre joined me again about twenty minutes later. A relaxed grin on his face as he patted my shoulder.

"Enjoying your party, Hijo?"

I plastered a smile on my face. "Of course, padre. Andre always delivers the most beautiful women."

He chuckled. "That he does. And you haven't even seen his masterpiece yet. Come with me."

He turned and I followed him back out to the hall, and down another wing of the house.

"As you know, arranged marriages are a tradition in our family. We don't always like the women we are chained to, at least not at first. I know Elena is a handful and not someone you would have chosen. We both know the real reason behind this deal. Soon, the Valdez family will be no more. This is just the first step towards taking over their lands and businesses. But that is not what I wanted to speak to you about tonight."

We reached the end of the fourth-floor wing and stopped outside of another room. This wing was not commonly used, it was more of a backup guest wing.

"Your bisabuelo felt bad for creating the first arranged marriage between his son and an influential family. It was purely business. It was the beginning of our family's success and growth. In order to make it up to his son, he started another tradition. He not only arranged for the first wife, but he also arranged for his son's first mistress."

I raised an eyebrow at my padre. That was not a story I had heard before.

Mistresses were common, they were no secret. I had many half-siblings. They held various positions, but, as my madre was his actual wife, I was the next in line.

If my madre had not had me, then the eldest of those siblings would have inherited. Besides fulfilling desires, mistresses provided additional heirs, additional stability, if needed.

"I contacted Andre after we made the marriage agreement with Valdez. He has spent months searching for what he refers to as his crown jewel. I did not make it easy on him. I insisted on someone who is both pure and innocent." My padre winked at me. "I know how you feel about sharing."

I stared at him in complete disbelief. "You bought me, my first mistress?"

That was odd. I was not sure how I felt about that. It was bad enough I was stuck with a wife I could not stand, now possibly a mistress as well?

My padre laughed joyfully. "I know what you are thinking, hijo." He shook his finger at me, still grinning. "This is not like Elena. You can get rid of this one whenever you like. This could be a one-night deal, one month, a year, ten years. Whatever you like. Personally, I kept my first for maybe a month and then added her to the family collection for my men. Your uncle Juan still has his first set up in a condo nearby his home. He visits her once a month. It is your choice how long you keep her, and how you even want to use her. I gave Andre specific orders. This one was not to be touched in any way. She is a virgin in every way. A blank canvas if you will. Now, enough talking. Go, enjoy your private party."

I smirked as he handed me the key to the room and walked away, leaving me to my thoughts.

I did love me a virgin. It had been weeks since I last had my needs met, and it had barely been satisfactory. Even longer since it was with a virgin. My best friends liked to tease me about my preferences, but I preferred clean water to bathe in. They wanted to get muddy, that was their problem.

I unlocked the door and walked into the darkroom. I locked the door behind me and turned on the lamp on a dresser nearby. I set the key down on the dresser while I looked around the room.

This was one of the larger guest suites. It held a sofa, a television, a large bathroom, and a king size bed. It had all been decorated in black and white coloring.

At first sight, the room appeared to be empty.

Then I noticed a pair of dark brown eyes peering over the arm of the couch. I huffed in amusement. She was trying to hide behind the couch. Innocent indeed.

"Senorita, you can come out. You have no reason to fear me. I will not hurt you." I waved a hand for her to come.

"Who are you?" Her voice was whisper soft, barely managing to hide her fear.

"I will tell you who I am when you come out from behind that couch." My amusement was quickly beginning to turn to frustration when she still did not move. "Either you come out on your own or I will come to pull you out."

A moment later she slowly stood up.

Andre did well. She had a small waist, but not like the overly skinny girls downstairs. It was a healthy kind. She was a head shorter than me. Her hips popped to the sides just enough that my large hands would be able to grip them. She had two long black braids cascading over her chest, which was barely contained in the white dress.

Andre not only dressed her in a way to show off her extensive attributes, but it made her look even more innocent. I couldn't resist licking my lips and rubbing my jaw as I stepped closer to her.

She was definitely the type I preferred. Far more than the herd of women down in the hall.

She tried to step further away, backing herself into the wall. I swiftly moved in and caged her between my arms. I hummed with approval as I looked down and got a full view of that luscious chest.

I traced her smooth jawline with the back of my finger, down her neck, and onto her chest. I pushed the braid over her shoulder and ran my hand down her arm. When I reached her hip, I grabbed it and pulled her into me. She yelped and goosebumps spread across her skin.

"An... Andre said no one was allowed to touch me. You need to stop before you get in trouble."

I chuckled. "Do you always follow the rules, senorita?"

"Yes." She squeaked.

I leaned back enough to look into her eyes, but I kept her hips against me.

"I'm glad to hear that. The better you follow the rules, the longer I will keep you to myself."

I already had no doubts I would be using her, but for how long depended on how well she could behave. The main reason I preferred virgins was because they had not yet been tainted by anyone else. If she remained solely mine, she could stay longer than one night.

"Wh... who are you?" She whispered.

"My name is Antonio, and you belong to me now. You are a gift from my padre, he bought you from Andre. What is your name?"

"Elizabeth."

"Tell me, Elizabeth. Did Andre follow his orders? Did you remain untouched in his care?" She stayed silent but there was a trace of fear in her eyes that raised my possessiveness up. "Who touched you and what did they do?" I growled, my fist tightening against the wall.

She was mine and they knew she was mine. She had been mine since the moment Andre chose her for me. Nobody touched what belonged to me.

Tear slid down her face and she began to tremble. "Nothing really. One of his men started to... to... Andre stopped him, just in time."

She couldn't even say what he did or almost did. She was more innocent than I first thought. She was perfect.

"Anything else?" I growled again. Her bottom lip shook. I removed my hand from her hip and placed my thumb on her lip. I worked to soften my tone, despite my anger. "I'm not mad at you. I need to know if I need to kill anyone for touching what doesn't belong to them. I am a very possessive man, Elizabeth. I do not share anything. Especially my women. Now, what else happened?"

She looked into my eyes, searching for something. "Andre made me clean myself in front of him. When I was done, he used a wipe and said I missed a spot. He had a hand on the wipe and a hand on himself. I was facing the wall and he was behind me. When he finished, he rubbed himself on me. I don't know if anything happened during the times I was unconscious, but I don't think so. He was very specific about nobody touching me."

There was a touch of venom in her voice by the time she was done. She may be innocent, but she had fire in her. I hoped it would make this more interesting. The domination game could be fun, but not in the long term.

"I will make sure Andre pays for that. He should have known better. Always be honest with me, never keep secrets from me. Entiendes?" She nodded her head slowly. "Habla español?"

"Si."

I smiled and traced my thumb along her bottom lip again.

Her body still shook against mine, but it had lessened a bit. Fear could be a powerful motivator, however, I didn't want her to fear me completely. I softened my voice another touch, gently rubbing my thumb along her cheek.

"You belong to me now, Elizabeth. You will obey me and only me. If anyone tries to lay a hand on you again, you are free to defend yourself and then tell me immediately. I don't care who they are, no one is allowed to touch you anywhere. As long as you behave, do not defy me, or lie to me, then I will keep you safe. Otherwise, you will be sent to join the family collection, and anyone can use you in any way they want. Do you have any questions?"

Her voice cracked as she asked, "Why am I here? Why did your father buy me?"

I smirked. "Tomorrow I am being forced to marry a woman I despise. Arranged marriages are a tradition in my family. Apparently, so is buying the first mistress." I pointed to her as I took a step back.

"So... I am to be your mistress?" She sounded partly incredulous, as though she was trying to fit the last few pieces of a puzzle together.

"No, you already are. You are mine. I will provide for you and protect you, probably better than I will for my own wife. Mistresses are quite common in my culture. This is a very dangerous world you have entered. Whether willingly or not, you are part of it now. Without my protection, a lot worse can happen to you. I am not a violent man... well, I do not believe in violence towards women. I will do what I have to in order to teach you your place, though only if you make me."

I took her hand and pulled her a few feet from the wall, then turned her around, her back to me. She followed my lead without a word. I put my left hand on her stomach, holding her in place, and began placing soft kisses along her bare shoulders.

Elizabeth stood still as I slowly unzipped her dress with my other hand. I slid my right hand inside the dress, onto her bare stomach, and slid it up. My fingers dug under the bra and carefully lifted it as my hand slid under.

She gave a small, shocked gasp and tried to move away. I growled and held tighter.

"This is your last warning. Do not fight me. You give me what I want. You will obey. I guarantee you will not like the consequences."

Using my left, not waiting for a response, I began pushing the straps of her dress off her shoulders. I unsnapped the bra and it fell to the floor along with the dress.

"Tell me no one has ever touched you like this. Tell me no one has ever had you." I commanded into her ear as I gripped tighter.

Elizabeth

O f course, no one had ever touched me. I witnessed too much evil in
this world attached to sexuality. I closed myself off from the world in
order to better protect myself.

While I really wasn't thrilled with this new path life had thrown me on,
at least it was better than the alternative. I didn't like the sound of the family
collection. I could only imagine it being similar to what I saw back in Andre's
warehouse.

As we left earlier, I caught a glimpse of a large room filled with women
laying on cots similar to mine. They wore rags, they looked like they were
starving and half-mad. I also saw Paul enjoying his job. He had flashed me a
grin and winked as we left, making his current girl scream louder.

Antonio did not seem as evil as Paul. At least he didn't plan on sharing
me with anyone or being mean. If I chose to believe what he was saying.

Then again, it wasn't like I had much of a choice either.

"No one has ever touched me anywhere. You are the first and only person
to ever touch me." I felt the vibration of his approving growl.

Apparently, he wasn't exaggerating about being possessive.

On the bright side, he was pretty handsome. He had muscles, the tanned
skin of his Mexican heritage, dark black hair, and a voice so deep you felt it in
your bones. If I played to his possessive side, I could at least make this easier
on me.

I would rather that than him feeling like I betrayed him.

I thought he was going to hurt me earlier when I told him about what
happened, he didn't seem to like me fearing him though. I have no doubts
that this could go very, very, bad for me if I was not careful.

Of course, the more he kissed me softly like he was, the more I didn't
mind so much. No one had ever done that before either.

I closed my eyes as he kissed towards the front of my neck, walking
around me. I let my head fall back, keeping him from bumping into my chin.

I gasped as his mouth was no longer on my neck.

Without thinking beyond the need to hold onto something for balance, I brought a hand up onto the back of his head and gripped his hair. His hand on my back pulled me in tight as he intensified what he was doing.

I felt an odd sensation between my legs, another thing I had never experienced before.

I moaned as his mouth moved to the other side and I felt his hands grab my butt and lift me up. I wrapped my legs around his waist as he continued his assault on my chest.

My other hand gripped his bicep to maintain that balance. Wow, he had large muscles.

The next thing I knew, I was laying on the bed, on my back.

He released me and sat up long enough to strip his shirt over his head and take off his pants. I watched him up until that part, then quickly looked at the ceiling.

He chuckled, "look at me, Elizabeth."

I slowly looked at him but kept my eyes on his face as he crawled on the bed and over me. His voice changed to the possessive demanding one again.

"Tell me I am the only man you have seen naked."

"You are the only person I have ever seen naked, male or female."

"Good. And it will stay that way. Just as I am the only person who is allowed to see you naked. Entiendes?"

I nodded quietly and tried to avert my eyes again as they kept slipping down. He had a very nice chest. It was decorated with a large red dragon, the long tail of which led down and ended below his waistline, not that I was looking that far down.

He chuckled again as he spread my legs apart with his knees.

When did he remove my underwear? I vaguely remembered the bra, but not the panties.

His hand slid down to my thigh, and oh hello! That was not what I was expecting.

He hummed with approval again. "You are very wet for me. That makes me very happy."

Wet? I felt something going on down there, but I didn't see what that had to do with him.

Oh... oh... holy cow. My legs and lower regions were acting odd now.

"What... what..." I couldn't finish the question as my body was reacting in a way I had never experienced before.

He laughed. Of course, he was laughing.

"Have you never had an orgasm before?"

I shook my head as my hips rocked forward on their own and I moaned as something exploded inside me. It was like fireworks exploding inside my veins. The wetness increased. I looked at him as he removed his fingers from me and slid them inside his mouth. He grinned.

"Innocent indeed. Andre chose well. I love that I am the first to make you feel that. But just wait, it gets even better."

Better than that?

He lowered himself over me completely now. His mouth attached to my chest again as I felt him moving something around lower on me. This was larger than his fingers, much, much larger. I had a feeling I knew what it was. And I didn't like it.

I was suddenly very anxious. All of this was new to me, and I didn't even know this guy. All I knew was that I belonged to him now.

I was having a hard time seeing that as a bad thing after what he just did to me though.

Suddenly I felt a lot of pain as he roughly shoved into me. I screamed. That hurt.

I went to push him off me, but he grabbed my hands and held them over my head in just one of his. The tears started falling. The more I tried to buck him off, the harder he pushed into me, keeping himself locked in.

"Stop!" He demanded as he stilled over me. His voice was very, very angry.

I stopped fighting, but the tears didn't. Seeing the tears, his face softened. With his free hand, he wiped the tears from my face. He lowered and started kissing my neck again.

"I don't want to hurt you. You need to stop fighting me. This can be pleasurable for both of us. Or I can take what I need by force. I would rather not do that for our first time together. It's your choice. Now, relax and stop fighting me." He continued leaving gentle kisses along my neck, the only movement he made.

He slowly made a path up to my face and whispered against my lips. "Have you ever even kissed anyone before, Elizabeth?"

My heart was pounding, confused, scared, and even a little turned on.

"No," I whispered back, my voice thick with the fear still.

He then slowly started kissing me. It wasn't long before I started kissing him back. I felt the fingers of his free hand lightly rubbing on my chest. I gasped from the feeling, he took the opportunity and slid his tongue in my mouth.

He carefully pulled my hands over his head, wrapping them around his neck. I recognized the sensations in my body this time, from what he had done to me prior to the pain. His hand playing with my chest caused me to moan into his mouth.

With that, his hips started moving again, slower this time. As that new feeling built inside me again, my hips rocked into him. I held tight to the back of his head with one hand, as he moved his lips to my chest again.

My other hand started digging my nails into those large biceps. I began screaming again, but differently this time.

"Say my name," he commanded in a hoarse voice.

"Antonio." It came out in a moan.

He started getting harder and rougher. "Again." This time it came out more as a yell, mixed with a few yeses.

Soon both our bodies were shaking, and his movements slowed. His lips met mine again, I welcomed them with more enthusiasm this time. I felt him chuckle against me, which made heat rise in my cheeks. He pulled back and smiled down at me.

"Andre did well in picking you. You are perfect."

I blushed harder and bit my lip, trying to block the smile, as I looked away. I wasn't used to getting compliments from people. The opposite actually.

Antonio used a finger and turned my face back to him. He pulled my lip out with his thumb and traced it again.

Chapter 4

Antonio

I stared down at this beautiful woman, completely transfixed on those plump lips. I hadn't planned on kissing her. I never kissed the women I was with.

I got so mad when she started fighting me. It took me by surprise, and I let my anger get the best of me. Then I saw the tears and the fear in her eyes. She had been completely relaxed when I kissed her neck earlier, I thought I would try that to relax her again.

The rest just sort of happened.

I leaned down and kissed her again, loving the feel of her lips against mine. Soon, I would have to teach her what else those lips could be used for.

Another day. She had already experienced a lot of new things tonight as it was.

I knew she was innocent. I knew she was inexperienced. I just hadn't realized the depth of it. Her confusion over the first orgasm was actually quite adorable, my need to be inside her took over. I should have been gentler, maybe she would not have freaked out the way she did.

As I deepened the kiss, I felt her arms tighten around my neck, and her fingers grip my hair again.

Yes, Andre did indeed choose well.

I didn't know why I enjoyed kissing her so much, possibly because I had no doubts that her lips had never been on anyone, anywhere, before now. I felt the effects of the kiss. She did too. I hadn't disconnected us yet.

Well, since I was already there.

I started out slower this time until her legs wrapped around me, and her hips rocked against me. I took pride in feeling her shake multiple times, as I purposely dragged things out. At least until I couldn't anymore.

Yeah, I was definitely going to be keeping her for a good long while. This had to be some of the best I had ever had, and she was still new to this. I could only imagine how much better it would be further down the road.

As long as she stayed purely mine, I wouldn't mind.

I didn't share.

I rolled us onto our sides as my legs collapsed out from under me. This time I didn't stay in, even though I almost hated to separate from her.

I loved knowing that I had been, and would forever be, the only one to be inside of her. Her waters would never be muddied. Always clean, always mine.

She was so tight. I was left with no doubts that I was her first. I'd had women claim to be virgins in the past and were anything but.

I held Elizabeth close to me as I steadied my breathing. She laid her head on my arm and left her other arm over my waist, holding me against her as well. I wasn't sure what to do from there. Usually, I was a one and done kind of guy. I'd never gone a second round so soon after the first and I certainly had never cuddled with anyone, period.

Not before, not after, not ever.

Maybe it was because I knew she belonged to me and only me. My possessive side just wanted to keep her right here, where no one else could taint her. Keeping her safe, just like I promised.

I felt her breathing slow and deepen. When I looked down, I realized she had fallen asleep. I guess I shouldn't be surprised. Who knew when the last time she really slept was? She had been through a lot over the last few days, at least.

I knew Andre, I knew how he got his girls. Human trafficking wasn't exactly something new to me. I knew we had an investment in his business. All of Andre's "collection" was taken without permission, including all the women downstairs.

Elizabeth and I needed to have a talk about that. I needed to know I could trust her to not run away. I could chain her to the room if I must, I just didn't want to.

I also needed to know if it would be safe to take her back to Texas with me, or if I would have to keep her locked up, so the cops didn't find her.

Would she be willing to act as though she came by choice?

Would there be anyone looking for her? Certainly not a boyfriend. But maybe family.

We still had a few days before we returned to the States. She would have enough time to decide what type of life she wanted to live and how much freedom I would be giving her.

A few days locked up in this room should help with that.

My mind floated back to what she told me about Andre, my temper flared up again. I slowly rolled her over, off my arm. I tucked the blanket around her and waited. Elizabeth didn't move an inch.

I quickly dressed and quietly snuck out the door, locking it behind me. I was the only one with the key to this room, she would be safe.

I pulled my phone out of my pocket, thankfully it was still there, and checked the time. Barely midnight. The party would still be going, which meant Andre should still be here somewhere.

By the time I made it back to the original party, the room was filled with smoke. It had a sweet tint to it.

Someone had pulled out the weed, lovely.

The younger men were still going with some of the women. Probably trying to make the rounds with as many as possible.

I looked around and spotted my dad with the older men, in a separate section of couches. Each of them held a girl in their laps. They talked and laughed, while their fingers continued to play. One or two girls were on their knees, facing the men.

I was glad that Elizabeth got sent to me instead of being part of this. She would never have survived. Many of them didn't. Girls like her were frequently drugged into compliance and eventually died of an overdose.

My padre spotted me and waved me over. I put on my mask of indifference, to hide the disgust, and approached him.

He grinned happily at me.

I focused on his face and not where his hands were currently. As her back was to him, the rest of us got a front-row seat as to what he was doing. The brunette of course played her part well. She leaned against his chest, with her head tipped back on his shoulder. She was making all the right sounds too.

As I approached, she began to climax. Either she was a good faker, or she had just gotten so used to all this that her brain let her body run the show.

I noticed her left hand clasped around my padre. My previous angle did not prepare me to see so much of him again tonight.

"Padre." I greeted with a slight bow of my head.

"Tell me, hijo. Was she worth the money?"

I felt a genuine smile cross my face. "Si. Padre. Well worth it. I believe I will be keeping her around for quite some time."

He laughed. "Glad to hear it. Nothing helps you destress more than a woman. We will have to congratulate Andre on such a great find."

"Si, actually I need to discuss something with Andre. Do you know where he is?"

My padre had survived as the head of our cartel for so long for a reason. He picked up on the slight irritation in my voice.

"I thought you said he picked well?"

"That he did. But it seems he didn't follow complete instructions. While he did stop one of his men from disobeying, he himself struggled with keeping his hands to himself. Not enough to warrant me killing him, but enough for him to need a lesson."

My padre laughed and then groaned in response to the girl on his lap. He grabbed her arm and turned her around on his lap.

"Check down the hall near the kitchen."

I turned quickly, trying not to see the girl positioning herself and sliding onto him. Somethings you just couldn't unsee.

Sure enough, I found Andre in the kitchen, eating, drinking, and laughing with some of the guards. They all stopped when they saw me enter.

He greeted me with a grin, spreading his arms wide when he saw me.

"Antonio! How did I do?"

I walked directly up to him and answered with a fist to his face. He fell off his stool as the other men stepped away. They knew well enough to not get involved.

"What was that for? If you don't like her, just say so. I will be more than happy to take her back." He chuckled at the thought.

I punched him again.

"I like her just fine. I would have had no complaints had you followed all the rules." I began pacing back and forth in front of him, flexing my fist. He flinched every time I got close. "One of the simplest of your instructions was that she not be touched. Can you tell me where you went wrong?"

He stood back up and brushed off his clothes while straightening them.

"Paul had already been warned. He gets a little over-excited with the new girls. I got there in time to stop anything from happening."

I stopped and turned to face him. He shrank back an inch under my glare.

"And what about you? Did you feel you were exempt from those rules?"

His face paled as he realized what I was talking about. "I... I hardly touched her. You watch a beautiful woman like that wash herself and not need some relief. I kept that wipe between my hand and her body at all times."

I sneered at him. "And what about when you rubbed against her?"

He had the brains to at least look ashamed. "I got a little carried away. I apologize." A spark of hope went through his eyes as he asked, "do you want me to take her back and find you someone else?"

I scoffed. "Is that why you did it? Were you hoping I wouldn't want her now and I would return her to you?"

"No, it was just an offer. I screwed up and I'm trying to make things right." He shrugged, "I wouldn't complain about keeping her either."

I sneered at him again. "No. I will be keeping her. And if you ever fail to follow instructions again, we will no longer be doing business together. This will be coming out of your fee."

I turned and walked out of the kitchen and back down the hall. I paused outside the party and debated telling my padre, but I had no desire to walk into that again. Instead, I climbed back up the stairs towards the third floor, where the family bedrooms were located.

I pulled my phone out and sent him a message.

Me: Andre has been warned. I also told him it would be coming out of his fee. 10 percent of your promised price should cover it.

Me: I'm turning in, I will see you in the morning.

I paused outside my bedroom door, my hand on the knob.

What would Elizabeth do when she woke up? Would she try to run? Would she be scared again?

If she ran, she would be caught. And the guards would take liberties. They didn't know she belonged to me yet.

All that waited for me in my room was an empty bed. Something I usually preferred. But tonight, it was not what I wanted. Which was interesting, since as of tomorrow, I would have a bride who I knew would insist on sharing a room. Not that I planned on sharing one with Elena.

I quickly turned back toward the stairs and made my way back up, toward Elizabeth. I unlocked the door quietly and snuck back into the room, making sure to lock it behind me.

I didn't trust most people.

I stood at the foot of the bed and watched her. She still hadn't moved an inch. I had been gone for nearly an hour, too.

I found one of the backup chargers we kept for guests in the drawer of a side table and plugged my phone into the wall. I pulled my clothes back off and slid under the covers. Slowly, I wrapped an arm around Elizabeth's waist and pulled her back against my chest. Her skin felt smooth under my rough hands. She moaned in contentment as my chest hit her. The feel of her against me, mixed with that sound had quite the effect on me.

I debated how I wanted to handle this. After a few minutes, I decided I didn't care. She was going to have to get used to this sometime anyway.

I carefully moved her head far enough up my left arm that my hand could access her ample chest. I lightly drew circles around, causing her to whimper in her sleep. With my right hand, I lifted her right leg just enough to slide in between. All the while kissing her neck and shoulders again.

I had barely gotten started when she moaned again, but deeper this time. She lifted her knee, giving me better access. I chuckled at how easily she was already responding to me in her sleep.

It was amazing what could happen when your brain stayed out of things. Like how her right hand just moved behind her and latched on to me. She wasn't the only one moaning anymore. Mine however seemed to wake her up.

She gasped in shock again and let go of me as she tried to jump away. I pushed her back into me and increased the pressure with both hands.

"Where do you think you're going?" I tried to hold back the laugh and keep my voice deep.

"I... I'm sorry, I didn't mean to... too."

I let the laugh go and stopped her talking. "Never apologize for doing that. Your hands are always welcome on my body, Senorita."

She pushed further into me as she reacted to what I was doing to her. Her hand slowly went back to me and picked up where she left off. I encouraged her by letting her hear how it was affecting me. As she increased in tempo, I bit down on her shoulder and started sucking on her skin again.

Soon I couldn't take it anymore and quickly maneuvered us, so she was under me. She gave a deep inhale, not expecting me to move in so quickly. I laid over her and started kissing her again, enjoying the taste of her lips and her tongue in my mouth.

Thanks to all the hand stuff, it did not take long for both of us to finish. This time we both fell asleep with her still in my arms. My last thought was that I could really get used to this.

Chapter 5

Elizabeth

For the second morning in a row, I woke up not knowing where I was. At least this time the place was cleaner, and the bed was a lot more comfortable. It was kind of hot though and I felt a heavy weight laying across my waist.

I lifted the blanket and looked down to investigate. My eyes widened when I realized that not only was I naked, but there was an arm around me. Every big arm.

Oh, boy, and were my girly parts sore. Both the top and the bottom ones. Almost like I had been mauled by a bear or something.

Riiight. Antonio. His dad bought me as a ... wedding gift?

I had always lived a boring and lonesome life. At least the last three years anyway. Since I aged out of foster care. I did what I had to do in order to protect myself. And yet, the one time I decided to go to a club and try drinking, I ended up kidnapped and sold as a mistress.

But maybe being Antonio's mistress wouldn't be so bad. Last night certainly wasn't. I could see why people liked having sex so much now.

Or was it just him?

Oh well. Guess it didn't really matter. Pretty sure he was the only man I would ever be with, whether I liked it or not. He did say he would take care of me and protect me. When had anyone ever done that? Not since my parents died that was for sure.

I felt him stretch behind me and pull me in tighter. I couldn't hold back the smile. People always talked about possessiveness like it was a bad thing. So far, I kind of liked it. It was certainly better than being ignored or cast aside like I didn't matter, a feeling I knew well.

I also liked it when I felt him kiss my neck lightly.

"Good morning, Hermosa." He mumbled into my shoulder.

"Good morning." I suddenly felt very shy. Pretty sure he knew that too. I felt the smile against my bare skin.

His hand moved down to my thigh and started rubbing it. "How are you feeling this morning? Are you sore?"

I nodded, keeping my promise to always be honest with him (I wasn't stupid enough to test what would happen if I wasn't), as I answered. "A little, I haven't tried moving much yet though."

His hand slid down and began massaging the sore area. I gasped at the unaccepted touch.

He chuckled again but did not stop. "The best thing for sore muscles is movement and stretching out."

Before I could form a response, he was on his back and had me laying on top of him. He pushed me up into a sitting position, the sheet no longer covering me. He licked his lips as he stared at me, the sun shining in the room left no space to hide.

His hand slid up from my waist and effectively said good morning to other parts of me as well. The momentary embarrassment disappeared and was replaced by a growing need. One I was beginning to recognize all too well.

His voice was hoarse as he spoke again. "Lift onto your knees."

I did as he commanded, another thing I was sure I would have to get used to. He grabbed my hand and demonstrated how to line us up. He then began giving me commands on what to do next, moving my hips along with me.

It didn't take long before my body began reacting naturally. For a controlling man, we stayed like that longer than I expected. I laughed when he quickly rolled us over, placing me on the bottom again.

My laughter soon turned to other sounds. Yeah, this life may not be so bad after all.

He laid back down next to me again, kissed the tip of my nose, and worked on slowing his breath. When we were both breathing normally again, he finally spoke.

"Why don't you go take a shower while I order breakfast to be sent up for us?"

"I thought this was a house. Are we in a hotel?"

He smiled. "No, this is mi padre's hacienda. However, we do have servants that can bring breakfast to us."

"Oh, alright."

I had never heard of servants doing that before, then again, I had never known anyone with that much money before. I began to sit up when a new thought came to me.

"I don't have any other clothes to wear."

"Don't worry about it. You can just put the same dress on for now. I will have someone buy you some clothes from the store, just make a list of your sizes and anything else you might need." He rubbed his knuckles along my arm softly.

I nodded and stood up from the bed and tried to take the blanket with me, he held onto it tightly and shook his head no with a smile.

I rolled my eyes at him, causing him to laugh.

There was no lock on the bathroom door either, which I thought was odd but let it be. The warm water felt like Heaven against my skin, so I stood under the pouring water for a few minutes. I was just about to start washing my hair when I felt a warm body come in behind me, wrapping his arm around me once more.

I stood as still as I could, not sure what to do. It should go without saying, but no one had ever been in the shower with me before either.

Antonio picked up the shampoo bottle and poured some into his hand, then he proceeded to wash my hair for me. Which felt really nice, his hands were talented in many ways. He then did the same with the conditioner. Once he finished with that, Antonio poured body wash onto a loofah and very slowly washed every inch of me. Once he finished, he handed me the loofah full of soap, wordlessly. I slowly washed him this time.

We both laughed when he had to lean down for me to get his shoulders, he got dramatic and squatted halfway. He thought it was even funnier to lick my chest, seeing as he was practically on eye level with it. I went down onto my knees in order to get his calves, he silently refused to lift them up, with a big cheesy grin on his face.

Before I could get back up, he placed one hand on the back of my head and his other lifted himself up.

"Open your mouth." I looked at him confused. "Do it. You need to learn this. I will expect you to do this a lot. Don't worry. You will enjoy it as well. Now, do as I say and open."

I followed his instructions, both verbal and nonverbal. I tried to move away when I felt something new in my mouth.

"Swallow it, all of it."

Oookay.

He shook but held my head firmly in place. It wasn't as good as some of the other things we had done, but it wasn't bad either. He helped me stand back up, then wiped the corner of my mouth with his thumb.

"See, that wasn't so bad, was it?"

I silently shook my head, knowing that was the answer he was looking for. His grin grew as he pushed me against the shower wall.

"My turn."

I had no idea about what he meant by that, or why he went down to his knees.

Oh, that was what he meant. Huh. Yeah, definitely liking this way much better.

It was a good deal of time after he was back on his feet, kissing me properly, the cold-water having long been turned off, when his phone began to ring. Antonio groaned but ignored it.

I giggled when he roughly picked me up and carried me out of the shower. I thought we were headed for the bed, but we didn't make it that far. He sat me on the bathroom counter and finished what he started under the water.

My yells were a bit echoey in this room. We were in the slow kisses while his shaking calmed phase when we heard the phone ring again.

He stepped back and put his hand up. "Come. Breakfast should be here. You need to eat."

I took his hand and let him help me down and lead me out. He handed me a towel – it was more for coverage than water at this point - and then took one for himself. I sat on the small sofa in the bedroom while he went and opened the bedroom door, where a rolling cart full of food waited.

My stomach grumbled when I smelled the pancakes and bacon.

Antonio

I hadn't planned on joining her in the shower, but after watching her walk away stark naked, it just couldn't be helped. As was the rest of it, it just couldn't be helped.

Not that I tried all that hard.

I saw what I wanted, and I took it. Just the way my padre taught me to do. I knew it was probably him calling on the phone, he was not going to be happy about being ignored.

Oh well. Somethings just couldn't be helped.

I made sure Elizabeth was situated with the food on the small coffee table before returning to my phone.

Sure enough, it was padre.

I looked at Elizabeth, who looked up at me, feeling my eyes on her. I put a finger to my lips, and she nodded as she turned back to her breakfast. I had ordered a lot of food, since I wasn't sure when the last time she ate was.

I hit the callback button and the other end began ringing.

"About time, where were you?"

Well, good morning to you too padre. "My apologies, padre, I was in the shower. I did not hear my phone."

His grunt sounded more amused than annoyed. "Where are you now?"

"I'm in my room, just starting breakfast. Do you need something?"

"Right, your room. The one I am standing in right now?"

I sighed. "I'm in the other room, padre."

Now he was all out laughing. "Andre may be stupid about some things, but I guess he still has a sixth sense about senoritas. Fine, we will talk later. You need to be down here in one hour. Elena is already here and getting ready. Guests will be arriving in two, you need to be ready to greet them by then."

I pinched the bridge of my nose. I had completely forgotten about the nightmare ahead of me today. Man, I hated her. I sighed and looked up. Elizabeth was still eating, not paying me, or my conversation, any attention.

Unable to help myself, and not liking the distance, I walked over and sat down next to her.

"Si, padre. I will be down in an hour." I hung up before he could say anything else.

I leaned back onto the couch and laid my head on the back rim, grumbling in frustration. Alright, it was more like whimpering than grumbling. When I felt a small hand lay on top of mine, giving it a small squeeze, I rolled my head to the side and looked at Elizabeth. Her partially dried hair was resting on her back, and the towel was tied around her chest, split open at her legs. She gave me a small encouraging smile.

"Is everything alright?"

I just stared at Elizabeth for a minute, then moved my hand out from under hers. I put my arm around her and pulled her against my side.

"Yeah. Everything is fine. I just forgot what was happening today." I rubbed my hand along her arm softly, reveling in the feel of her sk. My gaze returned to the ceiling.

"What did you forget?" Her voice was soft, almost soothing. Her presence was smoothing. Probably why I didn't like the distance between us.

I huffed. "I forgot that I am marrying the devil's spawn today."

From the stiffening of her spine, she had forgotten too. Elizabeth started to pull away, but I didn't let her.

She patted my chest and started to sit up again. "Come, you need to eat as well. Big day." I could hear the trace of sadness in her voice, not knowing what to do with that, I let her sit up and we both ate in silence.

"Elizabeth? Talk to me. Please." The only sounds I had heard from her over the last ten minutes were soft sniffles.

"I don't know what you want me to say." She leaned against the back of the couch and tucked her feet under her.

I picked up the dishes and placed them back on the cart, then sat on the small table, directly in front of her. I placed a finger under her chin and lifted her face up to mine.

"I want to know what has you so upset." I did not like the way it made me feel.

"Nothing, I just forgot for a moment there that you weren't actually mine. I am just the mistress, just the side piece. Bought and paid for." The cutest little grimace came from her mouth as she said the last part.

I scooped her up and sat her on my lap, facing me. "Technically that is true. But trust me. I belong more to you than I ever will to her. I am not marrying her by choice."

"You didn't exactly choose me either."

I chuckled softly. "Yes, I did. It was my choice whether I stayed. It's my choice on how long I keep you. And I am choosing to keep you for as long as possible. You belong to me, not because you were paid for, but because I want you here with me." I smirked. "I have never spent this much time with a woman, Elizabeth. You have had an effect on me already. I can't seem to leave you. I left last night for an hour, I had to go teach Andre a lesson in following orders, then I came straight back to you. I've never slept next to a woman, held a woman, showered with them, hell" I snorted "I rarely ever kissed one either. All of those things I have done with you, who I just met 12 hours ago."

I placed a palm on her cheek and stroked it with my thumb. I slid my hand to the back of her neck and pulled her to me for a kiss. She met my lips eagerly, her arms wrapping around my neck. I removed the towel that was barely hanging on as it was and threw it to the side.

I felt one of her hands leave my neck and untie the towel around my waist, moving it to the sides. I chuckled and then groaned as she literally took things into her own hands. She pumped me good before moving onto her knees and then slowly sat down again. She went very slow too, torturing me in the best way possible.

Unlike earlier, I let her maintain control. I had no regrets, not at all. I hugged her tight against me while my climax subsided. She was a fast learner.

"So, what happens now? What is my life going to be like?" She quietly asked over my shoulder.

"I don't really know honestly. We will stay in Mexico for a few more days, then we will all head back to Texas."

She leaned back and looked at me in surprise. "We're in Mexico?"

I laughed. "You didn't know that?" She shook her head. "Where did you think we were?"

She shrugged and seemed to shrink into herself. "I wasn't sure. I met Andre in New Orleans. I figured I wasn't there anymore, but I didn't know we left the country."

Right, that reminded me of what else we needed to talk about. It would have to wait though, now was not the time. That was going to be a longer conversation than I had time for.

"I wish I could take you around to show you some of the countryside. We are in the middle of Mexico, where it is pure Mexican culture, with very little influence from the U.S. Next time we come out, I promise to take you to the market."

She gave me a soft smile. "I would really like that. But..." she bit her lip as she prepared to ask an uncomfortable question. "What about your new wife? She is not going to like you spending time with me."

I shrugged. "Elena will get over it. This is the way it is in our world. Wives are part of business, nothing more. Padre has had many mistresses over the years. I have many siblings from them. My parents get along fine, but I rarely see them together."

"Does that mean Elena will have a man on the side as well?"

I snorted in amusement. "No. If she does then I am allowed to kill them both."

"How is that fair?" Elizabeth raised an adorable little eyebrow. I leaned in and kissed it before I even knew what I was doing.

"It just is what it is. The same goes for you. If you were to ever sleep with another man, I could kill you both."

"So, you don't have to share me, but I have to share you? Well, that stinks. I'm a bit possessive myself, ya know? I already don't like the idea of you having a wife and me being on the side. Now, I hear I might have to share you with whomever you want, to?"

I threw my head back and laughed lightheartedly. I liked the sound of that. I had never had anyone be possessive of me. I pulled her close and kissed her again.

"I feel no need to have anyone besides you. Elena is nothing more than a business arrangement and not one of my choosing. I cannot stand the woman. I am only marrying her out of duty, nothing more. I am fairly certain I am going to be playing favorites, with you being the favorite." I lightly tapped her nose, creating a small smile on her beautiful face.

Elizabeth wrapped her arms around my neck again. "I do like being the favorite." Her smile shrank. "But you are still going to have to sleep with her, aren't you? Consummate the marriage? Have children? And what if down the line you do decide you like her? It's not like you knew you would like me." Her voice shrank as she added. "If you like me that is."

I could see why she had stayed innocent for so long. She had so many deep-seated insecurities. I was going to have to do something about that. I stroked her long black hair, which was nearly dry now, running my fingers through it.

"First off, I do like you. After last night and this morning, that shouldn't need to be said. I don't see her and I ever trying for kids, at least not any time soon. And trust me, it will be very rare that I actually sleep with her, let alone have sex with her. I have known Elena for quite some time, we have never gotten along, and I have never been attracted to her. Whereas the moment I saw you hiding behind the couch I wanted to throw you on top of it."

We sat in silence, both lost to our own thoughts. She jumped when the alarm went off on my phone, reminding me I only had ten minutes.

I laughed at Elizabeth's surprise and then kissed her again before standing up and putting her back on her feet. I found her dress on the floor and held it for her to step into.

"I would much rather you be in here naked, knowing you are waiting for me, but I would prefer you be dressed when they bring you lunch and dinner later."

"Will I be seeing you again today?"

"I don't know. I will try to come back tonight. If I come any earlier, I may never leave. I am not one for large parties."

She smirked. "Me either. I was always more of a homebody. The one time I left my house to go out... well... here I am."

I zipped up the pants I had just put on and pulled her in for a hug.

"I am so glad you stepped out then."

She gave me a small smile and looked up at me. "Despite all the extra drama, I think I might be too."

I gave her another kiss before I pulled my shirt on.

I put a palm to her cheek. "Stay in the room. Until I have found a way to mark you as mine, I don't want to risk anyone messing with you. Stay here where it is safe. Entiendes?"

"Si, El jefe."

I laughed and kissed her one more time. She called me the boss. I loved it. Most of my men called me that but coming from her made it harder for me to leave. Against my better judgement, I closed the door and locked it behind me, putting the key in my pocket. I quickly walked downstairs to the room being used for the men to put on their tuxedos.

Chapter 6

Antonio

The first floor was buzzing with teams of people setting up for the wedding and the reception that would follow. The latter would take place in the dance hall, the same place the party had been the night before.

I stepped into the changing room, where my two best friends were. One was also my half-brother, Miguel. He was only a month younger than me.

"About time! Where have you been? I was starting to think you had run off and I was gonna have to marry the shrew."

I laughed at my brother and gave him a hug. "Not a bad idea, wish I had thought of it sooner."

"Soo, where were you?"

Nosey mutt. Oh well. I would have told him eventually anyway.

"I was hiding out with my new mistress." I answered nonchalantly as I pulled my monkey suit out of the garment bag.

The room went so quiet you I half expected to hear crickets. I let them stew on that for a moment while I changed. It was just a basic black tux. I didn't agree to do anything special. I purposely refused to participate in any of this mess.

I was tucking in my shirt by the time one of them managed to speak again. Francisco came to his senses first.

"When did you get a mistress? And where?"

I laughed, which caused each of them to raise an eyebrow and share a confused look. It just made me laugh harder, which of course made their eyes widen more. They looked at each other and then back to me.

Yeah, okay, I was already laughing more than I normally did. I was typically a serious man, and today of all days was expected to be a living nightmare. Laughing was the last thing I would normally be doing.

"Did either of you notice that I was not at the party last night?"

They looked at each other again, then back at me. They both answered "no" at the same time.

I chuckled, shaking my head. They were not as picky as I was. They were happy to fill any hole that opened for them, willing, or not.

"Padre pulled me aside after dinner. Apparently, there is a family tradition of buying the doomed groom his first mistress when he gets married. Kind of like a consolation prize. Padre had put a special order in with Andre, who delivered her last night."

"And?" Miguel pushed for more when I stopped talking.

I shrugged, trying to keep back the smile. "And Andre lived up to his reputation. I will be keeping her for a very long time. If I had my way, I would be running off with her and letting your ugly mug marry Elena."

"She must be one good lay. I thought you didn't like using Andre's women?" Francisco voiced the real confusion for both of them.

I poured myself a drink from the decanter on a side table, shaking my head. "I don't. Padre knew this and requested someone pure and innocent."

Miguel laughed and pumped a fist. "Virgin! Nice! I always love myself a good virgin. Nothing like it."

I shook my head. "She is more than just that. I plan on getting more details from her later, but I am fairly certain she has never so much as kissed anyone before."

The room went deathly quiet again. What did I say now?

Francisco, always the one to break the silence first, answered that question for me.

"You kissed her?"

Oh, right, that. They knew I didn't do that. It wasn't like anything was really all that private in this family.

I smirked and shrugged again. "I can't help it. I see her, and I want to kiss her. I did it once, to calm her down, and just couldn't seem to stop."

"Elena is going to hate this. She thinks she is the queen of the castle. You are already putting her behind a mistress." Miguel chuckled softly. "This is going to be so much fun to watch. Is your girl going to be able to handle it?"

I sighed and sat down on the small sofa in the room, clasping my hands together between my knees. "I think so. She has some fire in her, but she also has insecurities that we might need to work through. I honestly don't think she realizes how gorgeous she is. And I mean, she is gorgeous. How she stayed innocent this long is beyond me."

There was a knock at the door. Before Miguel could open it, I added, "let's keep all this between us for now, please. One thing at a time." They both nodded, understanding my meaning and agreeing.

We were soon ushered out the door to start greeting guests. The wedding wasn't set to start until two, another two hours away. Why guests had to start showing up three hours before it started, I would never know. I was sure it had something to do with strengthening ties, putting on a performance for the underlings, time for business dealings, etc. I don't know they couldn't do all that at the reception though. Shorten the nightmare for me, at least a little bit.

Around one, I sent Francisco to the kitchen to order a lunch tray to be sent to Elizabeth. He begged to be the one to deliver it. I wasn't going to let him, but then he made the point that I could trust him over any of the staff and strangers walking around the hacienda.

He came back down a little later, giving me a giant grin and a fist bump. I laughed. Apparently, he approved.

I caught sight of him whispering to Miguel a few minutes later. From the hand gestures he was using, he was describing how well stacked she was.

My mind wandered to how soft she was and how good she felt in my hands. Thankfully my padre drew my attention to new arrivals before my pants gestured to where my thoughts were. My luck, the guests would start teasing me, saying I was thinking about my wedding night with my bride.

Uh, no. That usually had the opposite effect on me.

When two o'clock came around, I stood near the preacher. Feeling like I was standing in front of a firing squad. Did the same rules apply? Would this dying man get a last wish?

Probably not. We all knew what that wish would be.

The ceremony itself was taking place outside. There was a buttload of flowers everywhere. Especially on this half-circle thing I had to stand under. This place would be killer for anyone with seasonal allergies.

I was half wishing we would get a random thunderstorm or a hurricane right about now. But... no. It was a bright and sunny August day.

The music started and I watched while Miguel walked down the aisle with some chick I didn't know. He was then followed by Francisco and another broad. Finally, Elena strutted down like she was walking a runway.

True to her princess attitude, Elena's dress was fluffy and sparkly. I had a feeling those were real diamonds sewn into the dress. I never thought a dress could be so puffy and so slutty at the same time. Yet, she managed to pull it off. Her chest was practically falling out of the dress.

I politely watched as she walked towards me, wishing it was Elizabeth. Not that I was in love with her. Far from it. I just liked her a whole lot more than the shrew coming towards me.

At least I was attracted to Elizabeth. I hadn't been attracted to Elena since the first time we met. It lasted about 5 seconds.

Elena's padre placed her hand in mine and then we both turned to face the preacher.

I only half-listened as we exchanged the traditional vows. I gave her a quick peck for a kiss, which she did not seem happy about. To hell if she was getting anything more than that from me. Who knew where that tongue had been last.

I held her hand as we walked back down the aisle together.

"Really? That was the best you could do?" She mumbled through her fake smile as we passed people.

"You're lucky you got that much." I mumbled back. She huffed and sped up, half dragging me along.

We spent the next hour taking pictures. It was so hard to smile and not grimace every time I had to put my arms around her. This marriage was going to be hell.

How was I ever going to procreate with this woman when I couldn't stand to touch her?

And what about the fact that we had to consummate the marriage tonight? Just the thought of it was making me shrivel and gag.

The reception was annoying. We had to dance together, multiple times. Some idiot decided to start the whole chanting for us to kiss thing, too. Had to have been someone from her side, or someone that hated me. Same thing in my opinion.

One time she tried to hold on and deepen it. Yeah, I wasn't having that.

I held her close, like I was hugging her, and growled in her ear. "Try that again and I will refuse to kiss you in front of everyone next time. I don't do kissing, learn to deal with it."

She glared at me but did not try again. In fact, the chanting stopped pretty quickly after that as well. Verifying for me that it had been from her side.

The party went on for quite some time.

At six, I let Miguel take a turn in delivering food to Elizabeth. I was at the bar, again, when he came back with a big smile.

"Vato, she is fine!" I laughed at my brother's version of dude. He went to college in California, where he obviously spent too much time with surfers. "Elena is going to hate her. Especially if you kiss her in front of her." He gasped dramatically. "Vato, you have to kiss her in front of Elena! Please! And let me be there for it!"

I chuckled. Yeah, that would be a disaster, but totally worth it. My smile shrank, thinking of Elizabeth up there all alone.

"How is she?"

He shrugged. "She seemed fine. She was watching a movie on the tv. She asked about you though. Told her you were about ready to strangle the woman already, she seemed happy with that thought. Looks like she is just as attached to you already as well. That's good."

He was silent for a moment before he got brave enough to ask. "Do you know how long she was with Andre before here?"

"I'm not positive, but I'm pretty sure it was just a few days. She didn't even know she was in Mexico. He took her from New Orleans, drugged obviously."

Miguel nodded. "That's good. I've met some of his men, they are pretty cracked. No way they would have left her alone for long."

I shook my head. "They almost didn't. Andre walked in on one of them, just in time from the sounds of it. Not that he did much better, but he only barely touched her. I paid him back for that last night, seeing as they had been instructed to *not* touch her at all."

Miguel laughed. "Are you going to be as possessive with Elena? We all know she has had her own side pieces over the years."

I sighed and scratched my jaw. "In some ways, yes. I will not allow her to disrespect me in that way. However, Elizabeth is my main focus. As will be yours and Francisco's. No one will ever touch her. When... if... she ever leaves the house, it will be with a guard. Elena's guard will be more like a babysitter."

"Basically, we treat your wife like the mistress and your mistress like the wife?"

I knocked back the last of my shot of whiskey. "Yes. They both deserve that treatment." He nodded. "I also need help thinking of a way to mark Elizabeth as mine. Something subtle enough that the men know not to harass her, but my enemies will not know of her importance."

We were both silent as the bartender refilled my drink and gave one to Miguel as well. After he left, Miguel spoke up.

"How permanent do you want the mark? I assume that if you ever feel done with her, that she will not be going into the collection."

I shook my head. "No, if that time comes, I will put her up somewhere safe. Similar to Tio Juan's old mistress. She has her own place, her own life, but he still provides for her and visits once in a while. Whether Elizabeth will become permanent is too soon to tell."

He held a breath then let it out like he was lifting weights with that one breath.

"All of our men know your tattoo. That dragon is pretty unique. They have all seen it when we work out or at the house during pool parties. If you got her a matching one, somewhere they would see, that could work."

That was not a bad idea. It would be a permanent mark, which was fine as I didn't see her ever going anywhere, not even to live separately. I wouldn't tell Miguel that though. Something permanent and unique like that would probably help her feel more secure in her position with me. I had my tattoo specially designed and contracted to keep it unique.

I would never allow Elena to get one. Wearing my ring was bad enough. Oh, there was an idea.

"What about having it done on her ring finger? I can't give her a ring, that would be too hard of a slap to the Valdez family."

Miguel smiled. "I like it. Subtle too. If she ever feels the need, all she has to do is scratch her face, showing her finger." He finished the last of his shot before adding "you should buy her a necklace too. All the wives have rings with GPS in them, just in case. No one ever does it for the mistresses, so no one will realize it is in her necklace."

I noticed Elena walking over towards me. I put up a fist and he bumped it.

"Good looking out, hermano. We will take care of all that when we get home."

"There you are husband."

Why did it feel like an insult when she called me that?

"Elena? What do you want? I was in the middle of a meeting."

She frowned and looked at Miguel. "You're drinking with your brother. I fail to see the importance of that."

I glared at her. She had the brains to at least step back. I grabbed her arm and pulled her close enough to whisper in her ear.

"You need to learn your place, senora. This is how meetings typically go and how business is done. Next time you can signal me if you need me. I will come to you when I am ready. Otherwise, wait until I am done. Never, I repeat never, assume it is not important. Miguel is one of the heads of this family, therefore, most of the time we talk, it is important. Entiendes?"

She ripped her arm back out of my hand, I let her. She glared back at me.

"¿Entiendes, Elena?"

"Si!" She snapped back.

I smirked spitefully.

She was going to have a lot of hard lessons to learn. She has been spoiled for too long and gotten away with too much. She was in for a rude awakening.

Unfortunately, she was probably going to target Elizabeth for retribution.

"Good. Now, what did you need?" I calmly asked her as I leaned back against the bar.

She took a slow breath, pulling herself back together, then gave me her fake smile. "It is after seven. It is time for us to leave, is it not?"

I grimaced. I didn't care if she saw it. The plan had been for us to leave after dinner, and head to our room for the next few days. When we got back to Texas, she would have her own room. I already had it set up for her.

Of course, I had no idea that Elizabeth would be joining us. Now the debate was whether to let her stay with me or give her a room of her own. I had plenty of them.

I sighed, dramatically, on purpose. "You're right, it is time for us to retire." Maybe if I got this over with, I could sneak into Elizabeth's room after. "Go say goodbye to your parents, we will be done in a few minutes."

Elena nodded and stalked off. I sighed and looked back to Miguel, who looked to be holding back a laugh. I waved the bartender over.

"Give me the whole bottle please." He smirked and handed me a brand-new bottle of whiskey.

Chapter 7

Antonio

Elena kept a death grip on my arm as we walked out of the reception and up to the third floor, to my bedroom, where we would be staying.

Well, she would. I had no intention of staying there with her.

"Is that bottle really necessary, Antonio?" She hissed as we turned off the stairs.

"That depends, Elena. Were you interested in a platonic marriage? I won't argue with that, however, you still wouldn't be allowed to sleep around."

"What's that supposed to mean?" She looked at me with a snarl.

"Exactly what I said. I have no problems with never touching you or consummating this marriage. Whether we sleep together or not though, you are not allowed to sleep with anyone else. Did you really think we didn't know about you and all your little boyfriends? Please." I scoffed at her as I opened the bedroom door.

As soon as I closed it again, I opened the whiskey and drank straight from the bottle before setting it on the table.

She smirked haughtily. "Same goes for you. As your wife, I will not allow you to sleep around either."

I bent over laughing at her audacity, nearly spitting out the alcohol. She was not happy with my outburst. Once I caught my breath, I responded to her.

"That is not how this works, and you know it." I raised my hands out to the side. "The joy of being a man in this world. I can have as many mistresses as I please." I lowered my hands and picked the bottle back up. "You, on the other hand, you step out once, and I will have both of you killed. Did you not read the contract? Are you really that naive?"

I took another long drink, the buzz of all the alcohol finally beginning to set in.

Elena huffed and stomped into the bathroom. I took off my tie and jacket, throwing them over a chair. I took another long drink before taking off my pants as well.

I should probably stop drinking or I was liable to pass out in bed with her. Knowing her, she would take it the wrong way. And, if I was going to wake up next to anyone, it was going to be Elizabeth.

I gave a resigned groan as I capped the bottle and sat down on the bed in my boxers. They at least would be staying on. I opened the nightstand and pulled out one of the condoms I stashed in there.

There was no way I was doing this without protection.

I laughed to myself. I hadn't even thought about it with Elizabeth. The idea of not being able to feel every inch of her felt wrong and I was pretty sure she never had a reason to be on the pill.

We may need to talk about getting her some. I wasn't sure I was ready for a kid yet. Although, that would put her ahead of Elena. And would definitely tie Elizabeth to me permanently.

I looked up as the bathroom door opened. Elena leaned against the door frame wearing a white negligee. If it wasn't for her personality, I probably wouldn't mind this so much. She was a very attractive woman; it was only her personality that was ugly.

She was trying to be seductive, and it wasn't working. No doubt it did with most males out there. But I wasn't like most males.

I stood up and put a hand up to her. She smiled and took my hand demurely. I struggled to not roll my eyes. I led her to the bed. She climbed into the middle, while I reached over and flipped off the lights. There was still a faint light from the moon outside, but it was dark enough that I wouldn't have to look at her too much.

She scoffed. "Really Antonio? I can barely see you?"

"Yeah, so? Mood lighting." I opened the package and she grumbled again.

"I'm your wife, do you really think *that* is necessary?"

"Do you really expect me to believe that you didn't sleep with someone else last night or even this morning?"

She gasped. Did she really think I was that stupid?

"I have a thing about sharing women. I don't like it. Until I am ready to have children, we use these. *If* this ever happens again."

She grumbled quietly, but I let it go.

After another handful of minutes, I realized I had a problem that I had not foreseen, nor was it so easily solved.

The woman did absolutely nothing for me. I just knelt over her, trying to keep as much space between us as possible.

She scoffed again but before she could say anything I cut her off.

"If you want this to happen at all tonight, you best keep your mouth shut. That is not going to help any. I have made no secret of my dislike for you, which seems to go deeper than I originally thought. So shut up and give me a minute. Do us both a favor and don't speak again for the rest of the night."

She finally listened to reason and kept her mouth shut. I closed my eyes tight and imagined it was Elizabeth wearing the negligee. I remembered waking up to her, the feel of her in my hands, the feel of her lips on mine, and in the shower.

Yup. That did the trick.

I kept picturing her in my mind as I covered up, placed my hands on the bed, one hand on each side of my disgruntled wife, and then did what I needed to do.

I didn't know if Elena got anything out of it, nor did I care. All that mattered was that the deed was done, and our marriage was consummated.

I stood up and went to the bathroom to clean up. I locked the door behind me and took a quick shower. I hoped she would be asleep by the time I got out.

I wasn't that lucky.

The lamplight was back on, and she was sitting in the bed with a ticked-off look on her face. It swiftly changed when she caught sight of me in nothing but a towel.

I laughed to myself. Guess I had more of an effect on her than she did on me.

I grabbed clothes out of the dresser and went back to the bathroom to get dressed. Elena didn't need to see any more of me than she already had. I threw on the pair of sweats and t-shirt, then walked back out. I took a duffle bag out of the closet and started filling it with a change of clothes.

I made sure to grab an extra pair of sweats and a t-shirt for Elizabeth. She may look hot in that dress, but it most likely came with bad memories from Andre.

"Where do you think you are going? It's our wedding night!" Elena yelled angrily.

I huffed in amusement and waved it away. "That is just a matter of semantics. I did what needed to be done. Our marriage is official. I will be sleeping in another room." I stopped at the door before leaving. "Remember, you are always being watched. If you prove to be trustworthy, our relationship may change. However, if you disrespect me even once, we are through. I am possessive and I am mean. And I take them both to a whole new level. We will be leaving for Texas in two days. I suggest you spend the time with your parents and your girlfriends. If you so much as hug a man that is not blood related, I will take it as a sign of disrespect. You are in my padre's territory, there is no place you can hide. If I do not see you before then, enjoy your stay in our hacienda. I suggest you think over your choices and your behavior." I turned and left my new bride fuming on the bed.

I was laughing as I made it to the stairs. Unfortunately, I was caught by my own parents as they were just coming off. Their room was down in the opposite direction. Padre took one look at my clothes and the bag in my hand and started laughing.

"Your wife kicked you out already, hijo?"

I laughed. "I'm sure she wants to now. I did my part and now I am going to hide. It will take a long time and a miracle before I learn to stand that woman."

My madre frowned. "Hijo, you have to give it time, you can't give up already."

Mi madre, bless her heart, was a romantic.

"Madre, I will give it time. I will try to get along with her. But not now. First, she needs to learn her place. She needs to learn to respect me and my position. She also needs an attitude adjustment. Tonight, I was discussing some very important things with Miguel. She interrupted, no apology, nothing. She put herself above that and refused to believe we were in a meeting."

Madre gave me a small sound of surprise, covering her mouth. My parents had been married for thirty years. She knew her place. She struggled with the mistresses in the beginning, but eventually, they became friends. She raised their kids with them, as though they were her own.

She nodded her head. "Her madre and I will speak to her over breakfast. Where will you be staying?"

I smirked and looked at my padre who chuckled and answered for me.

"He is currently enjoying his wedding gift from me. I knew Andre chose well. I just did not realize it was this well."

I smiled at him and my still confused madre. "Si, padre. If he had not made the mistake he had, I probably would have given him a bonus. He really did choose well. Now, if you will excuse me, it has been a long day." I kissed my madre's cheek and shook my padre's hand. "Buenas noches."

As I took the stairs to go one floor up, I heard him begin explaining his gift. I practically ran down the hall as soon as I hit the landing.

I checked my phone before unlocking the door. It was just barely eight. I carefully opened the door and called Elizabeth softly, not wanting to startle her.

"Hermosa?"

I looked around the room and knew a small moment of panic when I did not see her. I let out a long breath when I spotted her laying on the couch, asleep.

I set the bag down and locked the door behind me. I walked over to the couch and squatted down in front of her. I softly moved the hair off her face, she didn't move at all.

Since she was on her side, I unzipped her dress, then slid it off the one side. I carefully slid one of my arms under her head and the other under her knees and lifted her up. I carried her to the bed and laid her on her opposite side, allowing me to finish removing her dress.

I stripped my clothes off, turned off the light, and climbed in next to her. Before getting too comfortable, I sent a message off to Miguel.

Me: I'm with Elizabeth now. Assign someone to keep an eye on Elena. She is not happy. I don't trust her.

Miguel: That was fast. Did you do the deed?

Me: yes, with the lights off and picturing Elizabeth. Only way it would work. Then I showered and ran out the door.

Miguel: *laughing/crying emoji*

Miguel: Now that the job is done, enjoy your wedding night. *winky face emoji*

Me: good night, Hermano.

I plugged in my phone and silenced it. Seeing as this was my wedding night, and technically my honeymoon period, they should all be prepared to survive without me.

Who cares if it was not with my wife? I certainly didn't.

I laid down on the bed and moved into the middle, wrapping an arm around Elizabeth, and pulling her to me. She gave a small sigh, bringing a smile to my face. I fell asleep imagining what this day would have been like had she been my bride instead.

Chapter 8

Elizabeth

It had been one long, boring day. I watched a few movies. I ate the food that was sent up, and that was about it. I did laugh with the men that brought up the food. They both had been in tuxedos and introduced themselves.

Francisco was the first one to visit me. He was a very thin and tall man. He said he was one of Antonio's best friends, one of the few people he trusted. Which explained why he delivered my lunch, and not some random person. I didn't need more time with Antonio to fully understand the depth of his possessiveness of his belongings.

Dinner was brought by another man, who bore small similarities to Antonio. Miguel had the same height and build as him. However, he was a shade lighter both in skin and hair color. He said they were half-brothers, only a month apart. His mom was one of their father's mistresses.

That statement left me with a lot to think about.

It was comforting to know that if I were to have any children with Antonio, they would not be tainted by my status. I didn't like the sound of the "one of" though. Antonio said I would be the only one, but who knew what the future would bring.

It was kind of depressing knowing that I was beginning to care for a man who got married today, just a few floors below me. We wouldn't even mention the fact that I had been drugged, abducted, sold, then given as a gift. To that same man.

Yep, I was pathetic.

After dinner, I couldn't help but wonder if they were alone already. Was he doing to her what he did to me?

So far, he had treated me well, and he promised too always do so. But I never in my life imagined having to share a man with another woman, or *women*. I always imagined that I would meet someone and fall in love with them. Neither of us would have any desire to be with anyone else.

That was not the hand that life dealt me though.

I needed to keep in mind that I should be grateful for how this had turned out. I got lucky with Antonio. I could have had to stay behind with Paul.

When I woke up, it was pitch black in the room. I began to stretch out, thinking I should probably move to the bed. As I lifted my arms to stretch, I heard a deep moan and jumped with a squeak.

It was then that I became aware that I was no longer on the couch, or even wearing any clothes.

I felt a light kiss on my shoulder, and I smiled.

"Did I scare you, Hermosa?"

I enthusiastically rolled over to face Antonio and wrapped my arms around his neck. He came back to me! And on his wedding night!

"Just a little. I thought I was still alone and on the couch. Did you move me?"

He gave me a soft kiss on the lips. "Yes. I thought you might prefer the bed."

I lifted my eyebrows even though he couldn't see me. "Did you also remove my dress?"

I felt the silent rumble in his chest as he laughed. "Yes, I wasn't sure the dress would be comfortable to sleep in. Besides, I prefer the feel of your soft skin against mine."

He pushed me against his bare chest, demonstrating his point. I hummed my agreement and kissed his jaw. I was so happy he was here, that I didn't even think about what I was doing before doing it. As I continued placing kisses on his jaw, his hand slid down to my bare butt and held it tight to him. He didn't let me go much longer before he crashed his lips to mine and rolled us onto my back.

I pushed aside any thoughts about him, his new wife, or how I ended up here, and focused on the moment.

He left her and came back to me, that was the important part. Antonio said so himself. He didn't kiss, he didn't actually sleep with anyone; yet he chose to do both with me. With those thoughts spurring me on, I let him do whatever he wanted to me.

As our breathing settled back down, I fell back asleep, wrapped in his arms, feeling safe and secure.

The next morning, I woke up to an empty bed. I frowned as I sat up and looked around. The sun was barely poking through the curtains, but it was enough to see that the room was empty.

Where did he go?

I jumped when I heard the bathroom door open and then felt silly thinking he had left. He strolled back over to me, a smile on his face, and climbed back under the blanket.

He wrapped me in his arms and kissed my head. "Good morning, Hermosa? Did you sleep well?"

I smiled stupidly at his handsome face, I really loved that he called me beautiful all the time.

"I did, except for this part where I dreamt someone was mauling me in my sleep." I laughed as he began tickling me in retribution.

As soon as I could escape, I jumped up and ran to the bathroom. His eyes followed me the whole way.

When I came back, he was sitting on the side of the bed, typing on his phone. He set it down immediately and put his arms out for me as I walked back. I was still self-conscious about walking around naked, but Antonio seemed to prefer it that way.

He pulled me between his knees and kissed my stomach. I ran my hands through his black hair a few times. He laid his head against my chest and hummed. After a minute, he moved back just enough and pulled me onto his lap, facing him.

"I just ordered breakfast. It should be here soon."

I smiled. "And who will be delivering it today?"

He laughed. "No one special. Francisco practically begged me to let him deliver lunch yesterday. He made a good point that I can trust him more than the hundreds of strangers walking around yesterday. It was only fair that Miguel got a chance later too."

"Why did they want to deliver food so badly? Were they that bored downstairs?" I found it confusing that they both wanted to deliver my food to me. I was nobody important, and that was servant work.

Antonio laughed again and shook his head. "They wanted to meet you. Apparently, I was still very happy when I met them downstairs, right after I left you. They had to come up and meet this remarkable senorita who had such an effect on me."

I tilted my head and looked at him incredulously.

"Hermosa, you do not see yourself properly." Antonio laid his hand on my cheek, and I leaned into it. "You have this light about you. It attracts everyone to you and brightens our day. You are beautiful both inside and out. You have a kind soul. I can already tell how good you are going to be for me. I rarely laugh, hell, I rarely smile. Somehow you have changed that already. I am closer to them than anyone else. They knew something was different from the moment I walked into that changing room."

No one had ever said anything that sweet to me before, or that positive, period. I smiled and leaned in to kiss him.

"Thank you. That was the sweetest thing anyone has ever said to me." I kissed him again.

We were just building up the heat when there was a knock at the door.

I quickly moved off him and jumped under the blanket. He laughed and picked his pants up off the floor. I listened as he spoke to the other person in Spanish for a moment, then came back into the room with the cart full of food.

He locked the door behind him, dropped his pants, and came right back over. Antonio curled his finger, telling me to come. I smiled and crawled over to him slowly, keeping the sheet covering me. He growled, ripped the sheet down, and yanked me up off the bed.

I laughed as I wrapped my legs around his waist. It wasn't long before we were back on that bed.

Breakfast was an array of pastries, eggs, juice, and fruit. We sat on the couch, with my legs across his lap. Antonio fed me some of the strawberries. I giggled when he licked the dribbling juice off my chin. He also tried feeding me some of the melon. I took it a step further and sucked on his fingers as he slid the melon into my mouth.

I laughed as his response never changed. "Mujer malvada, me estás tratando de matar." (Evil woman, you are trying to kill me.)

After breakfast, he cleaned up our dishes and pushed the cart back out the door. I expected him to have to run off, so I was surprised when he sat back down next to me.

"What time do you have to leave today?"

"I don't. At least I don't have any plans to. I plan on hiding out here with you all day." He raised a questioning eyebrow at me. "Do you have a problem with that? If so, I might just have to teach you your place."

I tapped my chin and made a show of thinking it through. I laughed as he started tickling me again.

"Okay, okay. You can stay with me." I laughed so hard; I barely noticed him lifting me onto his lap again.

As we sobered up, I decided I needed to ask. "Elena's not going to be upset about not seeing you?"

He turned me to face him and placed both his hands on my face.

"Hermosa. I do not care what she thinks. I can't even tell you how miserable I was yesterday. Yes, she is probably ticked. She had steam coming out of her ears last night when I left her." He sighed and kissed my forehead. "I'm not going to lie. When she finds out my preference for you, she is going to lose her mind. She is going to make both our lives difficult. That is one reason why mistresses rarely live in the same home as the wife. But I don't care. It's you I want by my side. I will do my best to protect you from her, but I can't be around 24/7. I need to know that you will be able to stand up to her."

I smiled softly at him. "She won't be the first drama queen I've had to live with. Or my first bully. Don't worry. I'm tougher than I look."

His eyebrows made this sexy little crease above his eyes as they scrunched together. "Tell me about it."

"About what?" This time, I was confused about what he could possibly want to know about me.

"About living like that. About your life. I want to know everything about you."

Um, alright.

We spent the next hour, sitting just like that, talking about my childhood. Antonio never interrupted. Unless it was to ask a question for more details on something. He listened too, he truly listened.

I told him about losing my parents when I was little more than a baby. I told him stories about growing up in foster care. Some homes were somewhat decent. Others were trash bins.

TJ LEE

There were almost always other kids who were bigger and meaner. I would hide in my room, reading a book, just to keep my distance. They were usually playing video games and watching tv. They would never want to share, and they were always mean when I tried.

As I got older, I was moved into a group home. Since I was so quiet, foster parents always assumed there was something wrong with me. They never believed that I wasn't hiding things or sneaking out.

As a teenager, it was the adults who were the mean ones.

When I turned 18, I took the money the state gave me to get started and ran. Other than working as a bookkeeper for a bookstore, I rarely left my apartment. And I did most of that work from home.

He was silent after I finished. His thumb stroked my cheek softly. Finally, he commented. "I'm sorry you had to go through all of that. That explains why you have a hard time believing how wonderful you are and how beautiful you are. I'm going to make sure you never doubt that again. If anyone tries to make you feel less than what you are, you better put them in their place. As my woman, no one will be allowed to do that. You knock them down and then tell me. I'll back you up. Entiendes?"

I bit my lip with half a smile and nodded.

"That goes for Elena too. She will try to make you feel like you are below her. You're not. You are so far above her, that she will never be able to catch up. For our own sanity though, we will just let her think you are on equal ground."

I huffed out a small laugh. He kissed me gently and rubbed my back.

"Miguel and I were talking last night. I wanted to find a way to mark you as mine. Unfortunately, all the men know Elena is my wife. She wears the ring, and she will be living in the house. I do not want to risk anyone thinking they can treat you however they want to or touch you. At all. We came up with an idea and I really hope you're okay with it. If not, we can think of something else."

Well, this oughta be interesting, he actually seemed nervous. Antonio didn't strike me as the kind to get nervous.

"What is it?" I had been tracing his tattoo with the tip of my finger. I looked up and saw hunger in his eyes. I smiled and went back to tracing it,

68

following the dragon's tail down and then moving back up. Teasing him. "El Jefe?"

He barely smirked, but I felt the real reaction he had to that. "We were thinking of getting you a replica tattoo. An exact copy of my dragon."

I looked down at his chest. The dragon took up nearly his entire chest. "That is one big tattoo. Unless you want me to walk around topless all the time, I'm not sure how that will show people I am yours."

He chuckled. "No, Hermosa. I was thinking of a much smaller version." He picked up my left hand and tapped my ring finger. "Right here. If they are one of my men, they will recognize the tattoo and where it is. Anyone who is not part of our family, will just see a tattoo and not see you as a target. Would you do that for me?"

"Does anyone else have a copy of your tattoo?" I hated feeling so insecure, but I needed confirmation.

Antonio shook his head emphatically. "No, my tattoo is one of a kind. You are the only person I would share this with."

I smiled and went further down the dragon's tail, stopping at its tip, which was just above somewhere else. I looked him in the eye as he held his breath. I slid my hand further, keeping my eyes on his.

"If that is what you wish, El jefe. Then I would be honored to have you brand me with your tattoo."

I released him and wrapped both arms around his neck. Standing on my knees, I leaned into his ear and whispered, "make me yours." That was all it took before his fingers found me again.

We spent the rest of the morning in bed. Once we made it there. We had taken our time on the couch first.

After everything he had done to me in the last 36 hours, he worried that he may have hurt me. Antonio filled the large tub up with hot water and carried me to it. We soaked in the tub together until the water turned cold.

We talked about many different things, most of which were unimportant but still gave us a chance to learn more about each other. After the bath, Antonio pulled clothes out of his duffle bag and handed them to me.

"I should probably let you get dressed. It might help me keep my hands to myself." I laughed and put on the sweats he gave me. "Yeah, no. That's not going to help. You look exceptionally sexy in my clothes." He pulled me into him again and kissed me hard. I started laughing and pushed him away.

"No more of that."

He growled and pulled me in again, throwing me on the bed. He was on me before I could even take a full breath. His hand was already inside the extra-large shirt and his lips on mine.

Before we could go further, there was a knock on the door.

He groaned and moved off me. I was really glad we were both dressed this time, as we had not put in a request for lunch yet, even though we were nearing mid-afternoon.

Chapter 9

Antonio

The interruption was probably for the best. I didn't have any clue how many times I had violated my innocent little senorita since I found her hiding from me. Her body needed the break. It was exceptionally hard to control myself, knowing the strong personality she had inside.

After hearing her life story, I had two different reactions.

One was to go on a killing spree, and two, was to show her all the love and devotion she deserved, and then some. As it would be too much work to find all those people who hurt her, and she would not like that if I did, I went with the second route.

Killing was fun, sex was better. At least it was now. A week ago, I probably wouldn't have thought that.

Alright, so sex with Elizabeth was better. That was hands down, my favorite thing in the world. I was right too. The more comfortable she got with it, the better it would be. And we were only on day two.

I sighed as I stepped away from her on the bed. I picked up my phone but there were no missed calls or messages. I walked over to the door and opened it warily. I was a little worried Elena had found me. I shouldn't have. Very few people knew where I was, and not one of them would have told her.

Color me surprised when I opened the door and saw mi madre and Miguel's madre, Sandy, standing there.

"Uh. Hi?" I greeted them, completely confused as to why they were here.

They both smiled. Madre leaned forward, and I kissed her cheek. I did the same to Sandy as my madre spoke up.

"We just wanted to stop in and talk with you for a minute. We brought some treats." She waved to the cart next to them, filled with cakes and tea.

I smiled and shook my head. "In other words, Padre filled you in on his little gift and you wanted to come meet her."

They both nodded enthusiastically. I laughed and stepped back, allowing them entrance. I pulled the cart in behind them. We could probably use the refueling anyway.

Elizabeth wasn't on the bed anymore. From the looks of it, she must have hidden in the bathroom.

Well, I guess that was a step up from behind the couch.

I signaled for them to sit down. "She can be a bit shy around other people, especially since Andre is the one that "found" her, so take it easy. Please."

They both looked at each other, a moment of understanding passed between them. They both knew of Andre and his reputation. They both also had big hearts. Which was odd considering I always felt like my padre was a bit heartless.

I walked over to the bathroom and knocked on the door before opening it. I took it as a good sign that it was not locked, then again, I purposely hadn't shown her how to lock it.

She was sitting on the counter, looking adorably scared.

I walked over to Elizabeth and put my arms around her. I kissed her temple and leaned back to look in her eyes.

"Hermosa, are you alright?"

She shrugged and kept her eyes down. "Yes. I just got a little nervous not knowing who was at the door."

I figured as much. "It's mi madre y Miguel's madre. They want to meet you. I ran into my parents last night as I made my escape to come to you. Padre had to explain to madre about you. He knew I was running to you, he thought it was very funny. I had a feeling she would want to meet you sooner or later. I wasn't expecting Sandy though. They are like two peas in a pod, the best of friends. Will you come out with me and meet them?"

She took a deep breath and nodded.

I stepped back and put a hand up to help her down. I gave her a kiss and then led her out the door and toward the couch. I sat her on one end, and I sat across from her on the little table, still holding her hand.

The mothers noticed this and smiled.

"Madre, Sandy, this is Elizabeth. Hermosa, this is mi madre, Maria, and Miguel 's madre Sandy. Elizabeth met Miguel last night. He was kind enough to ensure that dinner was brought to her for me."

My madre spoke first, reaching a hand over to Elizabeth. "It's a pleasure to meet you, Elizabeth."

Elizabeth shook her hand a bit awkwardly.

"It's nice to meet you too." Her voice was soft. I squeezed her hand, reminding her I was there.

"Where are you from dear?" Sandy asked.

"Um, mainly New Orleans, in Louisiana."

"Ooo, I've always wanted to go there, it seems like such a fun place." She laughed.

Elizabeth shrugged her shoulders. "I guess. If you like going to parties and stuff maybe. I'm not much of a party person." She smirked. "I only ever went to a club once, and that was for my 21st birthday. It didn't exactly go the way I planned."

I couldn't help the quiet laugh that came out of me.

"Oh, why is that dear?" My madre looked at me, curious as to why I was laughing.

"Well... uh." Elizabeth looked towards me, lost on how to say it.

"Because it happened to be Andre's club." I finished for her. Both the mother's clicked their tongues with slight irritation.

Sandy reached to put a reassuring hand on Elizabeth's knee. "I am so sorry, sweet girl. We've seen a lot of awful things happen over the years, but that man is the worst."

Elizabeth nodded her head slowly in agreement. "It was definitely a new experience for me, but I got lucky. I wasn't picked up just to fill his chains." She looked at me and squeezed my hand.

"I should feel bad that he only grabbed you because of me, but I don't." I laughed.

She pulled her hand back and smacked me before taking my hand again. When I looked back at the mothers, both their faces showed a mixture of awe, shock, and confusion. Slowly they started to smile.

Yeah, yeah. I knew what they were thinking. I was a cranky jerk before Elizabeth came around. I smiled at them softly, acknowledging their reactions. I then picked up Elizabeth's hand and kissed it. Nonverbally explaining the reasons behind the change.

We spent the next twenty minutes with them getting to know Elizabeth. She slowly relaxed, feeling more confident and comfortable. I brought the tray of snacks over and fixed her a plate.

Mi madre looked so happy, I almost thought she would explode. A few minutes later, I walked them both to the door to say goodbye.

"I don't envy the position Elena is going to put you in. But I like that woman in there. She is good for you. I can tell. It's nice to see you smiling and truly happy for once. Keep her close, don't ever let her leave. Treat her right too."

I kissed her cheek. "Trust me, I know. I'm not sure how all this is going to work, but I am glad she is here. I can't imagine my life without her, even though it's only been just over a day."

"Awe, psh, time doesn't matter." Sandy waved that thought away. "Time can strengthen or weaken a relationship. The stronger you start out, the better it will be. Just hold her close, and all will be fine."

"We spoke to Elena this morning. I doubt she heard a word we said. Don't worry, no one told her about Elizabeth, yet." Mi madre padded my shoulder as she continued. "We will let you deal with that can of worms. Good luck." They turned with a wave and left.

I closed the door behind them and locked it. I turned and looked at my beautiful girl sitting on the couch. She smiled at me and raised her hand, silently beckoning me. I walked over and took her hand as I sat next to her.

"They love you. I told you, you have a light no one can ignore." She blushed and bit her lip. "Do you want me to order lunch now, or are you good for a bit?"

"I think I am good for now. Maybe in a little bit." She gave me this sexy mischievous smile before she curled her finger at me. "I may need to work up an appetite first." She leaned back and I leaned forward, until she was laying on the couch and I was hovering over her.

"Hmm. I don't know. I'm thinking you have quite the appetite already, just not for food."

"What can I say? I've become strangely addicted to what you do to me."

I kissed her slowly and responded against her lips. "I understand completely. I've never felt this hunger for someone before. I just can't get enough of you." I pulled back and looked down at her angel-like face. "Are you sure you are up for another round?"

"Si, El jefe. I may not be able to walk tomorrow, but it will be well worth it."

My hands were already pulling those ridiculously large pants off of her as soon as she called me boss again. Man, I loved when she said that.

I tried to take it easy on her, honestly, I did. But once we got started, I just couldn't stop. She wasn't the only one who would be walking funny after all this.

After we finished, I dropped next to her on the couch and we both fell asleep. We slept for about an hour, then I ordered a late lunch for us.

As we finished eating, we heard another knock at the door.

So much for not being bothered today. Elizabeth giggled when I groaned. What? I was comfortable with her legs across my lap like that.

I opened the door with a scowl. Si, I had a feeling it was them this time. "What do you two want?"

"Hermano!" Miguel called out.

"What do you want?" I repeated in a whiney voice just because I could. They both started laughing knowing darn well why I wanted them to go away.

Francisco was still laughing when he handed me a small purple suitcase.

"The mothers went shopping today. They bought a few different things for Elizabeth. Sandy said that having this will help her with Elena. Not sure how..." He had a moment of trying to figure it out and then shrugged it off. "Probably a girl thing."

"Maria also requested you both come down to dinner tonight. She wants to have a family dinner before we all leave tomorrow." Miguel added.

I scratched my chin, making me realize I never shaved today. "Uh, yeah. Is that going to be such a good idea? Won't Elena be there?"

He nodded. "Si, but maybe she will behave herself with more people around. This is going to have to happen sooner or later. Might as well get it over with now."

I sighed. "Yeah, all right. We will be down later then."

"Bueno." Miguel nodded and stepped back from the door. "Mom said they bought a dress specifically for tonight, it's in there."

They both turned and walked back down the hall as I closed the door.

Elizabeth was still where I left her on the couch, biting her lip nervously. She must have heard. At least she didn't hide this time. Progress.

I lifted the suitcase up and placed it on the bed. Out of curiosity, I unzipped it and opened it for her. On top there was a small garment bag, I pulled it out and set it on the bed. Next were a pair of black boots and a pair of black heels.

How did they know her size? I never got around to her making that list. I shook off the thought. Who knew with women? Especially mothers.

There was an assortment of underwear sets, shirts, jeans, and a smaller bag that looked similar to my traveling shower bag.

"Looks like they got you just about everything. I still don't understand why they thought all this would help with Elena." I commented as she came up behind me, sliding her arms around my waist.

That was her first time doing that. I kind of liked it.

"I do. I only know what you have told me about her. But I am assuming Elena is vain and materialistic." I nodded, oh boy was she ever. "When we leave tomorrow, I would have been leaving in your clothes with no luggage. No matter what happened after that, she would always look down on me as less than her. Your mothers are arming me and helping me to create a better first impression, for my sake as well as hers."

She moved around me and unzipped the garment bag. Inside was a black dress with a silver chain circling the hanger. I turned and wrapped her in my arms now, kissing her temple.

"You're right. This will make a much better first impression and will help you put her in her place."

Elizabeth leaned her shoulder into me and sighed. I couldn't tell if it was resigned acceptance or contentment.

"How long do we have until dinner?"

"A few hours still, you have plenty of time to get ready."

I rubbed her back lightly, neither of us moving. After a few minutes we went back to the couch and turned a movie on. Killing time.

Eventually, she left me on the couch to go shower and begin getting ready.

Chapter 10

Elizabeth

I locked the bathroom door behind me, having finally figured out there was one (it was a tiny little push button hidden by the knob), needing some space to get my mind in order.

I'd never had anyone buy me such nice things before, or anything at all for that matter. The foster homes only bought me clothes because they had too, and those usually came from Goodwill.

I was really touched by the mothers' generosity. Even more so knowing that this was their way of silently supporting me and welcoming me to the family.

I never felt welcomed before either.

I opened the toiletry bag while the water heated up. The bag held small bottles of top-of-the-line shampoo, moisturizers, body wash, a razor, deodorant, perfume, etc. The feminine side of me silently rejoiced.

I enjoyed that shower immensely.

I took the time to apply the moisturizer to my legs and arms. Ah, the feeling of being hairless again! Really, I wasn't that bad. I had shaved before going out the other night.

How long ago was that exactly? I really needed to ask to see a calendar.

Inside the small suitcase, I found a black strapless bra and matching underwear. Then, I pulled out a travel size hair dryer and a small round brush. I dried and curled my long black hair at the same time, giving it a little bit of a wave. Using the small clips from the bag, I pulled up the top layer into a clip.

I found makeup and carefully applied a natural colored smokey eye. I had watched many YouTube videos and had lots of practice before going to that club.

I took a deep breath and pulled the dress out of the garment bag.

It was an off the shoulder number, knee length, ending in an A cut. It had just enough flow to it that I could spin, and it would fly up, it made me giggle. The necklace was just a simple gold chain with a white feather that settled over my chest.

I laughed when I found a small bottle of red nail polish at the bottom of the smallest bag. I quickly applied it and waited for my nails to dry before putting on my heels. Before leaving the bathroom, I gave myself a quick spritz with the perfume. It had a subtle floral scent to it. I stood near the door, feeling both nervous and excited.

I had never dressed up for a man before.

After ten deep breaths, I opened the door and walked out. Antonio was sitting on the couch, watching something on the tv. He jumped up when I stepped out.

"Hermosa, wow... you... wow."

I giggled at his sudden lack of speech. I did a little turn, letting the skirt flutter around my thighs.

He walked over to me slowly, taking it all in. "Elizabeth, you look maravillosa. Absolutely stunning. I want to just keep you here, all to myself."

I smiled as his hands landed on my waist. "You like? Really?"

"Hmm, I like it very much, si." I recognized the look that flashed through his eyes and took a step back.

"Oh, no you don't! You are not messing this up." I held a finger up between us as a grin spread across his face. "No, Antonio. Don't you dare."

I squeaked as he yanked me hard against him. "Did you just tell *me* no? Tsk, tsk, tsk. I thought you knew better than to challenge me." His voice was deep and threatening. However, it wasn't shivers of fear that made my legs shake in the small heels. He knew it too and his grin got wider as he whispered in my ear. "I wouldn't dream of messing up this masterpiece."

He walked me backward, until my back was against the wall. His finger traced the neckline as it dug its way in and popped one side of me out. His mouth landed on me, causing me to moan. Before I knew it, my skirt was around my waist and his pants were gone.

He kissed my neck sweetly before leaving to shower and get ready. I stood there for a minute longer, catching my breath. I couldn't help the smile.

I loved the effect that I had on him. And him on me.

Fifteen minutes later he came back out, showered, and dressed in his black slacks and blue button-down shirt. I straightened back up from sitting on the couch and walked over to him. I gave him a small smile as I made a show of checking him out this time. He laughed and pulled me in for a hug.

"Are you ready for this, hermosa?"

I shrugged. "Yes and no. Every bit of this is new to me. Even the family dinner. Not to mention I have to compete with your wife. Which just sounds weird and wrong on so many levels."

He kissed my forehead and held me tight. "There is no competition between you both. She will act like it, but you are the one I want. She is business, you are pleasure. We need to find a way for us all to live in peace, but that is going to take time. Tonight, is just the first step. Please, remember, you do not have to fight to prove yourself to anyone, least of all her. Just be yourself." He kissed my cheek and down to my collarbone. "And when dinner is over, we will come back up here. Together."

Yeah, I couldn't respond. I was a sucker for his lips on my skin and he knew it. I was barely able to give a grunt in response. I felt the smile cross his lips. Such a jerk.

Antonio stepped back with a restrained sigh and held his hand up to me. I took it and let him lead me out of the room. I stalled at the open bedroom door. He gave me a reassuring squeeze and pulled me out.

Andre had kept me blindfolded as we entered three days ago. I couldn't help but look around and really take in my surroundings this time.

Wow. No wonder I'd never heard anyone outside the door. I had been staying at the end of a long hall, and then four floors up. It wasn't until we reached the bottom floor that I heard other people.

The whole house seemed to be decorated in traditional Mexican decor. For the first time, I actually felt like I was in another country. It was beautiful. Antonio led me down another hall until we reached what looked like a living room, but larger.

"Ah, there you are, hijo. Nice of you to join us this evening." An older gentleman greeted us. I recognized the voice, but the last time I heard it I had been blindfold.

"Good evening, padre." Antonio returned his greeting formally and shook his father's hand.

He then leaned over to Maria and Sandy, giving them both kisses on the cheek. Each had been sitting on either side of Antonio's father.

"Sandy, madre." They smiled in return saying hello.

He lifted my hand and pulled me in front of him. "Padre, this is Elizabeth. Elizabeth, this is mi padre, Oscar Ortiz."

Oscar offered his hand to me, so I accepted. However, instead of shaking my hand, he turned it over and kissed the back of it.

"Pleasure to officially meet you, Elizabeth. Welcome to the familia."

"Gracias, Senor Ortiz." I replied softly.

Sandy and Maria stood up and kissed my cheek. I whispered to them both "thank you."

They both smiled and told me I looked beautiful. I blushed and looked down. That was definitely not what I was used to, nor what I expected. Antonio placed his hand on my lower back and rubbed his thumb back and forth.

We all sat down on the sofas in the room and the men talked.

We were soon joined by Miguel, who enthusiastically gave me a hug and kissed my cheek. Antonio raised a warning eyebrow at him, which made Miguel chuckle.

Ten minutes later you could feel the air in the room shift and thicken. Everyone stiffened as someone new walked in.

"Husband, how nice of you to join us this evening. I was wondering where you had run off too."

I felt Antonio let out a long deep exasperated breath, one that said he was trying to control his actions. Oh yeah, he *really* didn't like her.

He stood up politely as she walked over, pulling me up with him, holding my hand like a lifeline. He leaned in and kissed her cheek. She tried to turn, making him land elsewhere, but she wasn't fast enough.

"Elena." Was all he said in greeting. Although it sounded more like a warning to me.

She huffed and then noticed me, a frown on her face when she saw our hands. "And who is this?"

Antonio stiffened at her attitude. "Elena, this is Elizabeth." She waited for more but didn't get it.

All was quiet as she took me in. Everyone's eyes were on us. I gave a small glance to Sandy who nodded subtly, encouraging me.

I put my other hand forward. "It's nice to meet you, Elena. I have heard a lot about you."

She incredulously met my hand for a weak handshake, it felt like shaking a dead fish. She was obviously still confused.

Thankfully the awkward moment was broken up by a man in a suit announcing that dinner was ready. Oscar took each of his women on an arm and walked out of the room. Antonio moved his hand to my lower back and led me out after. Elena huffed and followed behind. I couldn't help the small smile.

He may not have verbally told her, but his actions were speaking much louder. I went first, before her. The mothers were given equal treatment, she was not.

I could hear a deep masculine chuckle from the back. I assumed Miguel was being entertained.

Antonio pulled my chair out for me and then helped push it in. I saw he did the same for Elena, but with a grimace on his face. He then sat between the two of us. He reached for me with his left hand, letting it rest on my thigh, giving me a small squeeze. Elena watched this carefully with a raised brow but didn't say a word.

I followed the example of Sandy and Maria throughout dinner. I stayed quiet as the men talked, I was sure it had something to do with business and whatever else they were involved in. Just because I had grown comfortable with Antonio did not mean that I was comfortable talking to others yet, so I was good with the whole "women are meant to be seen not heard" method.

I had a feeling Elena didn't get the memo. She interrupted a few times, asking questions. They were rarely answered or even acknowledged.

"Why are you ignoring me?" She quietly demanded her answer from Antonio after, once again, not getting acknowledged.

He frowned at her. "We discussed this. You need to learn your place, when to speak and when not to speak, Elena. If you are unsure, follow the example of the other women at the table. Do you hear them interrupting?" He then turned away from her and back to his father.

I saw the small smile Miguel was trying to hide from across the table. When he saw me look at him, he winked at me.

TJ LEE

Antonio saw it too and scowled at him. Miguel's smile grew too full blown. He had to be well aware of Antonio's possessive nature and obviously enjoyed poking at it. It was obvious to me that these two brothers had a good relationship.

Elena didn't say another word throughout dinner, or even dessert.

The dinner was delicious. Having lost my biological family so early, I was not raised within the Mexican culture. Meaning, I had only ever had the American version of Mexican food. They failed in comparison to the real thing. At least my parents hadn't spoken much English, so I mostly spoke Spanish the first few years. I used it often enough since, that I didn't lose it as I grew up.

We started our meal with a pork pozole and then pork enchiladas. For dessert, we had individual tres leches cake. While we were eating the cakes, Oscar decided to turn the conversation to me.

"Elizabeth, is this your first time in Mexico?"

"Si, Señor Ortiz."

"Call me, Oscar, hija. We are family now."

I smiled softly and blushed as I nodded. Antonio squeezed my leg again. He knew what that would mean to me.

Elena made a scoff under her breath. The kind that said it was supposed to be hidden but you actually wanted someone to notice. We all noticed, and we all ignored it.

"Next time you all visit, we will have to take you to the markets and show you around." Maria volunteered.

"Gracias, I would really like that."

Our dishes were soon cleared away. At some unseen signal, Oscar stood up, followed by the mothers. Antonio stood as well and held his hand for me again. I took it and followed.

We all walked down the hall, back into the previous room. Oscar and Antonio led us to the couches. Oscar left small kisses on both the mother's heads and left them sitting.

Antonio led me to them, kissed my cheek softly then whispered, "stay with madre and Sandy, I will be back soon."

I nodded and gave him a small smile before I sat down, and he left.

Elena sat down with a huff, having been completely ignored by Antonio as he left. She sat in a chair across from us, with an ugly scowl on her face. It resembled that of a toddler who had just been reprimanded and lost their favorite toy.

"Alright, who the hell are you and why is *my* husband paying more attention to you than me?"

No one answered, as servants came in then with a tray filled with coffee and cookies. Elena at least had the sense not to discuss private matters in front of the servants. Well, I assumed that was why no one spoke. I did read a lot (perks of working for a bookstore) and had a pretty good imagination. Although it never conjured up any of these recent life changing events as a possibility when I planned to go out.

After they left the room, Sandy spoke up. "Elena, you need to work on your mannerisms and attitude. We spoke of this over breakfast. You are a grown woman. You are no longer in your father's household. It is time you learn when to shut your mouth and mind your own business. If you want to survive in this world at all, you better learn that lesson fast."

Wow, Sandy had snark. Never judge a woman by her silence.

Elena's scowl stayed in place.

"I have a right to be upset. My newly wedded husband abandoned me on my wedding night. Now, 24 hours later, he ignores me and gives more attention to another woman than he ever did to me. I have a right to know who she is."

"Elena, you already know how this world works. Antonio is allowed to have as many women as he wants, and he has no need to discuss it with you. The sooner you accept this, the happier everyone will be." Maria explained politely, and tiredly.

Elena gave me a snarky smile. "So, you are one of his side ho's?"

I scoffed. "Ho implies that I sleep around. However, Antonio is the only man I have ever been with. Something he prefers. As you said, he is your husband, isn't this something you should know?" The insult was very subtle, but she still caught the implication.

"How dare you!" She leaned over to slap me, but I caught her hand and held her wrist away from me.

"I strongly suggest you rethink this reaction." I scowled back at her.

She yanked her hand out of mine and sat back down with another huff and look of superiority.

"As the wife, I have power and authority over the household. You are just property that I can treat as I wish."

"Ha! I belong to Antonio, not you. If you dare raise a hand to me, you will be disrespecting him. I'm sure you understand better than I how men in this family feel about being disrespected." I took a breath before continuing. "Elena, I would much rather we learn to live in peace, or at least accept the other woman's presence. As Maria said, the sooner we learn to do this, the happier we will all be."

Elena sat in silence, slouching back into her chair, her arms folded in front of her. Such a petulant child.

"Mistresses come and go, wives stay. I will be the one to give him an heir, I will be the one to grow old with him."

I took a sip of my coffee before responding. "Sandy, how long have you been with Oscar?"

She grinned, understanding the point I was making. "28 years. I also bore him a strong son who holds a high position, right along with Antonio. It makes no difference that he was born from a mistress."

"None at all. Elena, many mistresses don't last but some do. They can be one of your best friends or they can be your enemy. I did not always treat them well either, but Sandy has become like a sister to me. I was unable to have more children after Antonio. Thankfully, he was still able to have many siblings. Sandy and I were pregnant together, it made the journey easier and more fun. The boys have always been more like paternal twins."

I gave them both a grateful smile for their support. Elena maintained her pouty attitude, while the rest of us talked of other things. After a bit, I decided to broach some of my concerns.

"Have you two always resided in the same house?"

"No, I had my own place for a time in the beginning." Sandy answered. "I wasn't the first mistress. The others rarely last long. Once I was pregnant with Miguel, Oscar moved me into the hacienda. It was a little touchy at times. Both Maria and I were pregnant and hormonal." They both laughed at the memory. "We about drove Oscar nuts. Eventually we turned to each other, and everything settled."

Maria asked the next question. "Has Antonio decided the living arrangements for Texas?"

I nodded. "Yes, he wants us all in the same house."

"That sounds like Antonio. He has always been protective and possessive. Even as a child he didn't like to share. Oscar fed into it, making sure he never had too. The house in Texas is smaller than here, but it is still large by American standards. I'm sure you will love it."

I smiled softly. Compared to the tiny apartment I had back in New Orleans; everything was bigger.

Chapter 11

Antonio

I walked into the hall after leaving Elizabeth, feeling nervous. I was sure the mothers would help if she needed it. I knew she was going to have to face this sooner or later. I just had to hope that I had helped her insecurities enough already that she would stand up to Elena.

Miguel was waiting for me in the hall with a big grin on his face when I walked out. "That was harsh, man."

"que?"

"The way you just walked right by Elena and ignored her." He laughed, obviously entertained with my dramatic life.

"If she wants attention from me, then she needs to learn her place first." I replied as we walked into our padre's office.

"Exactly. Elena has been warned many times already. If she refuses to learn her lesson, you will have to find a new way to teach her." Padre added his opinion as we sat down across from his desk.

By his voice, you would have thought we were referring to the weather. I wasn't around when mother was learning her place, but I had seen him with his newer mistresses. I had my ideas. Madre was very docile when he was around, something she wasn't when he was gone.

"I will give her a few days to settle into her new home in Texas. If she does not fix this on her own. I will find a way to do it for her." I told him confidently.

He nodded his approval. "Elizabeth is a quick learner. I was impressed with her behavior tonight."

I smiled. Yes, she did very well.

"Elizabeth has had a rough life. The very opposite from Elena. She learned from a young age to keep herself invisible for her own safety. She is not completely comfortable around other people. I know it meant a lot to her that you treated her like family. She has never had that. Elizabeth will perform her position well." I gave a small laugh. "She will probably perform Elena's as well."

"Where is Elizabeth going to be staying?"

"With me. I want her close, for her safety and my preference. Andre made it very clear he would be more than happy to take her back. One of his men also had his eye on her. I wouldn't put it past them to try and recollect her and hide her."

Padre scoffed. "That would be very foolish of him." He sighed in frustration. "But I can see your reasoning. She is a beautiful girl, and she has this... thing about her that draws people's attention. You will need to watch her close and make sure your men know as well. I don't need you killing off half our men because they couldn't control their animalistic sides."

Miguel and I looked at one another. "Yes, we discussed this last night. Elizabeth has already agreed as well. I am going to take her to my personal tattoo artist and replicate my dragon on her ring finger. All my men are familiar with my tattoo, with the placement on that finger, it will symbolize who she is and her standing with me. In addition, Miguel and I were thinking of getting her a necklace with a tracker. If anyone were to take her again, I would be able to find her."

"You are placing her above Elena." It wasn't a question.

"Yes. Elena will need to earn her place. We were informed that Elena continued visiting with a man just hours before the wedding. Those visits should have stopped the moment the contract was signed. I do not trust her. Nor do any of us trust her family."

Padre nodded his head slowly. "They will not be happy when she complains about this, but they are lucky we did not cancel the contract. We had every right too." He sighed again and leaned back in his chair. "Alright, I trust your judgment. If she proves to be untrustworthy and breaks the contract again, then you have my permission to deal with it as you see fit. We have clauses in the contract for just such occasions. We will still benefit if this fails. What time do you leave tomorrow?"

"I told our pilot to be ready by noon. It will be a long flight."

"When is your next meeting with Sanchez?"

"We have a virtual meeting Sunday, the day after we get home. They have had a small hiccup with one of their cleaners recently. Thankfully the man kept them out of it, but he had been a highly profitable cleaner. That was a little over a year ago. The cleaner was released from prison on a technicality, but then disappeared. Sanchez felt it was necessary to play it safe. There were too many FBI eyes on them. He mentioned an American family located in Northern California that he has worked with in the past. They were involved in the incident last year, but they warned him of the danger in time for him to cover his tracks. They will have a representative on the call as well. I will let you know what happens from there."

"Good, good. California is mainly Valdez territory. Strengthen our hold up there, it will help with taking them out. Now, las madres wanted me to ask." I rolled my eyes with a grumble knowing what was coming. He chuckled. "When can they expect nietos? They both like Elizabeth. They came to me this afternoon and told me about the visit. Maria especially was happy with your interactions."

I laughed. "Madre is such a romantic. But si. Elizabeth makes me happy. As you said, there is just something about her. She has many deep-seated insecurities. I want her to feel confident in her place in the family. Most mistresses choose this life, she didn't get that choice. We also know not all of them can handle it. Elizabeth will, I have no doubts. As for nietos... I don't know. We haven't exactly been careful. Elena," I shook my head slowly, "I won't touch her without protection. I could barely touch her last night as it was. I only managed it because I kept the lights off and thought of Elizabeth. It was not a proud moment for me. Elena was very offended, and she doesn't even know what it took for me to get the job done."

Both of them busted up laughing. They were very familiar with my revulsion of sharing a woman with other men. It had never caused such a problem though.

As soon as my padre could speak again, he did so. "As long as you don't wait too long. You know both tus madres are hungry for nietos. They have been spending time with bebe Lydia lately. I offered to have them move in, but Veronica wanted to keep her own space."

Lydia was our newest sibling. Veronica was in her mid-twenties like us and was our padre's newest mistress. She was not one for the long haul but enjoyed the benefits that came with it.

I didn't know how my padre did it. The two women alone were already too much for me to handle. I knew he loved mi madre, and maybe even

Sandy, on some level, but he just couldn't resist dipping into every pool he could find.

Padre stood up and we followed him. "You all should get some rest. We probably gave the women long enough to try and set Elena straight. I'm curious to know how it all has played out." He walked out with an eager grin on his face.

Miguel and I both just shook our heads silently. We had been gone for a little over an hour. I was curious and nervous to know as well.

Elena was sitting back in her chair, a frown on her face. The other three women were talking quietly across from her. My chest warmed at the small laugh coming from Elizabeth.

From the looks of it, Elizabeth was holding her own well, and Elena was not.

"Come, my beautiful Senoras. It is time to retire." Padre put both his hands out for the madres. They took them and rose. "Sleep well, my dear." He said to Sandy and kissed her lightly before handing her over to Miguel.

"Buenas noches, hijo." I leaned down and kissed my madre's cheek. She whispered in my ear. "She did well. Put Elena in her place."

I chuckled softly at the pride in her voice. "Buenas noches, madre. I'll see you in the morning." The others quickly left, leaving me alone with my two women.

Yikes. How to handle this situation?

I walked over to Elizabeth first and helped her up. I pulled her in for a quick kiss.

"Hola, hermosa. Are you ready to turn in?"

She leaned her head on my chest. "Si, por favor." She covered a small yawn and I chuckled.

Elena cleared her throat aggressively. I turned with a sigh and offered her a hand as well.

"Elena."

She took it with a small smile. "What? No kiss for me as well? I am your wife."

"Then you should learn to act like it. As I told you yesterday, I rarely kiss." I shrugged and winked at Elizabeth. "She is an exception. Now, come. It is time we all retire. We have a long day tomorrow."

I removed my hand from Elena as soon as she was standing, but she grabbed onto my arm. I kept my other arm around Elizabeth's waist, holding her close to me. We walked up the stairs in an awkward silence. I brought us to a stop on the third-floor landing.

I not so gently removed my arm from Elena's tight grip. "Have a good night, Elena. Be ready to leave for the airstrip at 1130." She huffed as she walked away.

I turned Elizabeth on to the next set of stairs, leading us up to our room.

I unlocked our door and held it open for her. She quietly walked by me, but my grip on her arm wouldn't let her go far. As I closed it, I pushed her against the door and locked it while I kissed her hard. I slid my hands up her dress and onto her butt, lifting her up.

"You did magnificent tonight, hermosa. Even mi padre was impressed." I told her as I carried her to the bed.

"It wasn't that hard. I just copied the mothers." I unzipped her dress before setting her back on her feet. "Thank you for the way you put me first tonight. I can't tell you how much that meant to me."

"Hermosa, I told you. You always come first." I pushed her dress down to the floor, leaving her in nothing but her heels and underwear.

She stepped out of the dress and walked around me. I turned, keeping my eyes on her. She began unzipping my pants, then pushed them down before pushing me onto the bed. I groaned at her touch.

"Well, I think it is time to put you first now." She went down to her knees, and I went up to heaven.

We didn't go to sleep for a long while, but when we did, we were both exhausted and satisfied.

We really should talk about the baby thing. While I enjoyed the way we were, the more I thought about it, the more I loved the idea of my baby being in her belly. I just wanted to make sure Elizabeth was ready for that first.

Her life had completely turned around on her. I wanted her to settle in and for her to be comfortable before we took that next step.

Up until a few days ago, I never would have believed that I would prefer to sleep with a woman, rather than alone. I was horribly wrong. There was nothing better than waking up to a beautiful woman in your bed.

Well, to a certain beautiful woman in my bed. I have had many women try to get me to stay the whole night, I just always refused.

I already couldn't imagine not having Elizabeth next to me. Which was why I decided we would be sharing a room when we got home. It would just be a waste of time and space to give her a room of her own.

I laid there after waking, watching her while she slept, enjoying the sight laid out before me.

She still had the pure and innocent look. After the last few nights, I knew she was not all that innocent anymore. It was more her soul and personality that helped her maintain that purity. With everything she had been through, the way she was treated, most people would turn hateful and violent. Not her though.

That was just not Elizabeth. She was all heart. I just hoped that my world didn't taint her and harden her. I liked her just the way she was.

She slept facing me, her head resting on my forearm. I lightly moved a hair behind her ear, it was obstructing my view. Speaking of views. I lifted the sheet and blanket up just enough to look down.

"What do you think you are doing?" She mumbled softly, with her eyes still closed.

I gave a small laugh, not feeling the least bit of shame. "Enjoying the treasures gifted to me."

I slowly pulled the sheet back and down, revealing those assets I had been enjoying the last few days. And technically now owned. She laughed softly and then gave a small shiver.

"Are you cold?"

"Ya huh. Some jerk took my blanket and let the cold air hit me."

"It was blocking my view."

She shook her head and rolled onto her back. "Is that better?"

I hummed and swallowed. "Much."

Her body reacted to the cold air. I frowned. She really was cold. My frown quickly morphed though. Guess I should help her warmup then. I rolled on top of her and used my body heat and movements to warm her back up.

I wanted to wake up like this every morning.

I joined her in the shower after ordering breakfast. Why would anyone ever want to shower alone?

I pulled the breakfast cart in while she got situated on the couch, both of us still in our towels. She learned my preferences fast and had adapted to them.

Today's breakfast was French toast and strawberries, with syrup and whip cream.

Si...we were going to need another shower. We didn't even make it halfway through breakfast before I carried her to the bed and commanded her to stay.

I went back to the table and grabbed the whip cream and strawberries. I poured the whip cream on her various parts, she laughed and squealed as the cold cream hit her. I dipped the strawberries in the cream and fed them to her.

I then took my time cleaning off the last of the cream, one lick at a time. It only took one lick to get to the center of my tootsie pop, didn't mean I was done after that one lick though. Elizabeth took her turn with the whip cream on me next.

I was right, another shower was needed. It got a bit sticky.

As we finished our breakfast, I decided that it was time to ask about last night.

"How did it go after dinner?"

She shrugged. "It was fine. Elena got a little demanding and whiny. At one point she tried to slap me, but I caught her hand."

I growled. I did not like the sound of that. Elizabeth put her palm to my cheek, rubbing her thumb softly back and forth. She deflated my anger faster than I had ever been able to before. At least without violence anyway.

"She didn't touch me, and I put her in her place. I'm good, honestly." I kissed her palm and then she continued. "She did try to tell me that she is in charge of the household, and I was just property, so she could treat me however she liked. I reminded her that I belong to you and only you. If she were to raise a hand to me or treat me badly, then she would be disrespecting you. That would not end well for her. Mostly I talked to the mothers. They tried to give advice on how it would be easier if we could get along from the beginning. Elena was grouchy and mopey for most of it. She was scolded for her behavior by both of them."

Elizabeth explained it all like it was no big deal, just another night. I felt a bit ashamed for my concerns. She handled herself well, even defending herself against Elena. I hoped she could hold to that confidence without the mothers there to back her up.

I pulled her onto my lap and kissed her, I seriously could not get enough of kissing her.

"I'm proud of you for standing up to her. I will speak to her again today and back up what you said. She needs to know that behavior will not be tolerated. Thank you for telling me."

Elizabeth played with the hair on the back of my head, I practically purred. I loved when she did that.

"You told me that was what you wanted." She leaned in and continued with her lips brushing against mine. "I will always do as you wish, El jefe."

I closed the last space between us, my hands on her bare back holding her tight against me.

She was standing on her knees, my fingers down below, and my mouth enjoying what was right in front of me... when my phone started ringing.

I dropped my head on the back of the couch and basically whined in frustration. Why me?

I felt her small hands grab me and then slide her hips down carefully.

"Hermosa..." I dragged it out as I half-heartedly complained. "I have to answer that."

She leaned down and started kissing my chest as she moved back and forth. "So, answer it."

I laughed. Alright, we could play this game. I reached around her and grabbed my phone off the table.

"Buenos días, padre." It would have to be him. I barely swallowed the moan bubbling up in my throat as her teeth grazed along my chest..

"There is a storm headed this way. The pilot says you take off in the next hour or leave another day. You have business you need to get back for."

"Tell him we will be there. Please send someone to let my men and Elena know. We will be down in twenty minutes." I hung up the phone and joined Elizabeth. It would speed things along and be more fun.

"Time to go?" She asked breathlessly as we both sat still for a moment.

"Si, we need to get moving. But I need a minute."

She giggled and began softly peppering me with kisses again. Seeing as she had not gotten up yet, my body reacted.

I laughed. "Hermosa, do you know what you are doing to me?"

She picked up my hand and placed it on her chest. "Are you saying you want me to stop?"

I groaned. No, it was too late for that now. "If you can't walk, it's your own fault." I told her as I swiftly changed us to her back on the couch.

"It will be well worth the price."

Twenty-five minutes later we stepped on to the first floor. I held my bag over my right shoulder, and her suitcase in my hand, my left hand kept her hand prisoner.

Miguel and Francisco were both waiting with knowing smiles.

I handed them the suitcase and my bag. "Shut up and put these in the car. Is everyone else ready to go?"

"Si. The men are outside. They are finishing loading up all of Elena's bags now. The plane has been loaded with food for the trip and gassed up. We were just waiting on you." Miguel ended with a wink at Elizabeth.

She blushed and buried her face in my shoulder. Si, still innocent in many ways.

"Let's go then."

My parents stood near the door. We bade them farewell. Elizabeth hugged the mothers before we left. Elena stayed standing near the car, a scowl on her face.

We all loaded into the two SUVs and took off. I had only brought five extra men with me. We always travelled with enforcers for extra security, but my padre had plenty roaming the hacienda, we didn't need to bring many.

The pilot met us outside the plane. "How are we on time?" I asked him.

"Fine, sir. Right now, it is only a category two hurricane. They believe it will make its way through the gulf coast, should reach us tonight. I just want to be safe. With all the water between it and us, it could strengthen before then."

I patted his shoulder as we turned towards the stairs. "I agree. Thank you for keeping an eye out. We have precious cargo flying with us today."

He peeked around me to Elizabeth who was still holding my hand and to Elena standing behind her.

He smiled. "Looks like you are bringing home two treasures from this trip, sir." I laughed but did not comment.

One treasure? Sure. The other? Eh, maybe, maybe not. Time would tell.

The plane took off moments later, just long enough for the attendants to get the door secure. The flight was long and uneventful, thankfully. We only had a small level of turbulence for most of the flight.

Elizabeth was scared, so I held her close. I should have asked her before if she had ever flown, I had a feeling the answer was no. I would wait until later to talk to her about it though, without all the extra ears.

Dinner was an assortment of tacos. Which proved an interesting feat with all the turbulence.

The flight lasted for nearly seven hours. A little longer than our pilot's normal time, but it was to be expected. It was still faster than some commercial airlines.

With us leaving nearly two hours earlier than planned, we barely made it back at our scheduled time.

Chapter 12

Elizabeth

Never want to fly again. Nope. Nuh uh. Never.

I didn't mind the part where Antonio kept his arm around me and was trying to comfort me. That was sweet.

I *really* did not like the turbulence though.

I heard them talking about the incoming hurricane. I felt the rush to get back to land and in the house before it hit. Growing up around New Orleans, I had been through my fair share of them.

Katrina even took my parents from me. They didn't survive the flooding. I didn't like talking about it because when I mentioned it as a kid, my foster parents would always scowl at me and say everyone lost things because of Katrina. My parents weren't *things*. They never liked it when I would say that.

Antonio kept me on the plane while everyone else got off. It seemed as though everyone was ready to get off that plane. I wanted to run down those stairs and kiss the ground, but I patiently waited. As soon as the last person stepped out the door, he turned to me.

"Are you alright?"

I gave him a half smile. "Yes and no. Not sure I ever want to fly again. That was pretty rough."

He pulled me onto his lap and gave me a gentle kiss. "The flights are rarely that bad. It was only because of the weather. You were safe the whole time. If it had been too bad, we would have landed sooner. I will never put your life in danger. I promise you that."

I put my arms around his neck. "I know. Having you right next to me made it better. I trust you. Now, can we get off this plane and onto the firm ground?"

He chuckled. "Whatever you wish, Hermosa."

Everyone had already loaded up into the cars, in a hurry to get a move on it. The winds were heavy, the storm was definitely coming our way.

We had a fifteen-minute drive back to the compound, as Francisco called it. When we got there, we pulled through a large gate that opened after

Miguel put in the code. The driveway was just shy of quarter of a mile deep. The house was actually a Spanish style Villa. It was gorgeous in its different shades of browns. It was like stepping into the past.

From the size of the outside, I was definitely going to get lost in there.

"Welcome, home." Antonio whispered softly in my ear, for only me to hear.

Home. I had never actually had a real home. Definitely not a permanent one. And this was. This was permanent. I was forced into this new life, literally, but I was going to make the best of it.

Antonio got out of the car first, then helped me out, then Elena. I knew he had to give her some attention (even though I didn't like it), technically they were married. I was going to have to bite back any hard feelings and try to make this work.

Even if a big part of me was hoping she would screw it up so badly that he would send her on her way. He mentioned, over breakfast, what his father said and gave him permission to do. I wasn't sure I would be okay with it going that far, I just wanted her gone.

"Elena." He greeted her as he helped her out of the car. "Before we go in, we need to discuss something."

"Oh, and what is that? We've been on the same plane all day, and now you want to talk to me?"

A small frown formed on his face. "The plane was not an appropriate place to discuss personal matters. The men have no need to hear such details. You will do well to remember that. You would also do well to remember that you do not speak to me in such a manner." When she didn't respond, only continued to scowl at him, he continued. "I heard about what was said last night and what you tried to do. You do not run this household. I do. You were given the privilege to be my wife, but you have not earned the benefits. If you ever treat anyone in my household with disrespect, it will affect you poorly. And if you ever, I mean ever, raise a hand to Elizabeth again, you will not see mercy from me. You have blatantly disrespected me time and again. I will not take any more of it. I could have canceled our agreement the very first time you stepped out. When was that, by the way? Two hours after you signed the contract?"

Elena at least blushed and looked down in shame. Or maybe it was just embarrassment for being caught.

"The only reason I followed through was for business purposes. I suggest you think long and hard on what you want. If you want out of this deal, then say so now. If you choose to stay, then you better cut the attitude. You have been counseled by many people regarding this. It is time to set your pride aside and follow that counsel or return to your parents and your lover."

With that, he took my hand again and led me into the house. Was it bad that I found that kinda hot?

"Tomorrow, I will take you for a tour of the grounds," Antonio promised as we walked in the front door, his tone and demeanor back to normal, as though nothing out of the ordinary had just happened. "With the storm coming, I want you safe and in the house. My men have already been working on securing the windows and other parts of the house. We have a generator in case the power goes out. We also have plenty of water and canned goods. This house is two hundred years old but has been updated. It will survive anything. We are still only at a category two status, nothing to be concerned about."

"Yeah, that's what they said about Katrina." I mumbled as I looked around the entrance way.

Wow. The house was so beautiful. The roof had rows of wooden beams. The halls had those circular pathways. Most of the walls were made with stone. The furniture was modern, the floors were hardwood with designer rugs that continued the Spanish theme.

"Why do you say that?"

Oops. I didn't mean for him to hear that comment. When I didn't answer, he pulled my arm to a stop.

"Elizabeth?"

I sighed. "I lived through Katrina, Antonio. New Orleans, remember? I was still barely more than a baby. I may have survived, but my parents did not."

I looked around the room at the people coming in and out, preparing for the storm. My silent plea to not talk about this right now. A plea he heard, and respected.

Antonio pulled me into his arms. "We can talk about this later. I'm sorry, I did not realize that is what happened." He left a soft kiss on my temple, rubbed my arm, and started walking again. "Let's go get unpacked while we still have power."

We walked up a flight of stairs that were tucked along the wall. Then down a hall and up another flight of stairs. He pointed things out as we walked.

"The first floor holds the dining room, the kitchen, a gym, and two living rooms. As well as the laundry room, my office, and a guest bano."

When we reached the second floor, he pointed down each hall. "To the left, we have three guest suites, down the right, we have three more. Up here, on the third floor, is where we all reside. To the right, we have four rooms. Elena, Miguel, and Francisco are down there. To the left," he turned us down that way, "we have three more. Our suite is the largest, and the only one on the right. The other two are across the hall and share a bano."

At this point he opened the door to our suite and gave me a moment to take it all in. We had a fireplace on one side of the room, with a sitting area and a large tv. The colors were both cream and natural.

Another wall held floor to ceiling windows surrounding French doors. They led onto a large balcony. In the middle of the room was a California King bed, with curtains on the frame. I always wanted one of those.

I was vaguely aware of Antonio locking the door behind us, as I walked toward the last wall which held two sets of doors. The doors closer to the corner led into the largest closet I had ever seen. You could have fit my entire apartment in there.

The next set of doors was actually two large barn doors. I slid them to the sides, opening up a large spa-like bathroom. The tub could fit four people, same with the walk-in shower. One whole side of the bathroom was taken up by a counter.

I walked back out to the room, where Antonio stood near the bed, watching me with a smirk on his face. I went back to him and put my arms around him.

"This is absolutely gorgeous. I love it!'

He chuckled. "I'm glad you think so."

"Is this for both of us? Will you stay here with me?"

"Yes, I can't imagine not waking up to you every morning. It would just be a waste of rooms." I smiled at the sweetness of the thought but then frowned. He rubbed his thumb under my lip. "What's the matter?"

"I feel a little guilty."

His eyebrows displayed his confusion. "For what?"

I bit my lip. "A couple things actually, first. Most girls who are kidnapped and sold off like cattle are not this lucky. Second, I feel like I stole you from Elena. I just came out of nowhere and took her place."

He chuckled and held me in a tight hug. "I am the lucky one. Who knows who I could have ended up with? When my padre first told me what he did, I hadn't planned on keeping you. I have no interest in being a man whore like mi padre. The moment I saw you, touched you, felt you, I knew I couldn't let you go. As for Elena," he gave a short sardonic chuckle, "you haven't affected her at all. I already had her room arranged down the hall *before* I even left for Mexico. I would have treated her the same regardless of whether you were here. What you did was improve my life. I thought I was going to be miserable for the rest of my life because of her. Instead, you showed up and made me happier than I have been in a long time."

He laid his forehead on mine, and we both closed our eyes, just taking in the moment. Which he interrupted when he started kissing me. Which was also when someone interrupted with a knock on the door.

He grumbled as he stepped away from me. I laughed and sat on the edge of the bed.

"We have all the outdoor furniture locked up and most of the windows completed. We just need to do your balcony, sir. Oh, and we have your luggage as well."

"Gracias, Orlando. Just set the bags on the bed." Antonio stepped out of the way and three men walked into the room. "Caballeros, I would like to introduce you to Elizabeth. She is my mistress. Even though Elena is here, Elizabeth is the one you go to for anything. I expect everyone to keep an eye on her for me. No one is to harm her in any way. Entiendes?"

"Si, El Jefe." They all said.

I bit back the laugh at the term. They came up to me and introduced themselves, with a kiss to my hand. There was no way I was going to be able to remember all these names. I already forgot the names of the men who flew with us. Except for Francisco and Miguel, obviously.

"Bueno. Go ahead and finish up then." Antonio had walked back over to me, placing his hand on my lower back. "Shall we unpack, hermosa?" I nodded and turned to the closet with him.

It only took us a few minutes to get everything put away. The dresser was built into one side of the closet. Even with all of Antonio's clothes, there was still a ton of space.

"I will take you out after the storm passes to go shopping. Maybe the same day we take care of that tattoo."

"You mean when you brand me as yours?" I teased him. Antonio threw his head back and laughed.

He lifted my left hand and kissed my ring finger. "If I had my way, I would brand you many times over, so there was no doubt who you belong to. I also want you to pick out a necklace. I want to spoil you. Plus." He took a breath and looked into my eyes. "I want to put a tracker in the necklace. Just as a safety precaution. It will only be turned on in the event that you disappear on me."

I placed a hand on his chest. "So, not only are you going to brand me, but now you want to chip me?"

He laughed happily and leaned down to kiss me. "You are mine, hermosa. I will protect you in every way possible. I have many enemies. I need to know that if you get taken again, I can find you and kill any who dare to take you from me." His voice had that deep threatening tone again.

I was practically whimpering by the time he finished talking.

He chuckled. "What?"

"That voice, do you have any idea what it does to me? That possessive, dangerous voice?"

"Hmm, tell me."

I unbuttoned my jeans. "It would be better to show you."

He took the hint and slid his hand inside. I gasped at his gentle touch. He groaned and kicked the closet door closed.

"All that from just my voice? The voice that I use to scare people with, turns you on?" His tone sounded like a mix of pride and disbelief.

I nodded and moaned some more as his hand was still there. Using that same voice, he began giving commands of what he wanted, all the while still playing inside my pants.

As we laid on the rug in the closet a few minutes later, panting, he held me in his arms tight. It wasn't until we heard the bedroom door close that I remembered there had been other people in the room. I covered my face and he laughed.

"Don't be embarrassed, hermosa. I doubt they cared what we were doing in here. Come, let's get up off this hard floor." He helped me up before checking to make sure the room was in fact empty. "Are you hungry? We can go down and get a snack before bed. Most of the staff returned to their own homes to ride out the storm hours ago."

"A small snack, then bed sounds good. I am pretty tired." I blushed as he laughed happily. He was obviously not embarrassed in the least bit.

We pulled our clothes back on and made our way down to the kitchen. The setup of the house was fairly simple, maybe I wouldn't get lost too often then.

The kitchen had the same stone and wood around it as the rest of the house, but overall, it was a modern kitchen. All the amenities were in silver. There was a fairly large white and black marble island with stools circling it.

Antonio led me to those and then he walked to the fridge and started pulling out various items.

"Does a sandwich sound good to you?"

I nodded. "Yeah, that's fine."

He made quick work of it, even though he went all out with tomatoes, lettuce, avocado, and even sprouts. As he was finishing up, the kitchen door opened again.

"You make enough for all of us, hermano?" Miguel teased.

"Nope, you can fix your own." Antonio brought the plates over to the island and sat next to me. "Did you make sure everyone got settled in somewhere?"

Miguel answered as he began making himself a sandwich, Francisco walked through as he did so.

"Si, Luis chose to go home. He said it was close enough that he could make it. Besides, his wife is seven months pregnant with their first bebe. He didn't want her alone, just in case."

"Understandable." Antonio rubbed his hand on my lower back. "I would feel the same way." I knew his hand was subtly telling me that he would be there for me too.

Soon enough, the kitchen was filled with men of every size. Tall, short, skinny, and hulk size. I was surprised that not all of them were Mexican. Two were blonde, and one had red hair. They all appeared to get along well enough.

One of the men that I had met in the bedroom smiled and winked at us as he came in. I blushed as he set a bottle of water down in front of Antonio, reminding him to hydrate. I hid my face in Antonio's shoulder, which caused them all to laugh, including Antonio. He was such a brat.

"Francisco, what's the word on the storm?" Antonio asked him, trying to change the subject for me.

"Reports say that it is hitting landfall about now. Still ranking as a category two. It might be a loud night, but it should be gone by morning. The house is locked up tight, cars are in the garage, windows are secure, all that jazz is done."

Antonio stood up, pulling me along with him. "Bueno. Make sure someone checks on Elena before you all turn in. See if she needs anything. Get it for her. She is a long way from home, and I don't know if she has been through a hurricane before. Oh, and Miguel. Make sure everyone is caught up on the change in authority."

"Will do. See ya all at some point tomorrow." Miguel responded with another wink. There were lots of chuckles around the room.

Antonio laughed. "Don't be jealous, hermano. We'll find you a senorita, too. She won't be as pretty as mine, but we'll find you something."

I blushed again and tried to walk out of the room as fast as I could. He followed and wrapped his arms around my waist, effectively slowing me back down, as we walked.

"What change in authority?" I asked him.

He kissed my neck. "You."

Ah, right. Change because they were only expecting a wife to come in, instead they got a wife and a mistress. And on top of that, we flipped the roles.

We slowly made our way back up the stairs. It was slow moving because he kept his arms tight around me. His hands slowly made their way under my shirt, onto my bare skin. When we hit the second set of stairs, one of them started inching higher.

I laughed as it started digging under my bra. "Hungry again, already?"

He kissed my neck, and his answer came out mumbled. "I seem too always be hungry for you."

As we turned down our hall, his hand made it all the way up and started massaging me. I laid my head against his chest and let the moan ripple out. His other hand started making work on my pants.

He had to stop that though when he unlocked our door. He refused to let go of me with his other hand. After we heard the click of the lock moving into place, we used the last of our energy reserves in the bed.

I woke a few hours later to the sounds of the wind banging around the house and tree branches breaking and flying. I jumped and screamed as it startled me.

Antonio held me tighter and tried to soothe me.

"Shh, hermosa. It's just the wind. You are safe right here with me." His voice was soft and smooth, despite being ripped out of a deep sleep. I looked up into his face, and he kissed my forehead. "What can I do to help?"

"I don't know, distract me. Talk to me about something, anything."

He stayed silent as he thought about what to say. "Alright, well. I've been meaning to talk to you about something, but it hasn't been the right time. I guess now is as good a time as any." I looked at him quizzically. "How do you feel about ninos? Are you ready for that or do you want to wait?"

Well, that was one way to distract me. "I hadn't really thought much about it. I have always just focused on the moment and trying to survive. It's only been the last year or so that I have focused much on the future. Why do you ask? Are you ready?"

He shrugged. "I don't think anyone is ever really ready, even if they think they are." He stroked my stomach with the back of his hand. "I do like the idea of my seed inside you, mixing with you, creating a bebe that is both you and me. It is expected that I create the next line, but we don't have to rush if you are not ready."

I kissed his jaw. "I would be honored to carry your child one day. But I'm not sure when that is. Things are going to be tense for some time, the way they are now. We just met and are still getting to know each other. Plus," I paused for effect as I began tracing his dragon. "Babies have a way of interrupting certain moments."

Antonio let out a slow deep breath, his body responding to my light finger. "True, but we can afford to have a nanny."

I shook my head. "No, no nannies. When we have children, we will be the ones raising them. No one else." I was a little passionate about that.

He rubbed my lower back, carefully pushing our lower regions together, promising me what would be coming soon. "Okay, no nannies. I love that you said *when*, not *if*."

I huffed. Oops. "What brought this on? Do you want to start trying for a baby already?"

He cupped my butt in his hand, then lifted my upper leg, resting it on top of his. "I am always up for trying with you. But no. I wanted to talk about it because we have not used any counter measures, not even once."

Oh, oops again. "I didn't even think of that. Then again, I don't really think much beyond the need to have you inside of me."

He groaned at my words and rolled us on to my back. He hovered over me, his parts hanging right against my matching piece.

"I have had the same problem. I don't want to use anything either. I need to feel every bit of you, I don't want anything to come between us."

I raised my arms, placing them around his neck and pulled his head towards me. "Then let's just forget about that then. Let's enjoy what we have, while we have it. If something comes of it, then we will deal with it. Until then," I reached down and aimed him in the right direction.

Neither of us spoke again for a while. The only sounds were of pleasure drowning out the sounds of the storm.

Sometime later, we were nearly asleep when a new thought came to me. "When are you and Elena going to try?"

He held me tight. "I don't know that we ever will. I won't touch that woman without protection any time soon. Besides, I couldn't even consummate the marriage without imagining it was you."

I laughed. "So, the one time you had sex with her, you had to picture me?"

"Yup. It took me nearly ten minutes to get it up, in a pitch-black room. I got it over with as fast as I could, showered off, and ran to you."

"Awe. Sucks for her. But awe."

He huffed in amusement. I fell asleep completely confident and assured in his devotion to me. Maybe one day we would fall in love, it could only make things better, right?

Chapter 13

Antonio

Elizabeth fell back asleep, no longer scared by the storm raging outside. I ran over everything that we discussed tonight, engraving it into my memory bank. There had been a moment when I had to bite my tongue, to keep it from saying one more thing.

I had never been an emotional man, or even a sensitive one. Those men didn't last long in this life. But this woman was doing something to me.

Right in the throes of passion, I had to catch myself from telling her I loved her.

Did I? I'd known her for all of four days. Given, they had been the best four days of my life.

I was a possessive man. I was that way with all things. Just ask Miguel what growing up with me was like. I knew I liked Elizabeth. I felt protective of her. I was sensitive to her emotions and her feelings.

I definitely did not feel that way about Elena. Couldn't stand that woman. I was only being possessive of her to make a point. It was all about pride with her. Not a desire or a need for her.

If Elizabeth were to betray me, I would be hurt, confused, and in a very murderous mood. The idea of someone taking her away from me turned me violent. Having someone look after Elena was an afterthought tonight.

No, I cared about Elizabeth. That was all. One day, maybe it would grow to be more. With the way things were, it was certainly possible. If that was the case, she would need extra protection. It was a good thing she didn't like to go out much. She would be much safer here.

Elizabeth stirred under my arm, her arm tightening around my waist. Why did I feel like she just tightened her grip on my heart?

Man, I was so screwed.

It took me longer to fall back asleep than it did for her. By the time I woke up, the sun was shining through the cracks between the boards on the windows.

The storm was over, thankfully.

107

I looked down and realized Elizabeth was gone. The bed was completely empty next to me.

Uh, no. No, no.

I looked around the room, but there was no sign of her. I got out of the bed and walked briskly to the bathroom. It was quiet, but the light was on.

I was happy to see that we didn't lose power in the night. Or rather I would be, once I found Elizabeth.

I pushed open the barn door and sighed with relief. Then I just stood there, watching her beauty as she soaked in the tub. I quietly walked over to her and squatted down to her level. She smiled at me.

"Good morning, sleeping beauty. I was wondering when you were going to wake up."

I chuckled quietly. "Sit up." She did as I said and I slid in behind her, she laid down against my chest. "How long have you been awake?"

She shrugged. "Half an hour or so. I'm sorry I woke you last night."

"I'm not." I snorted as I started drawing circles on her stomach. The image of her swollen with my prodigy was in my mind. "You never need to apologize for needing me, physically or emotionally. Especially not physically. You can wake me up any time for that." She laughed. I loved the sound of that laugh. "However, you should apologize for making me wake up alone this morning. Nearly gave me a heart attack."

"I'm sorry, mi querido. I did not mean to worry you. You were so peaceful, and this large tub was calling my name."

"Uh huh. Next time, wake me. I'd rather lose sleep then wake up to you being gone." Yup. I was screwed. Just lost my man card right there. I was dependent on a woman.

"Hmmm, I can't promise that. You have a lot of responsibilities. It would not be safe for you to lose sleep just because of me." Her hand slid behind her and gripped me hard. "But I can promise to always make it up to you. Would that be a fair trade?"

I lost track of the conversation. I agreed, even though I wasn't exactly sure what I had just agreed to. She turned around to face me, without letting go.

"Sit on the edge of the tub."

Ya huh, anything you say, mi amor.

Si, I was just going to keep biting my tongue before that came out on its own. As soon as I was on the edge, and out of the water, she made up for leaving me alone alright. It really didn't take long either.

After the bath, we moved to the shower and got ready for the day. As much as I hated no longer being able to stay locked up in the room with her, there was much that needed to be done.

"I'm sure you have a busy day. I know you have been gone for a while. What do you need me to help with?"

That, right here, was why I was falling for this woman. "I do. As long as the internet is up, I have a virtual meeting with some contacts today. I do not know how long that will take. Would you mind working with Francisco on checking the house and grounds for damages? The servants won't be in today, they will need to take care of their own familias and properties. So, we will be on our own."

Elizabeth wrapped her arms around my neck. "You are a great man. I'm glad to know that you care so much for your employees and their lives. It says a lot about your character." She gave me a quick kiss and stepped back. "I will do my best to help in any way I can. Will all those men still be around in case we need help with cleaning up?"

"Si, they will stay as long as needed, or until the roads are cleared."

"Okay. I will also take stock of what we have in the kitchen and make plans for dinner. We have what ten people in the house?"

"More or less. Do you know how to cook?"

She laughed and started pulling me from the room, probably a good call as I was already thinking about paying her back for the tub.

"Yes. I may not be a professionally trained chef, but with the help of recipes, I can cook most anything. Now, feed me breakfast. What I ate this morning did not fill me up, although it was quite a bit."

I threw my head back and groaned out a very manly whimper as she laughed. We made it to the stairs right as Elena was coming up.

"Good morning, Elena." Elizabeth greeted her with a smile. Elena looked at her like she grew a third head. "We are headed down for breakfast. Have you eaten already?"

"Yes. I have. I was just headed back to my room to continue unpacking."

"Wonderful. When you are finished, I will be checking the house and property from the storm, seeing what we need to clean up. If you would like to come help, we would appreciate it."

Elena made a face of disgust. "Yuck, no. That is servants' work."

"Unfortunately, they will not be in today. We must take care of ourselves. If you change your mind, come find me. I have no idea where I will be. I will be cooking dinner for everyone as well, if you would like to help with that. I know it's been a long week for you, so if you want to rest in your room, that is fine too. Well, have a good day, see you later." Elizabeth pulled me along with her as she made her way to the stairs.

I was completely lost and confused now. Who was this woman?

I heard Elena's door slam closed behind her as we made it to the second floor. I pushed Elizabeth against one of the walls and kissed her.

She laughed. "What was that for?"

"I couldn't help it. Watching you take charge like that and owned your place here, well, if I knew which one of these rooms was still empty, I would be pulling you in there and showing you how much of a turn on that was. Where did all that come from?"

She rested her hands on my chest. "I don't really know. After our talk last night, and all the wonderful things you said to me. And the way you spoke to her when we arrived. I guess, I am just feeling more confident. I feel at home for the first time in... well, ever."

I kissed her slowly, expressing my feelings through that one kiss. As much as I would have liked to do more, she was right, I had a lot to do today.

"You are home. And for the record, I love this newfound confidence. I love the shy version of you too, the reserved side. I love all your sides." I knew what I was basically saying, and it was kind of scaring me, so I decided to lighten the moment. I lifted the collar of her v- neck shirt. "I especially love the sides that only I get to see, touch, and taste."

I heard a door open and close down the hall, someone started whistling loudly, announcing their presence. Before I could let go, she leaned into my ear and whispered.

"I love all your sides too, including the possessive and overprotective side. Later, I will show you just how much. Maybe even on your desk."

During my moment of fantasizing, she laughed and escaped. I quickly caught up to her and slid my arms around her waist again.

The kitchen was full of men eating breakfast, having made their own. We walked in just as a couple dropped their dishes into the sink and started walking away.

"Freeze!" Everyone in the room froze and looked at Elizabeth, confusion and shock written all over their faces. "Don't even think about walking away from the messes you are making. You make it, you clean it."

When no one moved, I laughed and backed her up. "You heard the senorita. Clean it up."

She beamed up at me. It was so easy to make her happy. I knew I had to back her up if I wanted her to keep feeling so confident.

I led her to a stool and had her sit down again. "Eggs sound good to you, Hermosa?"

"Perfecto, mi querido."

I really loved when she spoke Spanish. Don't ask me why, I just did.

Miguel and Francisco walked in as we finished eating the quick eggs and toast, I made for us. They saddled up next to us at the bar.

Miguel snagged a piece of my toast. Francisco went for one of Elizabeth's and got a smacked hand. She was really on a roll this morning.

Miguel snorted as Francisco dramatically yelled "ow." "I've got the call set up in your office, whenever you are ready. I already double checked with Sanchez, they didn't get much of the storm, so their internet is up and working as well."

"Gracias, hermano. Francisco, walk around the grounds with Elizabeth. Check everything that might need cleaning up. Do as she says. She's fiery today, so good luck." I laughed.

I started collecting our plates to take to the sink, but she put her hand on mine and stopped me.

"I got it, go do your meeting."

"You sure? I don't mind." I smiled at her, "I made the mess after all."

She laughed. "Yes, but you did it for me. We're a team, right?"

I leaned down and kissed her softly. "Si, gracias. I will see you later. Be safe, please."

"I will. Now go, shoo." She waved me off.

I laughed as I stepped away, then laughed harder as she smacked my butt. "Watch it woman!"

I walked out the kitchen door laughing, Miguel following behind. He had an odd look on his face.

"Que?"

He shook his head. "Nothing, nothing. Just a little weirded out right now."

I chuckled again. "por que?"

He pointed at my face. "That, that right there. I have never heard you laugh so much. Even the men noticed it last night. You are happy. And then watching you two joking around... and kissing." He mocked a shiver. "It's just not normal."

I grinned and patted his back. "Get used to it, hermano. This is just the beginning. I don't know what it is, or why. Being with her just makes me happy. And watching her grow more confident, that's just making it even better. We ran into Elena on our way down. Elizabeth was kind but firm. There was no doubt who was in charge. Took all the control I had to not carry her back to our room."

"Ah, man." Miguel shook his head. "She has you whipped already. You never even wanted to share a room. We have plenty, yet you put her in with you. What happened to you?"

I took a breath before answering, my voice quiet yet serious. "I think I found mi alma."

Miguel stopped walking and turned to study me. I took him by surprise. This was not what any of us ever expected from me, of all people. But it was true.

I found my soul.

He pulled me into a bro hug, patting my back. "Congratulations, hermano. I'm happy for you, I really am." We stepped into my office before he continued. "What about Elena?"

"I gave her an ultimatum yesterday. Apparently, she tried to slap Elizabeth after dinner the other night. Elizabeth stopped her and put her in her place. I backed Elizabeth up. Elena was not happy, and she has hardly left her room since. We shall see what she decides to do. We need to keep an eye on her. She is not to be privy to any delicate information. I want her movements to be watched. Her cell phone is still on her private line, unfortunately we can't do much with that. She is walking on a tightrope, let's see which way she chooses to fall."

He nodded his head as he listened. "Did you talk to Elizabeth about the grandbaby situation yet?"

I smirked and scratched my jaw. "Neither of us care to take precautions. We decided to enjoy what we enjoy and deal with whatever happens."

"And Elena?"

"Elizabeth asked about that as well." I sighed. "Elena is a beautiful woman in her own right. If only her personality matched. Oddly, I don't think that is my only problem. I've had many women I didn't care much for. I got what I needed and washed my hands with them. I had some time to think last night. I think it has more to do with the fact that all I want is Elizabeth. I have no desire to be with anyone else. I also know that no matter how strong of a front Elizabeth puts on, the idea of me with Elena is killing her. I told her about my wedding night. I think that might have something to do with the confidence she is feeling today. I don't like the idea of hurting her." I let out a deep exhale. "For now, let's just see what Elena decides. I will deal with the rest later. Let's get started, shall we?"

Miguel turned and pushed the call button on the laptop screen. Within moments, two small screens appeared.

"Buenos dias, Caballeros. Thank you for agreeing to meet with me today."

Chapter 14
Elizabeth

I watched as Antonio and Miguel left, then I picked up our dishes and carried them to the sink. I rinsed them off and added them to a nearly full dishwasher. I looked around the room to make sure all the dishes had been collected.

I picked up the pan Antonio had used to make me breakfast. I smiled to myself; it was sweet of him to cook for me.

When he first walked into the bedroom the other night, I was scared half to death. All I could think about was how Paul had treated me earlier that day. Antonio was sweet and kind as he helped me to calm down. I wasn't sure what to expect after that.

Then later, I completely freaked because it hurt, and he was no longer as gentle as he had been. I tried to fight back, but I couldn't. He was so much bigger than me and stronger than me. However, I understand now what happened. He just lost control for a moment.

Once he saw my tears, he became gentle again. I didn't mind so much when he wasn't gentle anymore.

"What are you smiling about? Or do I even want to know?"

I laughed. I was so wrapped up in my thoughts, I completely forgot Francisco was still there.

"Just thinking about how much things have changed over the last week." I laid the now clean pan in the dish drainer and started the dishwasher. "Are you ready to walk around the grounds with me?"

"Si, senorita. I will follow you anywhere."

"Ha! You may not want to let Antonio hear you say that."

"Nah, he knows I mean it in a strictly platonic way. You are El Jefa, the boss lady. Our men should be willing to follow you and protect you. You are part of our family now, Elizabeth. We will treat you as such."

I bit the edge of my lip. "Even though I am only a mistress?"

"That word has been given such a bad rep by the world at large. If it was still legal to have more than one wife at a time, you would be Antonio's wife.

In our corner of the world, you will be treated as such. You will be given the same respect, if not more, than his legal wife. You are already acting the part. Elena should be out here doing this. She should be mingling with the men. She has not spoken to anyone, unless necessary. She is not earning their trust or their respect. You on the other hand. They have already seen how you care for their El jefe. They have seen how he cares for you. From what I hear, some saw it firsthand in the hall this morning."

He laughed as I blushed and covered my face. I'd forgotten about that already.

"There is no shame in that. Never be embarrassed to show him how you feel. The men may tease you both about it, but that's because we are all men, and we will always have the mentality of twelve-year-old ninos. Besides, we have never seen Antonio as happy as he has been since you came into his life. None of these men knew he was capable of smiling. After you two left last night, it didn't take much for them to understand why you are to be protected."

"Thank you, Francisco, I really appreciate it. I am not used to family or feeling like I belong. I lost count of how many foster homes I lived in before I turned ten. They were rarely happy homes. Even Oscar made me feel welcomed the other night, and he doesn't strike me as the sensitive type."

Francisco huffed. "No, definitely not. Miguel told me how he welcomed you to the family. I'm sorry to hear that you did not experience that growing up. I'd give you a hug, but I don't want to get shot." He laughed. "But you are home now, and we will take care of you."

We spent the next two hours walking over the grounds, yes, it took two hours! My feet hurt.

The damage was minimal. Most could be done by the groundskeeper; however, I insisted Francisco call the men down and have them at least put the larger branches into piles. It wasn't like they had a lot to do right then anyway. We continued on as they began piling them up.

I tried to help by grabbing the smaller ones, but they all shooed me away. I laughed and complied.

We ended at the pool.

I heard no complaints about cleaning it out before the branches clogged up the filtration system.

I covered my eyes as a bunch of them stripped down to their boxers and jumped in. They thought that was quite hilarious. It gave me an idea though. But I would have to run it by Antonio first.

Once the grounds were cleaned up, and the men dried off, I sent them up to begin taking down all the boards on the windows. I told them I would get the key to mine and Antonio's room later and they could do it last.

We all ate sandwiches for lunch. I made a plate up for Antonio and figured I would deliver it myself.

Francisco walked me down to the office, since all the doors looked the same to me. He knocked and peeked in to make sure the meeting was over and safe for me to go in. Thankfully it was. He even held the door open for me.

"Hola, hermosa." Antonio smiled at me and opened his arms for me to come to him.

"Hola," I gladly walked toward him, setting the tray of food down on his desk. "I'm not interrupting, am I?"

He set me on his lap and stroked my cheek. "No, the meeting just ended. I have a few minutes that I can spend with you."

I heard a click and turned, the other two had quietly left the room, giving us our privacy. I turned back to him and smiled.

"Good, I brought you some lunch." I made to get up, but he wouldn't let me.

"I seem to remember someone saying something about showing me the sides they love, on my desk..."

I scratched my chin, "hmmm, nope don't remember that. Must have been someone else." I started to get up again, but he held me tighter this time and growled.

"Hermosa..."

"Si, mi jefe?" I asked, mocking complete innocence. "Don't you want to eat your lunch?"

He gave a dark chuckle that gave me the good kind of goosebumps. "Si, mi amor."

He leaned in and bit my neck, pulling in a small piece of the skin. I moaned and gripped the back of his head. His hand made quick work of opening my jeans and then sliding in. When he released me, I shivered.

116

"Take off your pants and your shirt." He growled into my ear.

I did as he said. He stood up and took care of his own pants. Soon he was kissing me and setting me on his desk. He completely devoured me.

He made me stay sitting just like that, while he sat in his chair eating the sandwich I made him. I laughed.

"Why am I sitting like this?"

He smiled with a dark twinkle in his eyes. "Because I told you too. You are my favorite sight. The best part of my day."

I smiled and blushed. His fingers lightly slid along the inside of my thigh. Then he moved them along my bra line. He was working me up and he knew it. He stood up in front me, between my legs and handed me his fingers. They still had a touch of mayonnaise and mustard on them. I slowly sucked them clean. He did ask for it.

That started us on a much slower and gentler version of what we had already done. I nearly lost my balance when I stood back on the floor again, he thought that was funny.

"Shush you." I told him.

Which earned me a smack on my bare butt. Ooh, that hurt, but I also kind of liked that. He caught that too, and from the wicked smile, he planned on doing it again.

I winced as I put my boots back on, he didn't miss that either.

"Hermosa? Are you alright?"

"Si, mi querido. My feet are just sore. We spent two hours walking over the whole property. I need to remember to pick up some tennis shoes when we go shopping."

Antonio picked me up and carried me to the sofa in a corner of the room. He sat on the opposite end and picked up my feet.

"Here, let me see." He took my boots back off and started rubbing my feet.

I laid back on the couch and enjoyed every minute of it. Too soon there was a knock at the door.

"Come in." Antonio called out.

Miguel popped his head in, a hand over his eyes. We both laughed.

"It's safe, Miguel." I told him.

He gave a dramatic sigh of relief. He eyed my foot in Antonio's hands. He looked confused for a moment, but at Antonio's challenging stare he shook it off.

"Are you ready to call padre now? He is waiting for your report from earlier."

Antonio grumbled, sounding like a put-out teenager. I giggled. He then tickled my foot for payback, knowing how ticklish I was. Such a butthead.

I sat up, pulled my feet down, then pulled the boots back on. "I better let you get back to work. Thank you for the foot rub."

I stood up, then leaned down to give him a kiss. He deepened it.

I couldn't help the laugh when Miguel started whistling a tune. Pretty sure Antonio was purposely tormenting his brother.

I picked up the now empty tray, leaving the bottle of water I brought him on the desk.

"See you later, mi querido." I called as I closed the door behind me.

By the time I made it back to the kitchen I remembered I had forgotten to run my idea by him. Francisco was sitting in a chair at the small table in the kitchen. I decided to run it by him instead.

"Francisco?"

He lowered his phone and looked up. "Si, Senora?"

I gave him a quizzical look at the title change, he only smiled back. Alright, whatever. He did say they thought of me as a wife, so why not?

"I forgot to ask Antonio if a barbeque would be alright for dinner tonight. I was thinking we could grill by the pool and have a small pool party. Do you think that would be fine? I thought everyone could use the break after all the traveling, then preparing the house, and then cleaning up."

"Si, that should be fine. El Jefe doesn't usually mind when we do that. Besides, I'm sure he'd love to see you in a bathing suit." He winked at me, and I blushed.

I could swear they all did that on purpose.

"Unfortunately, I don't have one of those at the moment. I will just steal one of Antonio's shirts and wear it with a pair of shorts."

He shook his head. "Nope, can't have that. The roads are clearing up. I can send someone down to grab one, just give me your size."

"No, really, I don't mind. I don't need anyone to go to all that trouble."

"Senora?" That sounded more like a warning than a question.

I relented and gave him my size. He sent a message to someone and said it was taken care of.

I pulled the freezer open and found a variety of meats. I decided to keep it simple for tonight. I pulled out a box of hamburger patties and set them on the counter to start thawing.

"Did Elena come down for lunch?"

"No. Did you want me to send something up for her?"

"No. I told her this morning that we had no servants for the day. Everyone else has been fending for themselves, she can as well. She is a grown woman. She doesn't have to be waited on constantly. She may act like a Princess, but that doesn't mean she is one."

Francisco snorted and nearly choked on the water he had just taken a drink of.

I cut up some potatoes and put them on to boil. A nice potato salad would go well with the burgers. While that was cooking, I sliced lettuce and tomatoes. I made a tray full of all the condiments, then stuck them in the fridge to stay cool. By then, the potatoes were done. I made quick work of that as well.

"Francisco? Will you please have someone start setting up a table and the grill outside?"

"Si, Senora." I saw him pull his phone back out and start messaging someone again.

A few minutes later, three men came downstairs and walked outside. When they came back in, they walked over to me.

"We are ready to take the boards down in your room, Senora. Do you have the key?"

Ha! That I did remember to get. I pulled it out of my pocket and handed it to them. Francisco, knowing how Antonio was, followed them up. They came back down ten minutes later, handing me the key back.

"Anything else, Senora?"

I smiled, that title was kind of growing on me. "Not at the moment, gracias."

An hour later, I had everything ready to go and the grill was hot. Antonio and Miguel walked into the kitchen as I looked around to see if I had everything. Antonio came up behind me and slid his arms around me, placing a kiss on my neck.

"What did you decide to make?"

"I thought a barbeque by the pool would be nice. All the men have been working hard to clean up and take care of the house. On top of all the traveling." I turned to face him, placing my hands on his chest. "You don't mind, do you? I meant to ask you earlier, but I forgot." I scrunched up my nose and he laughed.

"Sounds like a great idea. Do you have a bathing suit?"

"No, Francisco sent someone to get one for me. But they have been gone awhile. I can just steal one of your shirts, it's not a big deal." I smiled at him, and he chuckled.

The men helping me walked in again to get the food.

"What else do you need, Senora?" I laughed as the name threw Antonio too.

"Francisco started it. All the food is on the counter, just take it out to the table you set up. Gracias, caballeros!" I hollered as they were already on their way out.

A blonde female walked in a few minutes later carrying a small bag. She looked around the room until her eyes landed on Antonio, hungrily.

"Angela, thank you so much for going to the store for us. Did you have any trouble?" Antonio asked.

She gave a shy smile and blushed. I felt a little territorial and jealous at the way she was looking back at him.

"No, senor. The roads were not too bad. But there are a lot of people out."

"Bueno, bueno. Angela, this is Elizabeth. She is running my household now." He kept a possessive arm around my waist as I put out a hand to shake hers.

"It's nice to meet you, Angela. Thank you for running to the store for me."

She looked a little confused at his arm but shook it off. "My pleasure, welcome to Laredo. If you'll both excuse me, I need to get back." She turned and walked back out just as quickly as she came in.

I looked at Antonio. "Who is she?"

He seemed amused at something. "She is one of the women who hangs around once in a while. The men use her, I never did. I told you. I don't like to share."

"She seemed like she was open to the idea."

He sighed and stroked my hair. "Most of them are. They would love to be one of my women. They think they would be pampered and spoiled."

I raised an eyebrow at his "one of" comment. I knew he was allowed to have as many as he wanted. Didn't mean I liked it.

"Hermosa." He called me out of my thoughts soothingly. "You are all I need. You are incredibly sexy when you are jealous, but you don't need to be. Entiendes?"

I nodded, even though I was fighting back against those insecurities. He saw it in my eyes and kissed my cheek, whispering in my ear for only me to hear.

"Mi amor, you are the only woman for me. The only one I want. No one can compare to you."

It hadn't sunk in earlier, but that was the second time today he called me his love. I liked the sound of that.

"Go, change into your suit, and come back down. I will start grilling. If I go up with you, we won't be coming back down again tonight." He nibbled on my neck, and I giggled.

I took the bag from him and made my way up the stairs.

I paused at the top, then decided to go down the hall to Elena and let her know what the plan was. I knocked on her door and waited. She took her sweet time, but eventually she opened the door.

"What do you want?" She snarled.

"I am letting you know that we are grilling by the pool tonight for dinner. You are welcome to join us, or you can stay up here, it is your choice." I turned and started to walk off.

"You know you are just a phase, right? All mistresses are. I am the wife. I am the only permanent one. You are just a temporary toy to him."

I took a deep breath. She was playing on one of my fears. I had to believe that that was not true. She was just being a vindictive woman. I turned back around to her.

"That may be. But until that time. I am the one here. I am the one making the decisions. You can join us, or you can fend for yourself. Everyone else is being an adult about this. I arranged dinner for everyone. Antonio is grilling. No one will be delivering dinner to your room. Suck it up and be mature or continue skulking like a child." I walked off, ignoring anything else she might have to say.

I unlocked the room and then locked it again behind me. I took a deep breath and let a small tear roll out. I let myself have a minute, but I refused to give her any more than that. Elena was lashing out because she wasn't getting her way.

I still felt a little guilty about taking her place. But Antonio was right, my presence didn't change much. He hated her long before I showed up.

I pulled the suit out of the bag and then groaned. I should have requested a one piece. At least Angela had included a wrap to go around my waist. I wasn't the biggest fan of my thighs. Or butt.

I walked into the closet and changed out of my clothes and into the bathing suit. It fit perfectly. It was just a basic bikini, red. The wrap was sheer black. It didn't cover much, but it was a little better.

I brushed out my hair and quickly pulled it into a braid. I needed another minute, so I searched for Antonio's suit. I took that and two towels and finally left the room.

He could change down there. It would save him some time.

Chapter 15

Antonio

I hated how Angela's appearance affected Elizabeth. I loved the jealousy part, that was awesome. I just hated how easily she doubted herself. All I wanted was to follow her up those stairs and drill it into her that she was mine.

Literally. I loved drilling into her. I loved a lot of things about her.

I couldn't believe I slipped twice and called her mi amor. I knew she didn't catch it the first time, she was sufficiently distracted, but she did the last time. I needed to be more careful with that.

I grumbled childishly as I stepped outside onto the patio, the opposite direction that she went. Francisco was already working the grill. I walked over and put my hand out for the spatula.

"How did it go today?" I asked him.

He smiled. "It went smoothly. The men piled up all the branches like she asked, with only minimal complaining. There was no complaining when it came to cleaning out the pool. They all got a kick out of her covering her eyes when they stripped to their boxers."

I laughed. "She is still innocent in so many ways. I hope that never changes. What's up with the Senora bit? She said you started that?"

He laughed with his head falling to his back. "She made a comment to me this morning about only being a mistress. I explained to her that we see it as another wife, not a side piece like the rest of the world. I did it nicely and respectfully don't worry. After that," he shrugged nonchalantly, "I decided to stop calling her senorita to make a point. The rest of them just picked it up and ran with it. It's good. It means they respect her. They all do. They all see how happy she makes you, and how she respects you. They will spread the word, don't worry."

"Has Elena been down at all?"

He shook his head but smiled. "No. Elizabeth asked that as well, after she took you lunch. I offered to have food sent up. She told me no. Elena knew we had no servants. She can come and get it herself like everyone else."

Now I was the one busting up laughing. I noticed how the pool went quiet. I laughed even harder.

"Si, I know how to laugh. I figured out how to the day I met mi hermosa." They all joined in with the laughter and went back to messing around.

"Did you talk about anything else?"

"Only a little. When I explained about the mistress bit, she told me about growing up in foster care and never having a real family. I made sure to stress that she does now."

"Gracias, mi amigo. We've talked a lot about it. It is why she struggles with insecurities. I am glad to hear that things went well today. I made an appointment with Alejandro for tomorrow, I will need a couple men to escort us there and go shopping."

He raised an eyebrow. "Are you getting another tattoo?"

I smiled as I shook my head. "No, as she calls it, I am branding her. I wanted a way to mark her as mine. I want all the men to know who she is and the severity of messing with her. At the same time, I don't want to make her a target. I am hoping something permanent like this will help her to feel more confident in us."

He nodded his understanding. "Are you putting your name on her then?"

"Nope. She is getting a copy of my dragon on her left ring finger. Actually, I'm thinking of having the dragon above her wrist, with the tail hanging down the back of her palm and circling her finger like a ring. Think that will send the message?" I laughed as he nodded in confusion and was speechless.

I flipped the burgers, and we talked some more. I turned when the back door opened and out walked mi alma, my soul. Francisco had to reach around me and put a finger under my jaw, closing my mouth, as he laughed.

That need to whisk her away was getting stronger. She walked over to me with a dark blush on her cheeks and soft smile. She saw my reaction.

"Wow." I told her as I wrapped my arms around her.

"Gracias. I brought yours down with me. I figured you could just change in the bathroom or something."

"Gracias, hermosa. You think of everything." I kissed her temple, knowing if I kissed her anywhere else, I probably wouldn't stop. "Watch the grill, Francisco."

I pulled her along with me, ignoring the whistles and yells that followed us.

"Where are we going?" She laughed.

"You are going to help me change."

"I thought the purpose of us changing separately was so that we didn't do what you are thinking."

I pulled her into the guest baño and locked the door. "Sí, but the bedroom is more dangerous. And that was before I saw you in that. Now get over here." I swallowed her giggles as I crashed my mouth onto hers.

I pushed the bottoms down to the floor and set her on the edge of the counter. It took all my control to bite those three little words back again.

Why did they keep trying to come out?

She laughed as I worked to catch my breath again. "Woman, what are you doing to me? I've never had trouble controlling myself before." I held her close to me, my hand on the back of her head.

She kissed my chest softly. "Probably the same thing you are doing to me. I never cared enough about any of this. I hardly thought about it. All this was something future me would worry about. I just can't imagine not having you or not needing you like I do. You have filled up every part of me, Antonio. Parts I didn't even know were empty."

I winked at her, loving the blush that always followed. "I will always be willing to fill up your holes." She laughed and pushed me away.

"Get dressed you perv. I'm ready to eat." She jumped off the counter and pulled her bikini bottoms back on. "Oh, and in keeping with our open honesty. I stopped by Elena's room when I went upstairs."

Uh, alright. That was unexpected. "And?" I asked, pulling my own suit on.

"I wanted to let her know that we were grilling by the pool for dinner, and she was welcome to join. I'm trying to follow the mothers' advice and bring peace from the beginning."

Judging by the way Elizabeth got defensive; it obviously did not go well. I put a hand on her back and rubbed softly.

"I appreciate you trying so hard. What did she say?"

Elizabeth grimaced, which was adorable. "She called me a temporary phase and said she was the only permanent one. I told her that may be, but for now I was the one in charge and if she wanted to eat, she could act like an adult and either join us or make her own food. I didn't listen to anything else that came out of her mouth, I just left."

I smiled. "I am so proud of you, and so turned on right now that we need to leave before I take you again." She laughed and we walked out the door. "Tomorrow, we have an appointment with Alejandro, my tattoo artist." I picked up her left hand and kissed her ring finger. "No one will dare call you temporary after that."

She turned around and stopped in front of me, then crashed into my lips this time. I very nearly carried her back the other way, until I realized we were already standing in the patio doorway and there were a lot more wolf whistles this time.

I knew when she realized that too because her face hid in my neck again.

The night went smoothly. One by one the men carried dishes back into the kitchen. I had a feeling they were going to clean it all up for her as well. Soon enough, it was just her and I in the pool.

We took our time. I held her in my arms, her legs wrapped around me, as I leaned against a wall. We talked and laughed. She told me about her talk with Francisco. I loved that she was taking the honesty part seriously.

I told her what I could about my meetings. She didn't question the parts I obviously left out. We made out frequently. I took advantage of her small coverings and no one being outside with us.

With how sensitive she was to my touch I was really glad we splurged for the top of the line filtration system and cleaners.

"Are you ready for bed, hermosa?" I caught her trying to stifle a yawn.

"Yes, but I need a shower first. I need to get all this out of my hair tonight or my hair will be impossible tomorrow."

I gave her a mischievous smile. "Sounds good to me."

I set her down on the stairs and watched her walk up. Which reminded me of when I spanked her earlier. I saw the look in her eyes.

I would be nice and wait until we got back upstairs though.

We dried off and then walked in through the kitchen to check the damage. I was happy to see they had cleaned up but disheartened to see that it was not empty.

Elena had finally come down to eat.

"Elena. Why didn't you join us for dinner?"

Elena scowled at us. "If you want my company, then you will treat me accordingly. As your wife, I deserve respect. I deserve to be treated as your wife."

"As I told you yesterday, that is to be earned not awarded. If you want the respect of a wife, act like one. We are going to bed. I suggest you do the same. I will seek you out soon to hear your decision."

I took Elizabeth's hand and we quietly walked up the stairs. She unlocked the door, then handed me back the key. Our playful bubble had sufficiently been popped. I wanted to get it back, but I didn't really know how.

Leave it to Elizabeth to know what I needed.

She walked into the bathroom and started the shower, then came back out to me. She took my hand and dragged me in with her, both of us still in our suits. She leaned against the wall and brought me against her, while kissing me.

She reached behind her neck and pulled the string to untie the top. I followed her lead and untied the back. It wasn't long before I was ready to take over again. It may not have been as playful as it would have been before, but there was still a lot of passion.

I helped Elizabeth take the braid out of her hair and wash it. She helped me wash my hair and laughed when I shook it out like a dog, spraying her. I didn't keep it as short as some of the other men. It was just long enough to fly with the movement and throw water at her.

I sat on the edge of the tub, watching her brush out her hair and dry it. She was still only wrapped in a towel. We both had gotten in the habit of sleeping in the nude. It just made it easier, and I much preferred to not have any layers between us.

When she finished, I followed her out and watched as she dropped her towel in the hamper before climbing into bed. I did the same, mostly to keep her happy.

Once she was back in my arms, I held her tight against my chest, her back to me. I hadn't understood why she insisted on drying her hair before bed. Now I did. Wet hair would have been very cold against my bare chest.

As I laid there, listening to her breathing slowly deepen, I realized I was wrong before. I really did love her. I couldn't imagine my life without her.

Why else would I be willing to mark her in this way?

Why else would she be willing to allow me too?

The need to say it was growing in me, and it was eventually going to come spilling out. I wasn't ready for her to hear it yet though. I didn't know if she was in the same place as me. After all, I was the man she was kidnapped for, and my padre bought her. For me.

As a wedding gift.

He paid just shy of a million dollars, American dollars. He didn't tell me. He didn't need to. Elizabeth told me Andre had called her his Million Dollar Angel. It was easy to assume from there.

She was worth every peso. And then some.

I waited until I knew she was deep asleep. I even kissed her neck, with no reaction. It was how I knew she was out. I softly said what was in my heart, hoping it would help me keep a lid on it for a little longer.

"Hermosa, mi amor, mi alma. You are the esposa of my heart. I will find a way to remedy this. I love you. One day, I will tell you this when you are awake, I'm just not sure I'm ready for that yet. I do hope you hear me on some level, so you know this is not temporary for me. You are my everything, there will never be another woman for me. No mistresses on the side. You will not share me. I will not share you. I love you, Elizabeth."

I held her close to me, fighting the urge to wake her up and show her.

Chapter 16
Elizabeth

I woke up before Antonio again, but I stayed next to him this time. I rolled over carefully, watching him sleep.

I had an odd dream. I dreamt that he told me he loved me. If only that were real.

I had a feeling that he might, at least in his own way. He acted like it. Men like him though could have a hard time showing it, or even realizing it. I wasn't even sure what that would mean for us.

Would it even change anything? Elena was still his wife.

Something inside of me whispered "for now." Which was an odd thought. I knew he gave her the ultimatum, but I didn't see why she would walk away.

The longer I laid there, letting my mind wander and overthink things, the more I started feeling restless.

It was possible that my nerves about today were setting in. I always said I wouldn't get a tattoo. I thought they were ridiculous. I moved the sheet back enough to look at the dragon. This would tie me to Antonio indefinitely. I found I kind of liked the idea of that though.

Indefinite.

Permanent.

Solid.

All things I had never really known. Especially in regard to the people in my life, or with where I lived. Those terms never fit into any description in my life. It had always been about getting from one moment to the next. Or planning for what *might* happen in the future.

I began tracing the tattoo lightly, testing how deep asleep he was. I had covered nearly the whole thing before he started stirring. I was working my way down the tail, and then just a bit past that when he moaned.

I took that as encouragement and traded up to my whole hand.

The part I held twitched, and Antonio let out a small gasp. I increased and he moved with me. It all made me feel a bit giddy. His eyes opened and he looked down at me with a smile. He started to say something, but I made sure a different kind of noise came out instead.

He paid me back for that by rolling onto me. As he was still in my hand, I lined him up. He grabbed my hand and stopped me though.

"Not yet." I frowned at him, confused. "I want you to do something else first."

"Ok, what?" What else was there?

Antonio moved my hand from his lower regions to my own. "Do it."

I just stared at him, no clue what he was talking about, so he moved my hand for me. I laughed when I realized what he meant.

"Really?"

He deepened his voice the way I liked. "Do it."

So, I did. He told me what to do, and I followed his instructions to the letter. As my legs began shaking, he started working himself over me. When he was on the edge, he moved my hand away and slid inside to finish. He held off long enough to drag another one out of me.

Antonio laid down next to me and put his arm around me. "You are only allowed to do that when I tell you to. Entiendes"

I was still working on pushing out the breath that had frozen in my chest. "Si, El jefe."

"That's my girl." He leaned down and gave me a soft kiss. "Buenos Dias, hermosa."

I smiled. "Buenos Dias, mi querido."

We got up and got dressed. It was a good thing we were going shopping today. I was running out of the clothes Maria and Sandy had bought for me.

We walked down to the kitchen, following a wonderful smell. One of the men, I really needed to remember their names, had decided to make up a couple dozen pancakes for everyone, along with bacon and sausage. Another one was working on cooking two cartons of eggs.

"Good morning, wow that smells wonderful!" I exclaimed.

"Gracias, señora. We figured it was our turn to cook."

Another piped in, "that and no one wanted cereal again."

We all laughed and then enjoyed the wonderful breakfast. I insisted on cleaning up since they cooked and cleaned up for me last night. Antonio sat back through all of it with a prideful grin on his face. I suspected the fact that we were all getting along was making him happy.

After breakfast, he and I loaded into a small black Mercedes. Francisco and one of the blondes climbed into the front. I listened to them talking and discovered this one was Jerry.

Hopefully I would remember that after spending a few hours with him today.

Our first stop was the tattoo parlor. Antonio held my right hand as the needle invaded my skin and permanently branded me with his mark. He didn't seem to mind that I practically broke all of his bones. He claimed it was good practice for when I gave him a hijo one day.

The artist carefully positioned the dragon over the outside of my left wrist. The tail draped down the back of my hand and wrapped around my finger twice.

Antonio said this way it would not be missed by anyone. It hurt like the dickens though.

I would need to keep it wrapped in a bandage and dry for the next week. Antonio was kind enough to offer all shower duties so I could keep it dry.

The men all thought that was funny.

We then spent the next three hours in the mall. I argued about him buying too much, he argued it wasn't enough. He won. He also bought me more than just basic underwear from those sections.

Our little group stopped in the food court for lunch, we were split between Chinese and pizza.

The three men carried everything, not letting me use my hand. I didn't argue with that one, it still really hurt.

We made a stop at a jewelry store before we left. I picked out a basic heart shaped locket, made of white gold. It had a traditional rose engraved on the front and on the back Antonio requested they put mi alma.

When it was done, he slid a small chip inside and paid the man extra to seal it shut.

By the time we made it back home, we were all tired. I was both surprised and nervous when I saw a line of new cars, accompanied by a herd of new people walking around the house. Antonio put his arm around me and reminded me that all the staff came back to work today.

He introduced me to everyone we passed. They were all very happy to meet me. Like with Angela, he did not specify whether I was the wife or not. They all knew he had left to get married. He let them draw their own conclusions.

I thought it was asking for trouble later, when his actual wife decided to pull her head out of her butt. However, it was his choice.

I tried to focus on all their names, it didn't matter though. They all went in one ear and out the other. I hoped they would forgive me when I asked for them again later.

Or if I requested they all start wearing name tags from now on.

We took the bags filled with my new belongings upstairs and I put them away. I now had a little bit of everything. There was no doubt I now had more things than I had in my entire life, combined.

Antonio just sat on the bed, watching me for most of it. Letting me put them where I wanted them. He wanted me to feel comfortable in my new home. So far I was really liking having one.

"Hermosa? Is there anything you wanted to get from your old apartment? Anyone you want to call? I'm sure someone has reported you missing by now. We can run a security check and then set the record straight for you."

I walked over to stand in front of him. I lifted my right hand and ran my fingers through his hair.

"There is no need. I doubt anyone even noticed I was gone. Eventually, my landlord will sell all my stuff and be done with it. There was nothing there that was personal. Everything from my parents had been destroyed by Katrina. I never got to keep anything when I switched foster homes. Sometimes all I had was the clothes on my back. So, no. But thank you."

Once back downstairs, he went to his office, and I went to the kitchen. I spent time talking to the ladies there, getting to know them. Thankfully, they didn't mind when I asked their names again.

They were two older ladies, probably the same age as Maria and Sandy. I laughed as they told me stories about their grandkids.

The next few weeks passed in a similar fashion. While Antonio worked in his office, and anywhere else he needed to go, I worked with the different staff members. I wanted to get to know each of them and what they did for us.

I even spent a day outside with the groundskeepers.

By the end of those weeks, I knew each of the staff by name and what they did. We rarely saw Elena. Some knew she was there, but most did not.

My branding had turned out beautifully. I absolutely loved it. Antonio loved it even more. He kissed it every chance he got. It helped me feel tied to him on a whole new level.

Chapter 17

Antonio

We returned home from Mexico nearly a month ago. Elena had been haunting the house like a poltergeist preparing to strike the entire time. She had food sent up to her room regularly now that the staff were present again. She refused to lift a finger to do anything for anyone else, not even herself.

Very few people even knew she was there.

I knew I should go talk to her, force her to make a choice. But frankly, I didn't want to talk to her. Elizabeth and I were perfectly happy. The whole house had been.

All of my higher-ranking men in the area had met Elizabeth. She had perfected the art of showing off her left hand when she met them. She learned quickly that most were going to kiss the back of her hand, not just shake it, so she gave them the left one. She also used that hand to randomly play with the locket, keeping the dragon facing out.

They all had the same first reaction of shock and then acceptance. After only a few minutes with her, they all respected her. She was easy to love, easy to get along with, and easy to smile.

Her insecurities rarely showed anymore. She was confident and strong. She kept the house running and I could focus on all the different business avenues we had going. Everything was running like a perfectly oiled clock. And the feeling in the house had never been better.

I finished another virtual meeting with both Sanchez and Cooper, the American family in California, just moments before. Levi Cooper invited Sanchez and I out to California, to get an eye on their operation. He said this was the best time, seeing as their school was closed for some sort of renovations for the next month or so. It was an odd time of year for a school to close, but I was learning to trust the man.

Levi had explained their setup with the school, as we discussed their plans for our product. I was curious to see it. I did ask if these renovations would get in the way of our plans, but he promised we still had access to the parts I needed to see.

I got the feeling he was like me and didn't trust easily. While we would be seeing parts of his operation, we would not be seeing the entirety of it.

In the meantime, we worked out a rough deal, but Sanchez and I both needed visual confirmation. All of us were paranoid.

It came with the lifestyle.

I wished I could take Elizabeth with me, we'd never spent a night apart, but it was all business and should be a quick trip. Levi offered to let us bring our significant others. His wife would be more than happy to play hostess. But I didn't trust many people with her life.

I was tempted to chain her to the bed and lock her in the room. Alas, she would hate me for treating her like that.

On the bright side, she was due for that lovely female time when she would be extra cranky and not allow me to touch her, sometime in the next few days. The timing for the trip was perfect in that aspect.

Of course, I was basing this on the fact that she had not had one yet, and we'd been together for nearly a month now.

After dinner, we went for a walk around the grounds, something she got us started on after a week of being there. We frequently ended up making love against a tree, which kept me from complaining. I decided this was probably as good a time as any to break the bad news to her.

"Hermosa, I have to leave town for a few days."

She stopped walking and turned to face me. "Why? Am I going with you?"

I shook my head sadly. "No. I need to go visit the men I have been talking with. It will help solidify this deal. I wish I could take you, but I don't want to risk taking you into what could be enemy territory. I've never been to this place before, nor have I physically met the man. I know of his reputation, and it is good, but I won't risk your safety over a rumor."

I saw a tear glisten in her eye as she turned away and tried to start walking again. I held her hand firm, not letting her move away from me.

"Hermosa, speak to me. Please don't hide from me."

She cleared her throat and turned back to face me. "I don't like the idea of being separated from you. I fear for your safety too. I feel safer when you are around. I would feel much better if we were together."

I wiped her tears and held her close to me. "It will only be for a few days. I promise. I will talk to you every night."

She sniffled. "When do you have to leave?"

"I will be leaving early tomorrow morning. Miguel will come with me, but Francisco will stay with you. I can also have more men come and protect the house and you. Whatever you need."

She shook her head. "Francisco will be plenty, although I would feel better if you took them both."

"He is one of the few I trust with your life, and your virtue. I promise to come back as soon as possible." She looked up at me and I leaned down to kiss her. I took all that I could from that one kiss. "Let's go inside. I want to make love to you in our bed." She nodded and we walked back inside.

As soon as our bedroom door was locked, I picked her up and carried her the rest of the way, my need growing by the second. As our breathing leveled out, I decided I had waited long enough.

"I love you, hermosa."

"I love you too, mi querido."

Hearing her return my love, I was glad I had not moved away yet. What came next was the best we ever did. Knowing she loved me the way I loved her, it changed everything.

I kept whispering I love you to her. I could no longer keep it back. As she was climbing again, I added what she needed most.

"You are the only woman I will ever be with. No sharing, it is only you and me. No one else. You are mi alma. My soul. My other half. I have no need for anyone else."

She kissed me like she had never kissed me before. My words wiped away any leftover insecurities she had. I would talk to my padre and cancel this thing with Elena. I wanted Elizabeth to officially be my wife.

But I planned to hold back on telling her that until I knew it was even possible. I didn't want to get her hopes up just to bring them crashing down later. It would undo all the hard work I put into helping her become who she was really meant to be.

A strong and confident woman.

The next morning, I kissed her goodbye in the bedroom and then left. I felt like I was leaving a piece of myself behind. Miguel and Francisco were waiting downstairs.

"Take care of her for me. She is more precious than all the gold in the world."

Francisco gave me a small smile. "I will, don't worry so much. We won't even leave the house."

I nodded, that was true. Elizabeth hadn't left the grounds since we went shopping and tattooed her wrist. I felt a little better about leaving as Miguel and I loaded into the car.

Our flight was just over three hours. Levi and one of his men were at the airfield waiting for us. Although, calling Levi's backup a man was a bit of a stretch. While he was a good size, he still looked very young. Possibly only 16.

Half an hour later Sanchez arrived, and we were able to leave.

We spent the next two days getting the lay of the land. Levi's right-hand man, Mitch, took us around. He and Sanchez worked together before, which helped ease some of our tensions. I listened as Mitch filled him in on the missing cleaner.

"Has anyone heard from Miller since he got out of prison? I'm sure you understand why I want to keep tabs on him. No one has seen him in a few months."

Mitch cleared his throat. "Yeah, sorry, I haven't had time to call you yet. He showed up over here the day after he got out and took Emma back."

Sanchez rubbed his face. "Idiota! I assume there is a reason he is missing then?"

Mitch smirked. "It took us a week to get her back. He left us no choice."

Sanchez nodded silently before adding. "Well, at least we don't have to worry about him squealing anymore."

I thought about asking, then changed my mind. I really didn't care that much. It wasn't hard to put together. The cleaner kidnapped one of their women, sounded like it wasn't the first time. He had not been left alive to do it a third time.

Frankly, I would have killed him the first time he dared to touch Elizabeth.

I was already anxious enough because I had not heard from her or Francisco. No one in the household was answering the house phone. Something wasn't right.

Tomorrow I would be home, I would get to the bottom of it. I had to keep reminding myself of that.

Miguel was waiting outside Cooper's house with a long, pale face when we pulled up. I jumped out of the car and ran over to him.

"What happened?"

"The house was stormed by feds two nights ago. They kept all the staff in the house as they showed up for work the next day. You know the routine when this happens. Everyone goes silent. John just called me a few minutes ago."

I bent over, my hands on my knees, gasping for air. "Elizabeth?"

"I don't know. There has been no word. I'm sorry."

Mitch and Sanchez caught up to us and Miguel filled them in.

"We have a man who used to be FBI. He still has connections. He can find out where your girl is. He is extra sensitive when it comes to our women disappearing."

"Please." I gasped out, feeling like someone had sucked all the oxygen out of the air.

Chapter 18
Elizabeth

I tossed and turned in our bed, not being able to fall asleep. I couldn't sleep without Antonio. It was hard enough not to cry when I talked to him on the phone earlier.

It was nice to hear him tell me how much he loved me. I would never forget the feeling of him telling me I was it. No sharing. He really picked the right time for that little revelation.

I lifted up the collar of his shirt and sniffed it again. I reached pathetic mode about an hour ago. I had pulled a dirty t-shirt of his out of the hamper in the closet. I hoped the smell of him would help me relax, but it didn't. Technically I could blame it on the extra hormones, but I knew it was way too early for that.

I promised him I would always be honest with him, yet there was one thing I hadn't told him yet.

Two days ago, he asked when my period was due. I thought that was an odd question coming from a man, but he explained he wanted a warning for when I was going to turn sour on him. I laughed.

I looked at the calendar and realized I was actually a week and half *late*. Before I could answer, he asked if it was next week, since we had already been there for just over three weeks. I went with it.

Once he locked himself and Miguel in the office again, I turned to Francisco.

Biting my lip I asked, "Francisco, I need a favor, but I need you to not tell anyone... including Antonio. Is that possible?"

He looked confused and a little taken aback. "Senora, I can't keep secrets from him, you shouldn't either."

I sighed. "I don't plan on keeping this from him forever, just until I know for sure. Please?"

He studied me and then silently nodded. "What do you need, Senora?"

I looked around the kitchen, verifying we were alone. Then, I whispered, "I need a pregnancy test, one of those early detection ones." I saw the grin slowly begin to creep across his face. I put up a finger. "No. Shoosh. No one can know until I do. And then not until I am ready to tell Antonio. Entiendes?"

"Si, Senora! I will take care of it myself. I promise." With how happy he was, I knew I had better make this quick.

Unfortunately, that was only yesterday, when Antonio also told me he was leaving. Francisco went to the store last night. He impatiently waited outside the bedroom this morning, after Antonio and Miguel left, pacing in the hall like he was the expectant father, while I peed on a stick.

He swore to me that he would not say anything to Antonio. I also had to make him promise not to tell anyone else either. I could see he struggled with that one. The man was obviously struggling with not running down the hall, shouting it out to everyone he came across.

It wasn't until I helped him realize how upset Antonio would be if everyone else knew before him, that he finally got control of himself. He still struggled not to smile any time he saw me today though.

I was finally starting to succumb to sleep when I heard the shuffling of feet from the hall. I looked at the clock on the nightstand. It was three in the morning.

Who would be moving around on this floor, at this time of the night?

I heard the jiggle of the doorknob and reached into the nightstand drawer for the gun Antonio put in there that morning. I really thought it was a bit over the top, but if it made him feel better who was I to argue?

Now I was really glad I let him. Not that my disagreeing would have stopped him.

I jumped and screamed as something slammed violently against the door, causing it to fly open and partially hang off the hinges. I held the gun up, pointing it at the intruders. A light flashed towards me, not quite in my eyes but still on me.

At the same time, I heard doors all over the house being opened in the same manner.

"FBI. Put the gun down, ma'am!" Some man yelled from the dark.

"How do I know you are the real FBI and not just some creep who broke in here? Uh, uh, I've been down the kidnap and human trafficking road before. You can bet I ain't going through that again." I may have been just a tad on the hysterical side.

Was this Andre's attempt to recollect me?

I heard a few muttered curse words slip out from across the room.

A female voice, a lot calmer than the other, spoke up next.

"I am going to turn the light on and show you my badge. The men will stay back, it will just be you and me. You can keep your gun on me the whole time. No one is here to hurt you. I promise." She paused for a minute then added. "Okay, here comes the light."

I squinted as the light flashed on. But thanks to that annoying flashlight, my eyes didn't need as much time to adjust.

I studied them carefully. There were three people standing in my doorway, two men and one woman. All were dressed in black and wore vests that said FBI over the left breast,

Those could be bought at a costume store though.

The woman set her gun on a side table and walked slowly to me as she kept one hand in the air. Her other hand reached into her back pocket and pulled out her wallet. She carefully threw it on the bed and stepped away.

With one shaky hand holding the gun, I opened the wallet, and sure enough, there was a badge and her ID naming her as Special Agent Stacey Lennings, for the FBI here in Laredo.

I lowered my gun and they lowered theirs. She walked to me slowly and I handed her back her badge.

"Sorry, I am a little jumpy and paranoid."

"No worries, sugar. We will get you out of here and back home as soon as we can."

I shook my head. They misunderstood. "No, this is my home. I was already rescued from the trash who took me."

She looked at me quizzically. I knew they probably assumed Antonio was the one who took me. They were probably here looking for him.

Suddenly, I was glad he left.

"Where is Antonio Ortiz? We were told this was his room." A rough man demanded.

I scowled at him. "I don't know. He left on business this morning. Why do you want Antonio?"

"Do you know who he was doing business with?"

"No. I haven't known him for that long. Only about a month."

Agent Lennings sat down on the edge of the bed, obviously playing good cop.

"Tell me how you met."

"About a month or so ago, I decided to step out of my comfort zone for the first time. See, I don't do well in crowded areas, especially around strangers. I learned early on it was better to stick to myself. It was my birthday, and I didn't exactly have any friends, so I went to this club alone."

My voice cracked remembering the fear I felt. Man, I really did not want to have to relive this.

"Where was the club?"

I lowered my voice, not wanting it to crack again. "New Orleans. That's where I'm from. Anyway, I was really nervous and kept falling out of my heels. The bouncer was really nice, even wished me a happy birthday. I argued with myself, all I wanted to do was run back out the door. I probably should have. The bartender was really nice too though. I had never drunk anything before, so he said we would start light." I smirked. "He made me an Adult Shirley Temple. It tasted more like juice than anything else. Then this guy comes up to me. Says he owned the club, and he heard it was my birthday. He ordered me a few drinks, working me up to stronger ones."

I shook my head again. I still hadn't figured out how it all happened, not that I let myself think about it much.

"I don't understand what happened. I watched each drink carefully. The bartender handed them straight to me. I figured I was just a lightweight, only four drinks in and I could barely stand up. I wanted to lie down. Andre took me to a back room to lie down while he called me a cab."

I was full up bawling now. Lennings put a hand on my leg and rubbed it gently. Even the men started softening. There were some things you just couldn't fake.

"When I woke up, I was in some creepy room. My ankle had a chain around it. The room was cold, and I was lying on a cot with a dirty mattress. Eventually this big guy came in and started talking about how he couldn't wait to make me scream. He held me down and was just about to...to." I took a deep breath.

"Anyway, Andre came in right then and got onto him because I wasn't supposed to be like the others. But there were ten more new girls waiting for him in the other room. After he left, Andre made me clean up with baby wipes and watched me until he couldn't just watch anymore. He said I missed a spot. He told me how he wanted to keep me for himself. I could hear girls screaming from somewhere else. Later, Andre came back for me. He said I was going with him to a party. He didn't trust Paul to leave me alone, so he was taking me with him."

I made a few minor adjustments to the truth, so they didn't connect Antonio to Andre, not in that sense. Not in the sense that would get him arrested.

"He took me to this really big house. Andre led me into a different room. I saw girls stripping for a bunch of men in a large room we had passed. Andre locked me in the room and said he would be back later. I don't know how long I was there before Antonio came in. I was hiding behind the couch. I told him what happened, and he snuck me out of there. I asked him about the other girls, and he said they were paid strippers, they would be fine. Apparently, it was his bachelor party, but the party was more for the other men. He hates that stuff. He hated the bride he was being forced to marry, too. He promised to protect me from Andre, who nearly lost it when he saw I was gone from the room. I didn't even know we had left the country until two days later. Antonio said he was taking me back to Texas with him. He offered to contact someone and let them know I was okay, but I don't have anybody. He insisted on checking the missing persons list when we got back. I told him it was pointless. I had a dead-end job that employees frequently just stopped showing up for, and I mostly worked from home anyway. My landlord was a jerk and wouldn't care. I was paid up and he would just sell all my stuff when time ran out. I was worried Andre would come looking for me if I went back there. Antonio said I could stay, and he would protect me. My guard sleeps down the hall, but during the day Francisco is always by my side."

"What about your family? Surely, they are worried about you." Lennings asked softly.

I shook my head and scoffed while wiping my nose. "My parents died in Katrina. I was a foster kid tossed from home to home. Antonio and his family are the closest thing I have ever had. They welcomed me, made me feel safe, and took care of me. No judgements, no bullying... well except Elena and she is a real piece of work."

"That would be Elena Ortiz, his wife?" The other man said.

I nodded. "Married by name only. Antonio can't stand her. He only married her because it was arranged through their parents. She was sleeping with someone else just hours before their wedding. She's kept herself hidden in her room since we got here. We've seen her maybe half a dozen times. Each time she is snottier than the last."

I watched as they all looked at each other, some sort of silent communication going on. Lennings stood up and the men walked out of the room.

"Why don't you put some pants on and we will go downstairs. Alright?" I nodded. "What's your name sweetheart?"

"Elizabeth Martinez." I grabbed the first pair of pants I found and slid them on.

She stayed by my side until we reached the first floor. Francisco was sitting on the couch, his hands in cuffs.

"Elizabeth! Thank goodness." He stood up to come to me but one of the agents got in his way and pushed him back down.

"Stop it!" I yelled as I ran over to him.

The agent turned and blocked me next. "You need to stay back, ma'am."

I scowled at him then turned to Francisco. "Are you okay?"

He huffed and shook his head. "I'm fine. I was worried about you. Antonio would die if anything happened to you. Are you... okay?"

I knew what he was trying to ask and not ask. I nodded as I blushed. There were too many eyes, and they knew Antonio was married to someone else. While Antonio's men may see me as a wife, I doubted these guys would.

I sat down on the couch across from Francisco. We both sat in silence, leaving them to do whatever it was they came to do. Elena was led out sometime later. A haughty smirk on her face.

She stayed across the room from us, looking around. Her eyebrows creased in confusion.

"Where is Antonio? Did you arrest him already?"

Now I was the one confused.

"No, ma'am. He is not here."

"What do you mean he isn't here? You were supposed to come in and arrest him! He has to be here somewhere!" Her voice grew in pitch as she yelled.

"No, Elena, he isn't. If you ever came out of your hole you would have known that. He left this morning on a business trip." I snarked at her.

The stress and lack of sleep were obviously giving me more courage than I normally had.

"Why didn't he tell me he was leaving? I am his wife!" She actually stomped her foot!

I laughed. "His wife of one month and when was the last time you came looking for him? When was the last time you acted like a wife? Do you know any of the staff in this house? Do you even know where anything is besides your bedroom?" I scoffed sardonically. "You are no wife."

She screamed and stomped her foot again. I only said all that because I was hoping they would realize she knew nothing. Whatever she told them was a lie. Their whole investigation was built on a lie. I sat back and ignored any more outbursts from her.

Another agent came from down the hall, I assumed from Antonio's office. He walked over to Francisco and started asking questions.

"You claim to be hired security for Mr. Ortiz. Do you have any proof of that?"

"Si, senor. My wallet is in my room, on top of my dresser. My identification is there." The agent looked at another man and they took off up the stairs.

"Why were you hired by Mr. Ortiz?"

Francisco looked at me. I nodded. "It's okay. I already told them about Antonio saving me from Andre. Antonio was right, I need to talk about it more, get it out of my system."

He smiled softly, catching my meaning. "Antonio and I grew up in Mexico together. He frequently hires me for different security jobs. I don't work for any company directly. I'm an independent contractor. Last month, I was with him in Mexico to stand next to him at his wedding, to the shrew in the corner." He pointed to Elena with his chin.

She scowled back.

"It was also my job to keep him from splitting. The morning of his wedding, he told me he found a senorita the night before. She had been kidnapped by the guy who supplied the dancers for his bachelor party. I already knew he had disappeared during the party. Antonio was never comfortable in those settings. He is a unique man. He doesn't do the whole jumping from girl-to-girl thing. Which is one reason why he hates the shrew, she jumps from man to man. He said Andre might come back for Elizabeth. I helped him keep an eye on her in Mexico, we all took turns hanging out with her. When she decided to stay with us here, Antonio hired me full time. He hasn't told her, but he has been looking into Andre's business and trying to keep tabs on him. He worries about Elizabeth and wants to keep her safe."

I had tears sliding down my face. I wasn't sure how much of that was true, but it was sweet, nonetheless. And Antonio did worry about me, a lot. He may be possessive and controlling, but that was only because he was a big worrywart. If it was out of his control, he worried more.

Lennings came back into the room and approached the questioner with a tablet. She showed him what was on it before turning to me.

"Well, Miss Martinez, looks like last week your landlord reported you missing."

My jaw dropped. No need for acting now. I was legitimately shocked. "He did? Are you sure? I thought the man hated me. Then again, he seemed to hate everybody." My voice lowered to a whisper, mostly talking to myself now.

"Are you sure Ortiz ran that missing person's check on you? He could have just been saying that to convince you to stay."

I frowned at her, wanting to scowl, but also not wanting to look like Elena.

Francisco popped in. "I ran the check myself. I have a low-level clearance with my license. I used it to sign into NamUs. I did it twice. We figured if no one reported it after two weeks, no one would report it at all. She wanted to just leave her past behind and start fresh. We respected those wishes."

A few minutes later another man spoke up. "I have it right here, sir. They ran the check."

"Regardless. We still have evidence to sort through. Mr. Lopez we will be taking you into custody until we can verify your license and the depth of your involvement with Mr. Ortiz and his businesses. Miss Martinez, Mrs. Ortiz, you both will come with us as well. We will have more questions for you, and we will keep you in protective custody. Miss Martinez, think back to all you know about the people who took you. You can help us take them out while we are at it."

"It would be my pleasure to help you take down Andre, just keep me out of it. As for Antonio, you're sniffing up the wrong tree. She is just an unhappy shrew who realized she wasn't going to be treated like the princess she thinks she is."

Elena sneered at me as the main man responded. "We'll see about that."

We were all led to different cars. I could tell it was killing Francisco to leave my side. I held my necklace in my left hand and rubbed it, almost absentmindedly.

"I'll be alright, Francisco. Just take care of yourself and do what you are told. This will all be over soon." He nodded once and got into the police car.

Lennings stepped into a black car with me. I scooted over so she would have room. I kept the necklace in my hand, hoping it would help the movement look more natural. Last thing I needed was for them to take it away.

"That's a pretty locket."

I looked down at it. "Thank you. It's all I have left of my mother. I thought I had lost it the night Andre took me. I promised I would behave if he gave it back to me."

"What does it say on the back?"

I showed it to her. "Mi alma. It means my soul. I think my mom said my dad gave it to her on their wedding night. She used to let me sleep with it on when I was scared. It's one of the few memories I have of her."

"How old were you?"

"Three or four. It had tarnished in all the flooding. I didn't mind. It made the necklace look cheap and old. Otherwise, I would have lost it in a foster home. Antonio got it cleaned a couple weeks ago for me. I didn't even realize it was white gold until the jeweler told me. I cried as they washed it in front of me." I smiled softly. "I hated the idea of losing it again."

I fell silent after that, staring at my necklace. I didn't have much experience with lying. I hated it, but I needed them to see Antonio as the good guy and I needed to keep my locket.

He would find me. I knew he would.

I spent the next two days holed up in a dingy apartment, it was still steps above my old one.

The main agent came in and out a few times, usually with Lennings in tow. My guard dogs changed every six hours, the same four teams of two.

I answered question after question. I told them all I knew about Andre's club and where we stayed in Mexico.

It wasn't a lot on the latter, but the former I knew enough that they could find it. It wasn't until the third day that things changed.

Lennings showed up with someone new this morning, a box of donuts in one hand and a tray of coffee and juice in the other. She had a big smile.

"Good news, Elizabeth!"

"I can go home to Antonio?"

She shook her head and sighed. She had tried to convince me many times that it was all Stockholm syndrome. The man saved me from a fate worse than death, therefore I made him my hero and fell in love with him.

Neither of us were going to be swayed.

"Agents in New Orleans were able to get a warrant for the club. They busted the place last night. They got a confession out of the bartender. He slips drugs into girl's drinks without them knowing. Only the ones that Andre is interested in, of course."

Well, that explained why I didn't see Andre put the drugs in. "What about Andre?"

She sighed and sat down. "He wasn't there. They found records in his office for various warehouses in different countries. The man keeps meticulous records, even old video tape. We have him on video, walking you to a back room. There were even cameras in the alley behind the club. Everything was recorded. It was kind of stupid of him to keep all that. But some psychos like to watch their actions later, like a home movie. We figure they are his trophies. Anyway, we are moving you to a safe location. We can't let him come near you. We are going to need your statement. It will help put the nail in his coffin."

"Can't you just let me go back to Antonio's compound? I was safe there." I whined.

"We are still searching through everything. All the staff has been interviewed. We are hoping to talk to him when he comes home. Odds are he won't. I'm sorry honey, but that man is going to run for the hills. His friend has been released. We didn't have enough evidence to keep him. That whole crew will be in the Mexican wind by nightfall."

I knew Antonio would come for me. I just had to let it go until then.

"What about Elena?"

Lennings scoffed. "That woman is a piece of work. She called us in, claimed she could give us evidence to bring down the Ortiz Cartel. Said they had a local branch, and the son ran the crew. She gave us enough intel that a judge approved the warrant. As soon as she could she jumped the border back into Mexico. The higher ups let her go. Said she at least got us started. If anyone retaliates against her, it's the Mexican's problem."

"Figures." I scoffed and picked up a donut.

"Okay, finish that up and pack up. We are out of here in ten." Lennings slapped her thighs and stood back up.

By nightfall they had me locked up in a cabin in Oklahoma. I cried myself to sleep, and not for the first time.

That idiota was taking me everywhere with him from now on.

Chapter 19

Antonio

I paced back and forth in Levi's living room. It had been three days since Miguel got the call.

Five days since the FBI charged into my house.

Francisco called last night. He gave me a brief rundown of what happened that night.

Levi's man was able to make contact with someone in the FBI. They had Elizabeth in protective custody while they flushed out Andre.

According to her chip, she was near a small town in Oklahoma. She was safe for now.

While I was ready to run straight to her and grab her, Levi convinced me it would be better to wait and see what happened with the investigation. If I showed up beating down doors, it would add to more questions.

I was giving them one more day.

"I just heard something interesting." A man they called Freddie said as he walked through the front door.

Apparently, he used to work for the FBI. He had been undercover trying to bring down Levi and his father. They brought down the father, Freddie came back.

Family was family.

They had some interesting stories to tell around here. Out of everyone, Freddie understood my anxiety the most. It was his girl the cleaner had taken, twice. I decided to not give him slack on not killing the man the first time around, Freddie had still been a Fed at that point.

"What did you hear?" I asked him as I stopped pacing.

"Your lovely wife jumped the border after ratting you out. She is now tucked in safe with her parents in Mexico. She didn't give them much, but it was enough to get a warrant."

I laughed and pulled out my cell to call my padre. "She is so stupid. She won't be safe for long."

"Hijo, any news on Elizabeth?"

I smirked. She had a way with everybody.

"The Feds have her in a safe house in Oklahoma. They are using her to take down Andre. He can lead back to us, so you might want to find him first. But that is a whole other issue. We just got word. Elena is the one who called in the Feds. She gave them just enough to get a warrant. The good news, she ran straight home to mama y papa."

Padre laughed. "I'll take care of it from here. I assume you will not be needing me to replace her?"

I smiled for the first time in days, it was only half of one but still. "No, padre. I already got who I want."

"Bueno. Call me when you have more."

"Si, padre." I hung up and turned back around.

"Well, that is one problem down. Do you know how much they have on me?"

Freddie shook his head. "Not really. They have been searching your house for nearly a week, they talked to all the staff. In my experience, they are grasping at straws. They are hoping you will walk in, and they can arrest you like your guard."

"What would happen if Elizabeth were to leave protective custody?"

"They can't force her to stay. She has rights. If she were to leave, they cannot press charges against her or whoever she went with willingly. I still don't suggest you show up there. Why don't you let us help you? Call it a goodwill gesture towards a stronger partnership?"

I huffed. "I thought you were just a counselor at the school, and you stayed out of this side of things?"

"I am and I do. But you also know, we have a soft spot for damsels in distress around here."

Just then a toddler ran down the hall wearing nothing but a diaper. Laughing like crazy as three very tall men chased him down the hall. Between them walked a very pregnant woman, laughing.

I wanted this. I wanted a family with Elizabeth. I turned back to Freddie.

"Help me get mi hermosa back, Freddie." I pleaded, not caring about my man card anymore. That worry passed days ago.

"Got it. Let's go talk to Levi. I have a plan, but I need his approval."

Levi Cooper may run things in an unusual way, but there was no arguing that he was still successful, he had created a sense of loyalty and trust among his men and made a safe place for his family.

We spent the next few hours going over the logistics of Freddie's plan. I hated that I would not be the one to go in and get her, but I had to keep our future in mind.

Once I had her, they couldn't take her back. They wouldn't be able to get anywhere near her ever again.

No warrant for my arrest had been issued and she was a free citizen. She was smart enough to know that I would come for her, she just had to sit tight.

Francisco arrived that night, along with John. The rest of my men were hunkered down, waiting for the all-clear. We sat and listened as Francisco told us the whole story.

"That chica is smart. By the time they brought her downstairs, she already had them catering to her. She spun it as though Andre had taken her for his own purposes. You just happened to come across her and took pity on her. She played you up to be the hero, not the guy who bought her."

"You bought her?" A female voice yelled from the doorway.

Levi didn't keep secrets from his wife, Callie. He said it saved a lot of fights. She may have been a Fed herself for a short time, but she still supported her husband.

I shook my head. "No, my padre did. Apparently my bisabuelo, my great grandfather, started this ridiculous tradition of providing the first mistress to the son with an arranged marriage. My padre knows I don't like women who have been around the block a few times. He got the bright idea to contact a man known for human trafficking. He placed an order for someone who was pure and innocent. Andre has a reputation for pulling miracles." I smiled. "I may not agree with the man's methods, but he certainly gave me my miracle. From the moment I saw her eyes peeking over the side of the couch, she has owned me. She had a rough life, she agreed to stay with me, for both her protection and stability. It worked out better than either of us planned."

Miguel put a hand on my shoulder.

"Okay, that sounds better than. You can continue." Callie told Francisco as she sat on the arm rest next to her husband on the couch.

I laughed. She was a tough woman, just like my Elizabeth.

"About then, Elena came in and got all upset about you not being there and then demanded to know why you didn't tell her you were leaving." He chuckled. "You should have seen the way Elizabeth put her in her place. I think we were both suspecting by then that Elena had a part to play in it all. Elizabeth went off saying if she was your wife then she would have come out of her room more and talked to you instead of hiding away. She laid it all out there. All Elena could do was stomp her foot and screech. A little later a female agent came out, she was all soft spoken when she addressed Elizabeth. When they questioned my current job, I wasn't sure what to say. Elizabeth told me very sweetly that it was okay, she had already told them about Andre. She played it off as though I was trying to protect her privacy and you were always trying to get her to talk about what happened. She even said how it felt good to talk about it. Again, making it sound like you were trying to help her heal. I tell you; she is scared stiff they are going to connect you to Andre. The female agent verified that Elizabeth was reported missing. Her landlord did it last week. Elizabeth was shocked and started tearing up. She honestly thought he didn't care."

I shook my head. "She never sees herself in the right light. All those stupid foster homes made her feel small and useless."

"She's coming into her own though. She saw I was worried as they were taking her away from me. She rubbed her necklace, reminding me about the chip, and then told me to take care of myself and to do what they say."

"I think I am going to like this girl." Callie said.

Levi chuckled. "You should, she reminds me of you." I looked up at Levi, confused. "Callie went through trauma as well before we first met. It took forever to convince her of her worth as a teacher." Levi looked at her lovingly and moved a hair behind her ear. "She came around eventually."

The room was silent for a moment before Francisco broke it, seemingly unsure of himself. Something I had never seen in him before.

"There is one more thing, El Jefe. She made me promise not to say anything. But... under the circumstances, I think you need to know sooner rather than later."

I didn't like secrets. She knew this. He knew this.

"What?" I growled.

He sighed and looked at the floor. "She's pregnant. She took the test right after you left."

I felt my face pale. Elizabeth was pregnant? What?

My whole world just ripped out from under me. I no longer heard the rest of them talking. All I saw was mi hermosa. Mi alma. Alone, surrounded by men she didn't know. Scared, worried about me, and pregnant with my nino.

For the first time since I was a nino myself, I cried.

I was vaguely aware of Miguel moving to sit next to me. He didn't say a word, he just sat there so I wasn't alone. Not like Elizabeth was, again.

It was my job to protect her. I promised her no one would ever touch her again. I should have listened. I should have brought her with me on this trip.

If Elena wasn't already a pile of ash, along with her traitorous parents, I would put her in her grave myself.

"I don't know what to do, hermano."

"We follow the plan, just with a few small changes." Rick, one of Levi's top men answered.

I looked up at him. "Like what?" Before he could answer, we were interrupted.

"How far along would she be?" Callie asked, in a more serious tone than before.

I shook my head. "Not long. We only met a month ago." My voice sounded hoarse and dry. Miguel patted my back, trying to be supportive.

Callie turned to Levi. "That's too early. Emma wasn't much further along when she had her miscarriage. It wouldn't take much to push her into it. And if she's pregnant with the child of a known cartel boss, the Feds will do everything they can to keep her. She may not even know why they are keeping her. But she just became a much bigger prize to them."

I rubbed my face roughly and then held it in my hands. The room was silent for a time again. Things just changed.

"So, what's the plan, El jefe? How do we get our Senora back?" Francisco's voice shaky.

He had probably spent as much time with her as I had. If it wasn't for the fact that I knew he saw her as his little sister, I would be upset.

I cleared my throat. "Freddie had an idea, and we have created a plan. While it kills me to follow it, I understand the purpose of it. We are waiting a few more days to give the agents watching her time to get comfortable. Rick's girlfriend, Rachel, has agreed to help out. She used to be a Park Ranger, still has the uniform too. She is going to try to make contact with Elizabeth, let her know we are coming."

I explained the plan from there. It was an odd one, but it should work. My men were more of the sneak in, shoot if necessary, grab what they came for, and leave type.

This was not that kind of plan. With Elizabeth in a more sensitive position, maybe this was better.

Chapter 20
Elizabeth

I sighed as I pushed myself in the porch swing. I was bored. I missed Antonio. I really didn't care much for these agents either. They were rude and rarely spoke to me.

We'd been in this stupid cabin for a week now. If Antonio were here with me, instead of these men, I would probably think it was the perfect getaway.

I was really beginning to feel antsy. I needed to hear his voice. I needed to talk to him. I needed to talk to a girl. I didn't feel comfortable enough talking to the men in that cabin.

I hadn't seen Antonio for nearly two weeks now.

I looked up as I heard a jeep pull up to the cabin. The agents came bursting out of the front door and tried to push me back inside. I refused to move.

Andre's people would be stealthier than this.

The agent trying to push me back inside scowled at me. I scowled back. I wasn't exactly here by choice. He could shove his badge up his rear.

I looked back to the front when I heard the car door close. A tall woman with black hair pulled into a short ponytail, wearing a dark green uniform strolled up. She carried herself in a way that shouted confidence and toughness. She certainly looked tougher than me. I bet no one would be able to hold her hostage... twice.

"Morning folks. My name is Rachel. I'm with the local ranger station. We like to make rounds every now and then, check on the residents and make sure all is well. This far from civilization, we only got each other, you know."

The agents relaxed. "Morning, Rachel. We appreciate the concern and all, but we are fine."

Rachel looked over the agents and then at me. "Miss, are you good? You don't look very comfortable. Do you need help?"

The agents looked at me, scowls still on their faces. Nice way to protect your cover.

"I'm fine. Thank you, Rachel."

She continued to walk closer to me and put her left hand out. I took it with my left and shook her hand.

"Nice to meet you, ma'am. What's your name?"

"Elizabeth." She looked down at my hand as I answered.

"I like your tat, Lizzie. Mind if I call you Lizzie?" I shook my head as she rolled up her sleeve. "I got this one when I was still in the service, most Marines get it. Something about tats, they help us feel closer together, like we've been branded as part of a family. Know what I mean?"

Branded as part of a family? Was she saying what I thought she was saying?

I nodded, a real smile sneaking across my face for the first time in weeks. "Yeah, I think I do."

She nodded. "I met a man once who had a giant red dragon across his chest. He was a cranky sucker. The man just could not sit on the sidelines and let someone else run the show. Course, he had loved ones he couldn't get to, but still. Eventually, he listened to reason and let my troop help. Everything was smooth sailing from there."

Holy crap. Please let that all be some sort of weird message. I could totally see Antonio not wanting to sit on the sidelines. What could I say back?

"Sounds like a man I once knew, well a lot of them actually. Men in general seem to be impatient and want to run the show. They don't realize they can get a lot further with the right partner, as a team. If only they would shut up and listen to the advice of others, we probably wouldn't have so many wars."

Rachel laughed. "True that! Well, if you need anything, you let me know." She eyed the agents carefully as she walked backward toward her Jeep, then loaded up and left.

"What was that all about?"

"That is what we women folk like to call being friendly with one another. You might want to try it sometime."

I sat back down and started pushing myself again. One of them stayed outside with me this time. I sighed and closed my eyes, letting the cool breeze calm my nerves.

If I understood right, Antonio had some friends helping him out. Good, they would keep him out of trouble. It also had to mean that he wasn't far away and would be coming for me soon.

Antonio

We all jumped as the phone rang. My men and a few of Levi's were all camped out in a cheap hotel room waiting to hear back from Rachel. Rick answered his phone and put it on speaker.

"Alright sweetheart, you're on speaker, give us some good news."

"It was easy. She was sitting on the front porch swing when I pulled up. I saw two male agents. They both came running out. They tried to push her back inside, but she wasn't having it. They tried to brush me off after I gave them my checking in spiel. The way they were keeping her back gave me the excuse I needed to get closer. I made it sound like I thought she was being held against her will. Ha! They didn't like that much. I shook her hand with my left then commented on her tat. I showed her mine and started talking about how we use them in the military, branding ourselves to show we belong to our family. Her eyes lit up like Christmas morning. To be sure, I started talking about this cranky guy I knew who had a large red dragon on his chest. I told her how he had a hard time sitting on the sidelines but eventually listened to reason and let us help. She came back with a message of her own. Basically, she said men need to learn to be patient and listen to the advice of others. Work as a team and we would have peaceful solutions."

I chuckled quietly. "Sounds like mi hermosa. How is she, Rachel?"

"She looked good, bored but good. She didn't seem very happy with the agents though."

We hung up a few minutes later and they started preparing for stage two. At least now she knew we were coming. One more day, one more day and I would get to hold mi alma again.

My pregnant mi alma.

Chapter 21
Elizabeth

After another half hour with the grump agent standing guard, I started getting a bit grumpy myself.

"You don't have to stay out here you know. I highly doubt she works for Andre. It was perfectly safe to talk to her."

He huffed. "It's my job to keep an eye on you and make sure you stay safe."

"Really, because I feel more like you are keeping me prisoner than protecting me." From the small change on his face, I knew I was right. "That's it isn't it? You all aren't just keeping me safe from Andre. You want to use me as bait to catch Antonio. And here Lennings had me believing you all thought he was going to ditch me while he ran for cover."

He smirked and turned away. Great. Now I was worried this was all a trap.

Not much later, my attention was drawn to the small dirt path again as another car pulled up. This time it was a black Toyota Camry. I watched as two more men climbed out.

Before they even made it to the porch, the agent who had gone back inside came out carrying my bag.

I stood up and looked at them, feeling a touch of panic. "What's going on? Are we leaving again?"

Agent grumpy pants stepped to my side and grabbed my arm. "Yes, we can't take any chances. There are rumors that there may have been a leak, with that Ranger showing up, we just can't be too careful. It's time to move on."

Oh, no. Not again. Antonio just found me too! I picked up my necklace and started rubbing it for comfort.

What had started as just covering my signal to Francisco had turned into a real deal habit. So far none of them had asked about the necklace again, or the tattoo. I'd like to keep my lies to a minimum if possible.

As a newbie at all this I was worried I'd slip up.

I obediently followed them down the few stairs and towards the car. But I was stopped by one of the new agents.

He raised his right hand up to stop me. "Hold on. I'm the paranoid kind. We are going to do a bug sweep before we leave."

He raised his left hand up and waved a small black wand looking thing. My heart started pounding.

"Bug? What do you mean by bug?" I was really hoping they misinterpreted where the fear was coming from.

"These guys are smart. They hide trackers on things they place value on. With all these coincidences, I want to play it safe. Just raise your arms out to your side, this will only take a minute."

I did as he said and waited for him to get to the necklace on my chest, already thinking of what I would say.

For one, I had to stick to my lie about it belonging to my mother.

And two, they couldn't know that it would bring Antonio to us.

Sure enough, as soon as the wand passed over my chest, it began to beep. The new, and apparently paranoid, agent lifted it up and looked at it closely.

"Where did you get this? Did Ortiz give it to you?"

I shook my head. "No, it belonged to my mother. My father gave it to her on their wedding night. It's all I have left of them. I never take it off."

He lifted an eyebrow. "You have never taken it off once? You never had it cleaned? You never let someone else hold it while you showered? It has never left your body?"

I took a breath, pretending to contemplate his question. "I have only taken it off twice in the last 17 years. Once when Antonio had it cleaned for me," a small smile started crossing the agents' faces. "However, they kept it in front of me the whole time. I was anxious about taking it off, the jeweler never left my sight."

Ha! Their smiles quickly turned to frowns.

"And the other time?" The grumpy pants agent asked.

"The other time was Andre. He had taken it off of me while I was drugged. He bribed me to behave when we left the warehouse that night by giving it back to me."

That was the story I had given Agent Lennings. I at least hoped I stuck to it well enough.

The agents all looked at each other, a silent conversation going on. The paranoid agent looked back to me, a look of apology on his face.

"My apologies, Miss Elizabeth. But I am going to need you to give me that necklace. It seems Andre may have bugged it in order to keep tabs on you. The only reason he hasn't come for you yet was because you were always on that compound. Surrounded by much stronger and violent men than him. Right now, he is on the run from us. Coming to get you just hasn't been an option yet. It sounds like he may have been planning too though." He put his hand out, silently asking for it.

I took a step back and held it tight, a tear sliding down my face. I needed to keep this with me. How else was Antonio going to find me?

"No, you can't. It's all I have left of my parents. Everything else is gone. If he is so afraid of Antonio, why don't you just let me go back? I am safer there."

He shook his head sadly as another agent walked up behind me and unlatched the necklace.

"I know you want to believe that. Ortiz saved you. He was good to you when no one else was. But, in time, you will see straight again. I promise. It's time to go now. That Ranger could have been working for Andre, we need to leave immediately."

He put a hand on my arm, and I let him lead me to the backseat of the new car.

I finally felt defeated. I finally felt lost. I sat in the car and watched as the grumpy agent hung my necklace on a nail that was sticking out of the porch, before heading for his hidden car.

I folded my fingers together in my lap and looked down. Through the tears in my eyes, I saw the red dragon possessively holding my wrist and finger. My only hope now was that the right people would see this and would let Antonio know they saw me.

I had to hold on to hope. If not for me, then for the sake of our baby.

I sniffed and took a steadying breath. When I first woke up in that warehouse, I was prepared to fight back, to find a way out. Turns out, I didn't need to.

Now, however, I would do everything I could to get away from these men and return to mi querido.

The two new agents loaded into the car and backed out. The old set followed us until we were on the main highway, and then for a few more miles. Eventually, they took a different exit and we continued on.

I already learned from before, there was no point in asking where we were going. They wouldn't tell me anyway.

Antonio

I sat on the cement curb outside of our cheap hotel room, watching the sunset, wondering if Elizabeth was watching it right now too. I felt so lost at that moment.

The door was open to the room, and I half listened as the others discussed the plan.

I had never felt so useless in my life. It was a good thing Elizabeth liked my possessive and overprotective side before, because it was going to be a hundred times worse when we got out of this.

The room went silent as Freddie spoke on the phone with one of his contacts, receiving an update. We all waited in silence until Freddie rejoined the room. As soon as I heard him ending the conversation, I stood up and went back inside to make sure I didn't miss anything.

"Alright, here's the gist. First, yeah, they are using her to get to you, Antonio. Apparently, her little speech, proving that Elena knew nothing, backfired. In time, they put two and two together. She had been found in your bed, and she knew more about your whereabouts than your own wife. When they decided you had been trying to protect her before, well... why would you stop now? Technically speaking, she is still being held in protective custody; however, they are doing it off the books. Procedure is that the witness in custody signs an agreement that they will exchange their statement for protection. They also agree to all the rules, yada yada yada. They skipped all that. They have no legal rights to hold her. That being said. I contacted an old friend. He was my handler once upon a time. Now he is a field supervisor. I helped bring down two mafia heads and get a three-month vacation, he gets a promotion and a raise. Democracy at its finest." His voice turned sour and sardonic. Irritated with getting a raw deal.

"Focus, Freddie." Rick warned him with slight amusement.

"Right, sorry. Anyway, Samson says he will vouch for me if need be. I brought my old badge just in case. All I need is a partner. Official orders will be sent to my email, I can print those in the office of the hotel."

Yes! Finally, something we could work with. I jumped up. "When do we leave?"

"Calm down, papa. We have to wait for the orders to come through first."

I smirked. Papa. I was going to be a papa! Maybe, as long as she stayed safe and calm. I heard all about how the stress could cause a miscarriage. I doubt she even told her bodyguards about the baby. She was smart enough to know better than that.

A few minutes later a loudmouth clown walked in carrying a bunch of pizzas. Freddie looked at him and started laughing.

"Hey, Garrett. How do you feel about going undercover again?"

Garrett set the pizzas down with a giant grin. "Will it be bloody?"

"No, but you get to rescue the damsel in distress again."

Garrett thought about it for a minute then shrugged. "Sure, beats hanging out around here. What do I have to do?"

"Be my partner, just like the old days, except this time it's for the other side. How does Special Agent Barney Rubble sound?"

Garret scowled and pointed at him. "No! No! We talked about this, no more Barney. It's bad enough Emma still calls me that, I don't need anyone else doing it."

"Awe, come on Barney!" Another man, Zack maybe, cajoled as he picked up a slice of pizza.

Miguel looked at me. "Do we really want to know?"

I shrugged. I really couldn't care less. Miguel apparently was intrigued enough, so he asked. Over the next half hour, the other men told the story together, each finishing each other's sentences, none of them caring.

From the laughter in the room, the story at least helped break the tension for them. The laughing was interrupted by Freddie's phone ringing again. The silence dropped faster than a jumper off a ten-story building.

Dark, I know, but such was my mood these days.

I listened carefully to Freddie's side of the conversation.

Unfortunately, either due to undercover training or time spent with the mafia, he learned how to keep his side to a minimum. Not allowing for eavesdroppers.

When he was off the phone again, he turned and looked at me. His face slightly paler and worry scrunching his eyes.

"What happened?" I growled out, no patience for anymore tiptoeing.

"I'm sorry, man, they're gone again. There were rumors of a leak, and then Rachel showed up. They didn't want to risk it. One of her new guards is of the paranoid sort, he brought a wand to search for bugs."

I waited for the count of three breaths, looked at Francisco and Miguel and walked out.

I had waited long enough.

Miguel grabbed a set of keys off the table and they both followed me out, along with John. The only men that actually belonged to me. I had told everyone else to stay put where they were, bunkering down until the heat passed.

None of Levi's men tried to stop us.

Francisco pulled the GPS app up on his phone, and we followed the directions to her necklace until we got to the small cabin in the woods. By now the sun had gone down, and the cabin was dark.

We pulled flashlights and guns out of the trunk and slowly approached the cabin from the back. There were no sounds of life taking place inside and no beams of light. It was completely dark and silent.

John and Francisco took the right side of the cabin, Miguel and I took the left. We all stopped when we met back up in the front.

The first two went through the cabin checking room by room. Miguel and I stood guard out front, a little off to the side, in case anyone came from behind us.

John and Francisco soon returned, looking defeated and frustrated.

"Sorry, El Jefe. There is no sign of them. They are gone." Francisco reported in.

I slowly drew my light across the porch, right to the swing where she had been sitting just hours ago. I felt my soul crushing in on me again.

I cleared my throat before speaking. "Check the app, does it say where the tracker is now?" My eyes never left the swing until Francisco spoke again.

"It says she is right here." He growled out in frustration.

We all moved our lights along the cabin, until something sparkled in the light. All four lights turned to it and stayed.

I walked up and lifted her necklace off the hook and held it in my hands. I turned it over and rubbed a thumb over my engraving.

All three men jumped back as my growl crescendoed rapidly, followed by a hard kick at the pole it had been hanging on, with all my might. It only took one kick for it to split in half. I felt heavy hands on my shoulders, pulling me away.

"Time for hiding is done. Spread the word. Tell the men their El Jefa is being held captive by the federales, against her will. Send out her picture, the one we took by the pool after her tattoo was healed. I want everyone on the lookout. Spread the word to all our contacts, anyone we trust. I don't care what level they are. Tell them there is a $100,000 reward for her return, safe and unharmed."

"Si, El Jefe." They all responded as Miguel backed the car out of the woods.

I picked up my phone and made the call I had been putting off. Despite the late hour in Mexico, I knew he would answer.

"Hijo? What's the matter? Did you get Elizabeth back yet?"

I cleared my throat again. "No, padre. They moved her again. They found the tracker in the necklace. That was all that was left. We are spreading the word to everyone. I am offering a reward, 100K. We have a picture of her tattoo. I will send it to you. Will you send it out to everyone on your end?" My voice cracked. I didn't care about trying to hide it. "Por favor, papá? She's pregnant, too. She found out the day I left. Francisco told me."

My father's voice sounded oddly hoarse when he responded. "Make it 500. Send me the picture. We'll get her back, hijo. Both her and the bebe. It will take time, but we will do it. The federales won't hurt her, they need her. Let's just hope we get her back before they realize the prize she carries."

"Gracias, papa." I didn't remember the last time I called him that, if ever. He always insisted on the more formal versions. I guess this was an appropriate time to be informal.

I hung up the phone and then updated my men on the new reward amount. The ride back to the hotel was silent.

As soon as we walked back into the room, Levi and his men jumped to their feet. I raised the necklace up for them to see and then collapsed into a chair. Curse words were thrown about the room.

"What's the new plan, Antonio? You know we will help where we can." Levi asked in a grave voice.

"The plan is to spread the word. We have a picture of Elizabeth showing off the tattoo I put on her wrist." I smirked. "As you know, she calls it her branding." I unbuttoned my shirt and opened it. "It is a perfect replica of mine. I had this drawn specifically and my artist knows they are not allowed to put it on anyone else. I need you to spread the word to all of your men, everywhere, and anyone else you trust. My family is offering a reward of 500,000 for her safe return. That should be large enough to get every level to open their eyes and pay attention. Other than that, you all should go home, go back to your familias."

"We can spread the word, that is not a problem. We will also help investigate any rumors or tips that come in. With that kind of money on the table, you can bet there will be many coming in. We have allies in various parts of the country, we will reach out to them."

I turned to Freddie. "Any chance the new agents have checked in or said where they are going?"

He shook his head. "No, they are playing it close to the vest now. If I hear anything though, you will be my first call."

I simply nodded my head.

Over the next hour, nearly every man in the room reached out to all those who worked under them and all those they trusted. Men, women, it didn't matter. Levi and I sat at the small table in silence, watching as our men did the duty we assigned them.

The next morning, we went our separate ways. The Cooper family returned to San Francisco. While my men and I found new lodgings and checked in under assumed names, until we had a better idea of where to go.

Levi's prediction proved true. Tips were coming in from all over. I was amazed with how many contacts and allies he had across the country. When this was all over, we were definitely going to be doing business together.

For now, the four of us moved around frequently. Sometimes we drove, sometimes we flew. It all depended on how credible the tips were, and how far away they were.

A pattern was beginning to show. Elizabeth and her agents were most likely traveling by car. They would spend a few days here and there in different places; however, we had no idea where they were headed.

Our best guess was North, but that was it.

Our hopes got up when we got a call, and a picture, of her at a diner just outside Fresno. She was practically in Levi's backyard. But they moved on too fast and slipped right through our fingers.

That was two weeks after they left the cabin. The weeks since then had been a living nightmare.

Chapter 22

Elizabeth

By the time we walked into a diner in Fresno, I was grumpy, irritable, and just done with it all. We had been on the road for the better part of two weeks now. Agent Sturgis wasn't kidding when he said he was paranoid.

If I didn't believe him before, I sure as heck did now.

When we left Oklahoma, we drove through the Northern tip of Texas, then New Mexico, Arizona, and from the bottom of California to the top. We spend all day in the car, then roughly two in a cheap hotel.

My back was sore from the lack of exercise, and the amount of time sitting.

My old babysitters used to call to check in with someone at least once a day. These guys rarely called anyone. At least they were somewhat nicer than the last set.

As it was still early - the sun was just coming up - the diner was mostly empty. We were met by a hostess, a young woman, possibly around my age.

Was it really just three months ago I walked into that club to celebrate turning 21? I felt so much older than that now.

I only realized we had hit October when we walked inside the diner.

The diner was decked out in cheap Halloween decorations, top to bottom. Each table had plastic pumpkins and skulls, the windows were outlined with orange and black lights. Paper skeletons were taped up on both sides of the entrance and on the bathroom doors.

The women's restroom had a skeleton with a dress on it. It was tacky but festive.

The hostess had spiky black hair, skull earrings in each ear, a spike in her eyebrow, and tattoos crawling up both of her caramel arms. As per my new habit, I raised my left hand and ran my fingers over my hair, as though I were adjusting my braid.

It took about five seconds before her black lipstick covered lips cricked up in a small smile. I tried not to get my hopes up. It wasn't the first time I had gotten some type of reaction, but nothing had ever come from it.

Then again, we didn't usually stay long enough anywhere for me to find out.

"Good morning! Just the three of you today?" She greeted us, her smile growing greedily. Her eyes raked my face and hand again.

"Yes." Agent Ryley's deep voice answered.

"Bueno, come with me please." She spun on her heel and began walking down the nearly empty walkway, a pep in her step.

We followed her to a booth directly in front of the main counter. She laid the menus down in front of us and then excused herself saying she would give us a few minutes. Through the break in the wall, where the cooks hand food to the servers, I saw her go in and whisper to a man dressed in all white. He looked through at us and then his smile widened like hers.

My hopes began climbing, despite my efforts to stay realistic. Just in case, I was going to try and drag this breakfast out as long as possible.

The hostess, who was apparently also our waitress, came back a few minutes later. Both agents ordered the meat lover's special, with a side of pancakes. I ordered an omelet with avocado and a side of fruit. The men drank coffee. I drank orange juice.

I may not have been able to get to a doctor yet to confirm the presence of my child, but the lack of a monthly visitor since I still lived in New Orleans was enough confirmation for me. And the not too cheap test Francisco had bought me.

In the meantime, I was going to do the best I could to take care of my baby.

My best guess was that I was between two to three months along now. I had no experience with pregnant women, so I wasn't sure when I would start showing. Unfortunately, I had begun to feel nauseous lately. Thankfully, the agents didn't seem to have much experience either. They believed I kept getting car sick or eating too much greasy food. Hence the occasional diner stop.

When we ordered, the waitress patted my left hand, right over the tattoo and smiled sweetly.

"Eres la jefa?" (are you the boss lady?) she asked.

I did my best to keep from grinning like an idiot. "Si, ayúdame, por favor." (Yes, please help me.) I responded.

171

TJ LEE

I was really hoping the agents had not lied about knowing Spanish. I tested them a few times, and they never responded. They could just be good actors though. She nodded once and walked away.

"What was that about? What did she say?" Agent Sturgis asked with a curious expression.

I shrugged nonchalantly. "Nothing really, she was just asking if I felt alright. I guess I look a little pasty."

They didn't seem too convinced of that, but let it go. I spotted the man in the kitchen picking up his phone and making a phone call. Please be calling Antonio.

The man turned and looked at me, then winked. I had to fight harder to keep my face neutral. The struggle was real, people.

How long would it take Antonio to get to me? Was he close? Were his friends?

Unfortunately, my babysitters seemed to be very observant this morning. No sooner had I finished eating before they began giving commands.

"Go use the bathroom, Elizabeth. We won't be stopping for a while. I will pay the tab. Agent Ryley will escort you."

I gave a soft, frustrated, sigh. I missed being able to use the bathroom on my own. At least they didn't insist on coming in there with me. At most, they would check to make sure the place was empty, then let me be.

As I walked out of the bathroom a few minutes later, I could see the waitress trying to stall Agent Sturgis. I acted like I tripped on something, twisting my ankle. Agent Ryley surprised me by picking me up and carrying me straight out the door.

Agent Sturgis threw some bills on the counter unceremoniously and we left. I looked over the agent's back and saw the look of devastation on her face. She mouthed a sorry as the door closed behind us.

That may have been the closest I came yet. She was at least the first one to address me. Which was something at least. Word had reached this far. Antonio was really spreading out his reach to find me. I just had to hold to that thought.

He was still looking. He wasn't going to give up.

We spent the next two weeks traveling through Nevada, Utah, and up into Idaho. We didn't sit down in a diner again either. They ordered ahead

172

and picked up the food. Sometimes we ate in the car, sometimes we pulled over and ate outside.

During those times, I would walk laps around the car. Frequently, they joined me. We were all tired of sitting inside it. When this was over, I had a feeling I would never want to be in a car again.

Things changed on October 25th. We pulled into an airport around eight one morning. According to the sign, it was the Billings Logan International Airport.

When did we pass into Montana?

I followed the agents quietly to the check in desk for Delta Airlines. Another man in a suit was standing near the desk, he turned when we walked up. The agents greeted him and shook hands, before turning to me.

"Elizabeth, this is Brandon Jones. He is an Air Marshall. He will be escorting you to your new home." Agent Sturgis informed me.

I scowled. "I don't need a new home. My old one was perfectly fine."

They all chuckled tolerantly and turned away from me, ignoring me, as per usual. They spoke to the lady at the counter and received two airline tickets. Without so much as a goodbye or a good luck, my babysitters left the airport, leaving me with someone new.

I was beginning to feel like the hot potato.

"Here, hold on to this until we board." Marshall Jones handed me my ticket and boarding pass. "Look, I don't know the whole story, nor do I need to know. From what I have been told, I am here to protect you from some pretty bad people until we reach our destination. This is going to be a very long day for both of us, so please, try to behave and remember that I am not the bad guy here."

I felt a little bad for him. He wasn't part of all this, he was only doing his job. However, that didn't mean I wasn't going to run at my first chance. And since he didn't know much, this might be easier.

I just had to keep my eyes open for the perfect opportunity to present itself.

I sighed and looked at him, no time like the present to start testing my boundaries.

"Habla español?"

He shook his head with a small smile. "Sorry no, that is about all I know. I'm sure you would be more comfortable if I did, but I only speak English and Japanese." I raised an eyebrow at him. That was an odd choice for a second language. He chuckled. "It's a long story. I lived in Japan for a while."

At that, we started walking towards security. I walked next to him. He made sure to stay at my speed, not letting me in front of or behind him. While we waited in line, I took the opportunity to look at my tickets. It would be a nice change to know where we were going.

According to the plane ticket he gave me, we were flying to Nashville but would have a two-hour layover in Colorado City.

If I was going to make a run for it, that layover would be my best option. We would arrive there around lunch time. I could copy after one of my favorite book characters, Bella Swan.

In the book *Twilight*, she pretended to be looking for food and then paused to use the bathroom. It was so busy, that her friends didn't see her come back out. Given, her bathroom choice had two entrances/exits, but I couldn't count on that being an option for me.

We eventually made it through the long security line and headed to our gate. Marshall Jones, who told me to call him Brandon as his identity on flights was actually a secret, bought me some breakfast. I chose a fully loaded breakfast burrito. The meat and melted cheese smelled divine.

We only had to wait an hour before boarding for our flight began, then another half hour sitting on the tarmac waiting to take off.

It was only my second flight, the first one being when we were trying to beat a hurricane. Thinking about it made me miss Antonio and the way he comforted me.

I didn't realize when the tears started sliding down.

Brandon leaned over and whispered, "Are you alright?"

I wiped my face and cleared my throat. "Yes, I'm just a little scared. I've only flown one other time and it wasn't exactly smooth."

There was no point in talking about Antonio. I already knew how all the cops felt about him and their opinion on our relationship. Besides, that might make him pay more attention to me when I tried to make a run for it. I needed him to think I would continue along like a good little puppy dog.

He patted my shoulder awkwardly, but softly.

A few minutes later, the morning sickness decided to fully kick in for the day. I quickly grabbed the small bag that was hidden in a pocket behind the seat in front of me.

I regretted that burrito now.

An older female flight attendant, she looked to be in her forties or fifties, came over then, looking concerned.

She patted my back gently and ran her fingers through my hair. "Are you alright sweetheart?"

I simply nodded my head. She reached over and took the filled bag away. Twenty minutes later, I used Brandon's bag too. After disposing of the new bag, the flight attendant came back with a bottle of water and some crackers.

"This isn't a full flight, and we have a small section open in first class. Would you like to move up there? You will be more comfortable and have a bit more privacy."

I shook my head. "No, that wouldn't be fair to the rest of the passengers." I looked around at those near us. Our section was obviously fuller than first class, but not overly full.

The flight attendant patted my shoulder. "No offense, but I think they will all be okay with you not throwing up in front of them anymore." Her voice stayed soft and gentle, in a soothing manner.

I looked around at the other passengers again, a few of them sitting close by smiled and nodded their heads. I turned to Brandon, who decided to answer for me.

"That would be better, thank you."

We stood up and followed her to the front of the plane. I had to admit, these seats were bigger, and softer. No sooner had we buckled up again, then a new flight attendant brought over a blanket and a pillow for me.

My jaw nearly dropped when I saw her. She fumbled for a minute too, then looked at Brandon, who had missed both our reactions. Thankfully.

She carefully put the pillow behind my head and then put the blanket over me. I laid my hands on top of the blanket, ensuring she could see my tattoo.

I hadn't seen Angela since the day she brought the bathing suit to me.

"That's a lovely tattoo you have there. I have one very similar on my shoulder." She turned and pulled down her shirt just enough for me to see the top of a familiar red dragon.

I looked at her with my confused look and she gave me a grin that could only be described as mischievous.

"My boyfriend insisted I put it on my shoulder," she dropped her voice, as though she was telling a secret. "He likes to come from behind and wants to see it every time." She raised her voice back to normal. "Let me know if you need anything else dear, there are more bags in the seats and the bathroom is right there." She pointed to a small door just a few feet away before walking off.

I watched her carefully. Antonio said that I was the only one besides him to have that tattoo.

When she came in that day, he told me that he never touched Angela. I didn't know how many times both he and his friends told me how he didn't like to go where every other man had gone before.

Did he lie to me?

Was everything a lie then?

I felt my heart shattering the more I thought about it. Maybe I shouldn't go back to him after all. I was starting to think I needed time for just me, to help clear my head a bit. I needed time away from both sides. With no one trying to convince me that their own agendas were the right ones.

Those thoughts of course caused me to use two more bags before we landed. On the bright side, all the throwing up gave me a good reason to sneak off into the bathroom for a while.

"Do you want to try eating something before our next flight? We have time." Brandon asked politely as we disembarked the plane.

I pretended to think about it for a minute before responding. "Maybe if we can find a place that serves soup. That should be light enough."

He laid a hand on my upper back and led me down the terminal towards an area full of restaurants. We found one that looked promising, it was located diagonally from the bathrooms.

"Would you mind ordering me something that is close to a chicken soup? I want to freshen up in the bathroom, maybe brush my teeth." I grimaced, showing a disapproval for the taste in my mouth.

He chuckled. "Sure, I'll be right over here. Go there and back, nowhere else."

I nodded and smiled at him before turning around. I said a silent prayer of thanks for my luck so far and for help with this next part.

I entered the bathroom and waited in the short line. Once I was in the stall, I pulled a new shirt out of my small carry-on bag, all I had with me, and changed. After I left the stall, I washed my face and brushed my teeth.

I wasn't lying about wanting to do that part.

Up to now, my long hair had been pulled back in a braid. It pretty much lived in that braid for the last month and a half. Less hassle.

I pulled my hair into a ponytail and then wrapped it up into a bun. These were all just small changes, but hopefully enough to keep him from noticing me right away.

I knew I was running short on time before he started getting worried, so I stood near the entrance and peeked out. I could see Brandon sitting at a table nearby, the food having not yet come. I sighed with relief, hoping he wouldn't get worried until after.

As expected, I did not have Bella Swan's kind of luck. There was only one entrance and exit.

The bathroom had become busier and the line longer. Another girl was standing near me, waiting for her friends. They looked to be teenagers still and wearing jerseys.

"Are you all on a team?" I asked her.

She nodded enthusiastically and smiled. "Yes. We just got back from a soccer tournament. We won!"

I laughed at her obvious excitement. "Congratulations! That's wonderful!"

Four more girls gathered around by then. "Thank you. Have a good day!"

I smiled at her and quickly walked behind them. "Hey, do you think you girls can help me find the baggage claim? I've never been in this airport before, and I have a horrible sense of direction."

The girls laughed and the first one nodded. "Sure, come with us."

"Thank you! I can't tell you how much I appreciate this."

I made sure to keep them between Brandon and me. I chanced a quick glance at him. The food had come, and he was starting to get antsy. I forced myself to keep my breaths slow and my pace steady.

From behind, I would look different, and I would look like I was with these girls. Their presence in that bathroom was a stroke of luck, or a blessing. Same thing in my opinion.

I was also of the opinion that I was *way* overdue for one.

I thanked the girls when we reached baggage claim and practically ran out the door.

I found a bus nearby, the sign read long term parking. This would be the last place he would think to look for me, so I quickly boarded and walked to the back of the bus.

I sat down in an empty seat next to a woman in her mid to late twenties with short dark hair. She probably would have blended in with the soccer players better than I did. As the bus began to pull out, I saw her tuck her phone into her purse, which gave me an idea.

"Excuse me? Do you mind if I borrow your phone for a quick call? Mine died on the plane. I need to let my brother know I got home okay."

"Oh yeah, sure sugar, no problem." She reached in, pulled the phone back out and handed it to me.

I held back the threatening tears, stupid hormones must be kicking in. Mixed with the complete mental and physical exhaustion I was feeling settle in.

"Thank you."

I quickly dialed one of the few numbers I actually knew, and not the one I wanted to talk to the most. If I heard his voice, I would never be able to do this.

The phone picked up on the second ring, the voice cautious due to the unknown number.

"Hola?"

"Hola, hermano."

Two heart beats, then a tone of disbelief. "Senora?"

"Si." My voice came out soft and shaky.

Through the corner of my eye, I could tell my friendly neighbor was pretending not to listen.

"Senora, I can't tell you what a relief it is to hear from you, Are you okay? Is the baby okay?"

I cringed at his obvious relief, as the guilt of what I was about to do fully hit me.

"We're both fine, Francisco. I just called to check in with you. Are you okay?"

"Si, si, I am fine. Man, El Jefe is going to be so mad he missed you. He is going out of his mind worrying about you... uh... I had to tell him. I'm sorry, but with everything that happened, he needed to know."

"It's fine, I had a feeling you would by now. Listen, I am borrowing someone's phone, so I only have a minute to talk. I'm glad you are safe. Take care of Antonio for me, please."

"Senora, what are you saying? Tell me where you are, we will come get you. Are you still with the federales?"

I cleared my throat and lost the fight with the tears. "No, I got away. For now, I am in Colorado. I just got off a plane and managed to get away. I'm sorry, Francisco. I'm not coming back anytime soon."

His voice turned panicky. "Why? Please, just find somewhere and wait, we will have someone pick you up soon. We have had everyone we know looking for you, and then some. Antonio will be so relieved to hear that you are safe."

I shook my head quietly. "I can't. I'm sorry. You know what I have been through these past few months. I don't know, maybe it's the pregnancy hormones, maybe it was what Angela said. Or even what the FBI said, but I need space, hermano. Antonio will be fine without me. He has plenty of women to warm his bed." I didn't mean to snarl that last part; it just sort of slipped out.

"What are you talking about? What did Angela say? When did you see Angela? Senora, you know you are the only one for Antonio. He hasn't touched another woman since he met you. He even marked you to separate you from everyone else."

I scoffed and looked down at the biggest mistake in my life. "No, he didn't. Angela was only too happy to show me the one on her shoulder. She even proudly told me about why he chose that spot."

Francisco groaned. "Elizabeth, I don't know how she got that. But trust me, he's never touched her."

When I didn't respond, I heard his silent resigned sigh. "Where will you go? What will you do?"

I shrugged, realizing I did that a lot. "I don't know. I just know I need to find a place to settle for a while, see if I can create a second chance at life. The first one hasn't exactly gone so well." I huffed sarcastically.

Before I could say anything else, I heard a door open and another voice come in, one that brought memories of late-night talks and soft touches.

"I need to go, hermano. Te quiero."

"Señora, wait. Please."

I hung up before I could hear the background voice again. I handed the phone back to the girl as the bus began unloading in the parking lot.

She touched my arm gently. "This is going to sound weird, but... would you like to come home with me? I run a diner with my brother, in a small town an hour from here. I could use the help."

I looked at her cautiously before disembarking from the bus. "I don't know."

"I know you have no reason to trust me, but where else are you going to go? I can give you a place to stay and a way to make money for a time. If not for you, then how about your baby?"

I smirked. I knew she had been listening. "Where is it that you live exactly?"

She was the one smirking this time. "In a little town called SecondChance."

I laughed for real that time. Talk about coincidences. I nodded. She was right I had nowhere else to go. At least this time I would be disappearing with another female.

"That would be wonderful. Thank you. My name is Elizabeth by the way, call me Liz." I hadn't gone by Liz since my birthday. It was time to mix who I had been with who I was now.

"Anne. Follow me, my car is right over here."

Chapter 23

Antonio

I had just met with some cousins of Levi's in Seattle. We were hoping the Feds would head this way, but so far there had been no sign of them.

I left Elizabeth nearly two months ago, promising to be gone for only two days. She should be nearly done with her first trimester.

Was she sick yet? Was she getting cravings, back pain, or even showing yet?

Had she been able to go to a doctor for a checkup?

So, I had done a little reading on pregnancy, shoot me. I wanted to be ready for when she got back. And she *would* be back.

Freddie called yesterday and said the FBI finally released my house. Technically we could go home now, but it wouldn't be the same without Elizabeth. Nothing was the same without her.

I returned to the hotel with Miguel, feeling just as distraught as when I left. I growled when I walked in and said a few curses in Spanish as I threw my keys on the table.

That was when I noticed Francisco on the phone.

His face looked paler than I had ever seen it. A moment later he finally said something to the person he was talking to, and my heart stopped.

"Senora, wait. Please." I had never seen that look of utter sadness on his face before.

Was he talking to my Senora?

"Is that Elizabeth?" He sighed and hung up the phone as I reached for it. "Where is she? Is she okay? Why did she call you and not me?"

"Cálmate, El Jefe. I will tell you everything, but I need you to sit down and hear me out first."

I nodded slowly and sat down, even though I had a feeling I was not going to like what I heard.

"Elizabeth just got off a plane in Colorado. She managed to give the federales the slip somehow. She borrowed someone's phone to call me."

I sighed with relief and started laughing. "Perfecto! Where are we going to meet her? Do we have someone there who can get to her first?" He didn't answer and by the look on his face, that was not the real message. "Francisco?"

He took a deep breath and sat down on the edge of the bed, rubbing his face roughly with a growl.

"She must have been on Angela's flight. That's all I can think of how this happened."

"Angela saw her? Then why didn't she call? Did she help her get away? Angela loves money, I'm sure the reward would have been very motivating for her."

Francisco looked at me carefully, preparing to drop the bad news.

"There was something else more motivating. You. Alone and depressed. At some point Angela managed to get a copy of your tattoo on her shoulder. She showed it to Elizabeth. She told her you had it put there for a special purpose. Elizabeth is upset. She has spent months with the federales feeding her lies, Angela telling her that she was one of your marked women, and the pregnancy hormones. She was a mess." He took a breath and then looked in my eyes. "She's not coming home, Antonio."

I opened my mouth to speak but I couldn't. I could barely breathe. She wasn't coming home? No, that wasn't allowed.

My voice came out gravelly and hoarse, sounding more like a deep growl. "Where is she exactly?"

Francisco shook his head. "I don't know. She said she was going to find a place to settle down and create a second chance at life because the first one has kind of sucked. That's all I know. She did say she and the baby were fine though."

I nodded my head absently. There was that at least. I pulled my phone out and dialed Angela. She should still be between flights.

"Antonio." She purred. "How lovely to hear from you. It has been way too long."

"What city are you in?"

"Colorado City. I will be home tonight though. Would you like me to come by and keep you company?" Her voice was low and seductive, promising what kind of company she would be.

I huffed. "No. You are banned from the compound. And get that tattoo removed from your shoulder. If I ever see you again, I will kill you myself."

"What? Why?" She shrieked. "What did I do?"

"It's what you did *and* didn't do, Angela. You were told to help bring mi alma home. Instead, you fed her a bunch of lies causing her to run away. How stupid could you have been? Stay far away from her and from me." I hung up the phone and threw it on the bed as I stood up and started pacing.

"Angela says they landed in Colorado City. Elizabeth has to be somewhere near there. Miguel, pull up a map and see what is around there. Francisco, get us on the next flight out of here. We will drive to every town and city in Colorado if we have too. I doubt she has any money on her. I do not want my woman and our child living on the street."

I half expected them to put up an argument. Yes, she said she wasn't coming home. But that didn't mean I wasn't going to stop trying.

Thankfully, they were wise enough to just do as they were told.

Chapter 24
Elizabeth

Anne talked nonstop the whole drive back to her town. It was so beautiful. The town was tucked into the mountains, hidden from the rest of the world.

"Oh, wow." I said softly.

"Majestic, isn't it?" I nodded, with my mouth still open in amazement. "The town is so small, that everyone knows everyone else's business. The women to men ratio is way off, but I can't bear to leave it for long."

We pulled up to a little diner, simply called "The Diner."

"My parents left this place to my brother and I when they passed. There is a small studio apartment above it, you can use that. I live in a small house down the street, my brother has his own place as well. You will have some privacy. I say some because the whole town will be flocking in by tomorrow to meet you. They may be nosey, but they have a good heart. You aren't the first stray to be brought home, and I doubt you will be the last. Just let me check in with Daniel really quick and then I will take you up." She explained as we exited the car.

I nodded mutely and followed her through the glass door.

I stayed near the front as she walked back to the kitchen yelling for her brother. She said hello to a few people as she passed them, calling them all by name. When she came back out, she was hanging up the phone and her brother was behind her.

The brother walked up to me, not so subtly looking me up and down.

Lovely. He put a hand up to greet me politely at least.

"Hello, I'm Daniel. Welcome to SecondChance. Anne says you are going to be working with us and staying upstairs?" His voice wasn't as deep as Antonio's, but it was still pleasant enough.

"Liz, nice to meet you. Yes, she was kind enough to offer."

"Perfect, we could use the help. We don't usually get too busy around here, but it still gets tiring doing all the work."

At that comment Anne pushed Daniel to the side, with a rough smack on the chest.

"You only do half the work, butthead." She then turned to me and waved me forward. "Come with me, Lizzie. I'll show you to your new home. Hopefully you will have time to settle in and get comfortable before the first wave hits."

I again followed her, anxious about all these people she was sure were going to show up. I may have gotten better about being around people while living with Antonio, but I was still nervous about it.

Besides, I apparently was more naive and gullible than I thought. I could have read everyone wrong while I was there.

We walked up a hidden staircase at the back of the kitchen. There was one door at the top. Anne put a key in and opened the door. It was small, and definitely a studio. For one person it would be fine, but I would need to upgrade before the baby came.

Anne closed the door behind us and sat down at a small dinette set.

"I hope you don't mind, but I called a friend of mine over. Sam was the last stray to be brought in. Aunty Lee brought her home over a year ago. Since then, she has started dating the town sheriff. She helps out at Aunty Lee's hotel. Figured you two could talk." She put both hands on the table and pushed herself back up. "Anyway, she will be here in a few minutes. I am going to head home and get cleaned up. If you're up to it, come downstairs tomorrow and we can get you started on your training."

"Thank you, Anne. I can't tell you how much this means to me."

She waved my thanks away with a smile. "That's what neighbors are for honey. Us girls, we gotta stick together." With one more smile she walked out the door, closing it behind her.

I found a small dresser in a corner and unpacked the few things I had. I then took out the small shampoo bottles I had taken to hoarding from the hotels I stayed in with the agents and put them in the bathroom. I was grateful they were so small when we went through airport security.

Thinking of this made me think of Brandon. I genuinely hoped he didn't get into too much trouble for my disappearing act. He had been the nicest out of all of my babysitters.

I laid down on the twin size bed in the corner and sighed. Hearing Antonio's voice like that, even though the words had not been pretty, really did a number on my heart.

I missed him. Oddly, I had actually been gone longer than when we were together. We only had a month together, a beautiful month. Followed by the worst two months of my life.

By the time there was a knock on my door, I was full out sobbing.

I wiped the tears away the best I could as I walked to the door. I took a deep breath and then opened it. On the other side was a woman with short black hair, about my height, and skinny. Her smile shrank and concern filled it as she pulled me into a hug.

"Oh, sweetheart. It's going to be okay." She stepped us far enough inside to close the door. "I know it is hard right now, but it will get better. You'll see. Why don't we sit down, and we can talk, alright?"

I nodded as I pulled away from her and sat at the dinette table. She took the seat Anne had been in not that long ago.

"My name is Sam, short for Samantha. If you want to tell me your story, you can. But you don't have to. I lived here for a year before I spilled my guts. And that was just recently, like recently, recently. I'll tell you what, it gets easier every time. Now, mind you, I didn't tell anyone because I was afraid of being found and I worried about how the good folks of SecondChance would react when they found out what I had done. See, before I came here, I was living in Los Angeles with my now ex-husband. We had been married for ten years. It took me about that long to wake up and smell the dead flowers. The man was emotionally and verbally abusive. I knew it wouldn't be long before the physical came in too. He was known for his temper. Anyway, for over a year I made my preparations. When my opportunity came, I took it and never looked back. Scariest time of my life. The next day, I met the noisiest old broad on a bus. She recognized the look in my eyes. She had been in my shoes once before. Told me to call her Aunty Lee, and that I was coming home with her to find my Sunrise." Sam gave a small giggle. "I found it alright. Jackson, my boyfriend, was my sunrise. He helped put me back together and to see my true worth. Don't even want to know where I would be if I hadn't met him. Without knowing he was doing it; he gave me the courage to step into the open again and file for divorce. My ex found me eventually, but by then, I had my backbone back. I slapped him and kicked him out! So, you see, life may throw us some curveballs once in a while, but gravity will always pull the ball back down. If you're lucky, someone special will catch that ball."

She reached over and rubbed my hand, giving me a small smile. Before I knew it, I was venting out everything that had happened since August. From my failed attempt to enter the adult world, all the way up to Anne bringing me home.

Sam didn't interrupt me once, she rubbed my arm and let me say everything I needed too. Knowing she hid from a bad situation too helped me to feel like I wasn't alone.

"I am so sorry that you had to go through all of that. But I am very glad that you decided to come home with Miss Anne. SecondChance is the perfect place to recover and let your mind heal. I hope you don't mind me saying so, but I think that Angela girl was full of horse manure. I don't know why so many women choose to step on each other." She shook her head sadly, then stood up and walked to the door.

"I brought you a few things I thought you might need. I well remember how little I had when I arrived." From the top of the stairwell, she pulled in a small beat-up duffle bag. "It's not much, just a few toiletries and some clothes. Miss Anne told me you were pregnant and alone. We'll see what we can do about getting you some maternity clothes soon. FYI, Anne is the town gossip, don't tell her anything unless you want everyone to know. She is a good friend and sweet as can be, but that mouth has a hole in it." Sam chuckled at her own joke.

I did a little too.

"I take it you have not had an exam yet?" I shook my head no. "No worries, I will call the town doc and get you in for tomorrow. Jackson is off for a few days so he can cover the hotel for me. I will go with you and introduce you."

"Thank you, I really appreciate the help."

Her smile was soft as she unpacked the bag. "It's my turn to help another woman in need. Eventually you will meet Aunty Lee. She's out of town right now, visiting her son and his family. She's the mother hen of the town and we all love her."

TJ LEE

We talked for a little longer, at some point Daniel knocked on the door. He had a couple boxes of food in hand, saying Jackson called and told him to deliver it to us. Hearing how sweet Jackson was made me miss Antonio more.

Maybe Sam was right, and Angela was full of it. I remembered the scowl on her face when she saw me with Antonio that first day. He hardly paid any attention to her. His eyes were only on me.

They always were. It always felt like I was the only person in the room that he saw, no one else ever existed.

The next morning, I woke up refreshed, having had the best night sleep in months. The privacy while I slept was a beautiful thing. Sam showed up on my doorstep at ten, ready to take me for my checkup. She was carrying a to-go cup of orange juice and a small breakfast burrito for me. I expected to be revolted by the scent of it because of the day before. I wasn't. Just the opposite, I inhaled that sucker.

I also expected us to drive but instead we walked. The doctor's office was only two blocks away. The movement felt wonderful, and the air was crisp. Sam had brought me two sweaters in the bag last night, with this cool air, I was eternally grateful.

She introduced me to many people on the street, saying I was a friend from out of town. No one asked for more details but welcomed me with open arms.

Literally. I got a lot of hugs, and not just from the women.

The town doctor was really nice. They ran a blood test and had me pee in a cup. Everything came back good. The doc decided I was far enough along, roughly ten weeks, that we could do an ultrasound and see the baby.

I cried as I saw my little bean. We would need to wait a few more weeks to know the gender. I cried as I walked back out to the waiting room, carrying the ultrasound picture. Sam pulled me into a hug again.

"It's okay if you miss him. I hate when Jackson covers the night shift. I don't know how you have handled two months."

I sniffed and wiped my face. "Did you miss your ex when you left?"

Sam snorted and we turned to leave the office. "No. But then, he had stopped being a husband to me years before that. He was more like a prison warden. I never felt even a fraction of what I feel for Jackson, for that low down dirty scoundrel. Having someone who accepts you for who you are, celebrates all the little things with you, needs to be with you every minute but not control every one of those minutes, that is what it is all about. If you have that, then that is all you need."

Antonio did that. He started out saying he was going to control so much, but he didn't. It didn't take long before we became more of a team in everything. He never failed to give me compliments. And not once did he ever talk down to me. No, he always did his best to lift me up. Not so he could carry me, but so I could carry myself. But I always knew he would be there to catch me if I fell. They all were.

We were about a block away from the diner when I finally got the courage to ask, "do you think I should go back to Antonio?"

Sam smiled at me. "I think that is your choice. I think you deserve the chance to get your head and your heart straight. If you had gone right back to him, you would have always wondered. Take the time you need, Liz. Don't make any permanent decisions until you are ready. And don't let anyone else make them for you." Her advice was sweet but firm. "When I first came here, Aunty Lee gave me a small picture frame with a quote. Basically, it said it was our choice how we felt and what we wanted to do. We need to choose what we want. Choose to be happy. Choose to live in peace. No one else can choose that for you. You have had a lot of people choosing for you lately, now it's your turn."

I spent the next few hours in my little home, staring at the picture of my baby, while my mind relived the last year of my life.

In the afternoon, I went down to the diner, where I was practically force fed a club sandwich. I met more people from town and then I started working.

My previous work experience rarely involved other people, so that was a challenge for me.

As the hours and days went by, I realized I actually enjoyed it. Sam came by frequently, bringing Aunty Lee with her. She really was a nosey old broad, but a fun one. Her opinion on Andre and what he did was always colorful and made me giggle. I even met our town Sheriff, Jackson Thomas. Apparently, everyone but Sam called him Jack.

I still had morning sickness at random times and not every day. It was weird. On one hand I was grateful that I wasn't sick all the time, on the other,

I wish I knew when it was going to happen so I could be prepared and work around it.

As the time went by, I expected my heart to ease up and let things start to go. It didn't. I still missed Antonio and thought about him all the time. Part of me wanted to call him and tell him to come get me. I just couldn't bring myself to do it.

When the debate kept me up at night, I would go for a walk around town. I never strayed into the woods, I always stayed on the street. Right under the street lights.

I was afraid to get lost in the dark.

Chapter 25

Antonio

Two weeks. It had been two weeks since mi alma called Francisco and said she wasn't coming home. We were all tired.

We sent John home to start getting the house cleaned up and to see what damage the FBI had left behind. I wanted it to be back to normal when we finally brought the Senora home.

Since then, it had just been me and my two best friends.

Miguel used the GPS on his phone and sectioned the state into quadrants, which would allow us to cover the most ground. We had already covered the Northeast and Southeast quadrants. This time we would be going through the mountain regions.

This area was harder with the GPS, so we decided to grab a physical map of the area.

Francisco and I leaned against the car silently, while Miguel laid it out on the hood and began taking notes of where to go. I was reliving my last night with Elizabeth (for the millionth time). I was rudely pulled out of them and brought back to him when I heard him utter a few curses and then start laughing.

I looked at him, completely confused. I looked back at Francisco who was equally confused. I couldn't remember the last time any of us had laughed.

"Hermano?" I called him carefully. If anyone was going to lose it and have a mental breakdown, it would be me.

Miguel scratched his jaw and looked at me with a sly grin. "There is this little town about a hundred miles from here. I never even saw it on the GPS. This town looks to be completely buried within the mountains."

"Si, and?" I prompted, not seeing what was so funny.

He laughed again and sighed. "It's called SecondChance."

It took a moment before a smile began to slide across my face. Irony at its best.

Francisco started laughing. "I could see how that would appeal to the Senora."

I slammed a fist against the side of the car, pushing myself off. "Bueno! Let's go bring our Senora home, caballeros!"

Francisco patted both my shoulders and then squeezed as we all climbed back into the rental car, feeling hopeful for the first time in months.

We got lost a few times, trying to navigate the roads through the mountains. By nightfall we were entering the small town.

We drove around and found a small Inn on one side, pushed up against the mountain. It was the sort of place I would love to bring Elizabeth one day, just the two of us.

We parked the car and walked inside the building. It was decorated to look like a cabin, just a lot larger. A tall man in a Sheriff's uniform sat in a chair behind the desk, one leg crossed over the other.

He looked up as he saw us come in and greeted us with a smile. "Good evening, gentlemen. How can I help you?"

Miguel answered for us. I was almost afraid to say anything to a cop. Last thing we needed was for the federales to find out where we were.

"Good evening, Sheriff. Are there any rooms available for a night or two?"

The man stood up and clapped his hands.

"How many do you need? Three?"

"Yes, sir, three would be perfect."

The man typed some information into the computer, we gave him our IDs, the fake ones we traveled with. We weren't sure if the federales were still looking for her, or us, but we had to be safe. Freddie hadn't even been able to find word on the fact that she escaped.

The Sheriff handed us back our things along with the keys.

"My name is Sheriff Thomas. My Aunt owns the hotel. If you need anything feel free to ask. We live in a cabin nearby. If it's an emergency we can come right over, otherwise, please wait until daybreak. Aunty Lee isn't as young as she thinks she is anymore." He had a jovial and relaxed smile. "Your rooms are on the second floor and to the right. If you hurry, my girlfriend still has dinner served for another half hour. Best cook in the county. Breakfast is served between seven and nine. There is also a diner about two miles down the road. Take your pick."

"Gracias, Senor." I thanked him as we took our keys and headed up the stairs.

We found our rooms easily enough. They were nicer than what I expected for a small town. The beds were all queen size, and the mattress were of the pillow top variety. The bedding was clean and fluffy.

Sadly, we had been staying in hotels on the cheaper side of things, trying to keep a low profile. John said they hadn't been bothered by the FBI at all; although, they did find a few bugs when they did a sweep.

I wasn't surprised to hear that. In fact, I would have been disappointed if they hadn't bugged the place.

Quite a few bedroom doors had to be replaced from when they had been kicked down, including mine. I was glad I wasn't there to see it. Just thinking about Elizabeth alone in that room when they kicked it in made me a little on the murderous side of things.

Had she been scared?

Did she scream?

Did she silently call for me to protect her?

Were they rough with her? If so, someone was going to pay for that.

We put our bags in the rooms and headed down to the dining room. None of us were in the mood to go anywhere else tonight.

There was a spread of enchiladas, rice, and beans on a buffet table. We were a mix of wary and excited. It had been a while since we had enchiladas, but the American version was never the same.

We weren't chickens though and it smelled really good. We loaded up our plates and sat down.

All three of us were pleasantly surprised. They weren't perfect, but they were much better than we expected. We polished off our plates and went back for seconds. The food was good, and it was something besides greasy and fast.

The three of us were sitting back, patting our satisfied bellies when a young lady walked in, a big grin on her face.

She looked at the buffet table and then us, laughing. "I take it you enjoyed the food?"

"Si senorita, that was very good. Where did you learn to cook enchiladas like that?" Francisco asked.

"My name is Sam. I've played around with them a few times. We get guests from all over and I want to be able to serve food that will help my guests feel more at home."

I smiled. "We thank you for that. We have been on the road for so long, I don't remember the last time I felt like I was home."

"Oh, that's a shame. How long have you been on the road?" She stopped her cleaning and came to stand near us. I got the sense that she was studying us.

"Over two months now." Miguel answered solemnly.

"That's a long time to be on the road. Any reason in particular? Work?"

I shook my head. "No, senorita. We are looking for someone. No one has seen her for many months now. We are concerned and want to take her home, or at least make sure she is safe."

I ended up having to promise both the boys that I would return home with them, if that's what Elizabeth wanted. As long as she was safe and happy, that was all that was important. I knew they didn't buy it though. I would follow that woman everywhere, as long as I could be with her again.

"I see." She said quietly as she looked at her feet. "Well, I hope you find her. Don't give up, you never know when she could be just around the corner or just down the street. I'm sure she is ready and waiting for you, whether she knows it or not. Have a good evening, gentlemen. We'll see you at breakfast." She turned and gathered up the dinner trays and carried them to the kitchen.

I watched her leave, feeling both confused, and touched by her words.

We got up to leave as the Sheriff walked out and picked up the rest. We waved goodnight and headed back upstairs, separating in the hall. I showered and laid in bed for an hour, not being able to get Sam's words out of my head.

No matter what I did, my body just refused to relax. Finally giving up, I sent the other two a message telling them I was going for a walk to clear my head and that I would be back, then left the room. As soon as I stepped outside, a cool breeze hit me. It was like that first breath after holding it for so long. It felt refreshing and exhilarating.

I turned down the street and started walking. I was about a mile down when I saw an angel walking down the street. I froze, sure I was seeing a mirage.

My dreams, coming into reality.

Maybe I had finally snapped.

Elizabeth

It seemed like I just couldn't sleep anymore without going for a walk. You would think after being on my feet most of the day, walking a couple miles at night would be the last thing I would want to do.

But when I wasn't working, my mind rolled to Antonio and wondering what he was doing, or *who* he was doing.

Was he still looking for me? Or did he give up and go home?

I knew there was no way he would ever be able to find me here. I lost my tracker months ago. And this town was so hidden, it would take divine intervention for him to find me here.

I pulled my hair down from its ponytail, running my fingers through it, loosening my hair. I pulled it over my left shoulder and played with it. I absentmindedly rubbed my growing belly. It was just a small bump, but it was there. Aunty Lee said I was now past the first trimester, and the bump would begin growing quickly.

Well, her belly did at any rate, but everyone was different.

She had been a big help. Sam, and Anne too. The whole town had been very welcoming and very nice. On my days off I spent time in the kitchen with Sam and Anne. Sam kept pestering me about the right ways to make different things, she was getting better.

She had Jackson deliver a plate of enchiladas to me earlier, definitely an improvement from before. I taught her the tricks I had picked up from the kitchen staff in Texas.

I kept my head down for most of my walk, having my regular path memorized. Suddenly I felt a presence, I wasn't alone tonight.

I looked up and saw someone standing about a hundred feet in front of me. They were completely covered in shadow, the tree blocking the moonlight from them.

I knew I should have been scared, but something about it gave me the feeling of peace. I kept my eyes on the shadow as we moved closer together.

A minute later I heard a soft "hermosa?" float to me in the breeze.

I stopped walking, completely shocked. It shouldn't be possible.

"An... Antonio? Mi querido?"

196

He laughed with relief and took the last few steps at practically a run. Before I knew it, he had picked me up and was spinning me around.

"I knew I would find you! I just never thought it would be like this." He set me back on my feet and laid his forehead on mine. He closed his eyes and breathed deeply, like he was inhaling my essence.

It took a moment, but I did finally find my voice. "How did you find me? They took my necklace away. I tried to keep it, honestly, I did." My voice quivered as I started crying.

He lifted a hand to my cheek and wiped away the tears, leaving only his palm. I leaned into it, loving the feel of his touch once again.

How had I lived so long without it? Whatever made me think I could?

Or that I would even want to?

With his other hand, he reached into his pocket and pulled something out.

"We were told you left the cabin about an hour after you left. I had to see for myself, and I found this hanging on the porch."

He walked around to my back and clasped the necklace back on my neck, right where it belonged. His arms slid around me, his hand resting on my stomach. He began laying gentle kisses on the back of my neck.

My mind flashed to that first night, when Andre delivered me to his home. The way he held me. The softness he used as he spoke to me. The gentleness of his lips on my neck.

"I missed you so much, mi alma. Did you miss me?"

I nodded, not being able to find my voice again. The emotions were running to strongly for me to be able to form coherent thought, let alone a complete sentence.

"Why did you not come home to me?" He seemed to be struggling with his voice too, as he leaned away from me.

I felt the pain in his words like a dagger to my heart.

I turned in his arms to face him, placing my palm on his cheek this time. My tears flowed freely.

"I wanted to. I waited every day for you to find me. Every time someone looked carefully at my wrist, I got my hopes up. The worst was in his one diner. I thought for sure the waitress there would be the one to rescue me and bring us back together, but the agents caught on and whisked me away. Then I saw Angela, and I thought that was it."

I stopped talking as he growled. Francisco must have told him what happened. I should have known he would.

"I was already feeling vulnerable, hormonal, and completely messed up. Every day for two months, I had those agents telling me that you didn't care, that you didn't really love me, and that you were too busy covering your own hide to come find me. I convinced them the tracker came from Andre, so they wouldn't use it to lure you into a trap." I sniffed. "Then Angela showed me the tattoo on her shoulder, telling me about you looking at it while you took her from behind... and... and..." he pulled me in and held my head against his chest.

"Mi alma, I don't even know how she got that tattoo. I told you. I've never even wanted to touch her. I haven't touched anyone since you came into my life. Don't you remember what I said that last night we had together? It's only you and will always be only you. I love you, Elizabeth. I know we didn't get much time together before this happened. But you are my everything. I felt like somebody ripped my soul out of my body when I heard they took you. We've been on the road ever since. We haven't stopped searching. That diner in Fresno about did me in. A friend of mine had people there just ten minutes after you left. The waitress described the car, even gave them a partial license plate, but they still couldn't find you. As for Angela, she has been banned from the compound. If she ever comes near me, or you, again, I will kill her myself. I need you, mi alma. You have the choice though. If you are not ready to come home, then I am staying here with you. I will follow you anywhere you want to go, for as long as you wish. But please, don't make me live without you again."

I looked up at him and saw a tear slide down his face. I was shocked that he was actually crying. I didn't know he could do that. I looked down towards the ground.

Those were all very sweet words, and they helped a lot, but there was one more thing I needed to know.

"Do you want me to come home because of me, or because of your baby that I'm carrying?"

Antonio chuckled then lifted my chin up. He lowered his head and lightly pressed his lips to mine. Before he put the full pressure on, he answered my question.

"For you, mi alma. You are the other half to my soul. The bebe is just a bonus."

Then he shocked my heart back to life by closing the distance and really kissed me for the first time in months. Just like that first night, it took no time at all for me to return it. It was like my soul had always recognized his as a safe harbor. As home.

I laced my arms around his neck and buried my fingers in his hair, which was longer than it had been before. His tongue didn't request entrance so much as demanded it. His arms held me tight against him, leaving no space anywhere. When we eventually broke for air, I finally answered the request he had made.

"Take me home, mi querido. I love you and I have been miserable since the moment you left for that trip. Which, by the way, is the last time you go anywhere without me. Entiendes?"

He chuckled, kissed me again, then said. "Nunca más, mi alma." (never again, my soul). "Now, I have a very important question for you."

I felt his hands begin untucking my shirt, giving me a pretty good idea of what he wanted. He gave me his mischievous smile, "your place or mine?"

I pulled his head down to my lips again. "If you are staying at Sam's Inn, then yours. The beds are bigger."

He chuckled then kissed me again, that one just as hungry as the last. Right as his hand was about to reach its desired destination, I stepped back and grabbed his other hand. I laughed as he groaned.

We half ran the rest of the way back to the Inn. He frequently tried to pull me back in, but I laughed and pulled away.

We quietly walked up the stairs to his room, being careful not to wake anyone. As soon as the door closed, he had me against the door and he was pressing some very serious need against me. He didn't even break the kiss as he began unbuttoning my pants and pushing them down.

"Take off your shirt." He demanded as he fell to his knees and placed his lips somewhere else.

It took me longer than normal to get my shirt off, I was too distracted. By the time he stood back up, his pants were undone. His lips met mine again as he lifted me up and carried me to the bed.

He gently laid me on the bed, then finished removing his clothes, not taking his eyes off me. He then kissed my baby belly softly, his five o'clock shadow tickling it. He traced kisses up, taking his time in my mountains, while his hand picked up where his tongue had left off against the door.

He had me shaking and moaning twice before he finally reconnected our bodies after their long and difficult separation. The next time I shook, he went with me. However, he did not leave my body.

Neither of us were ready to separate. We needed to feel that connection for as long as possible.

We talked for a while. He told me about the Coopers and how they had been trying to help find me. I told him how I escaped from Brandon.

I felt what that story did to him, apparently it turned him on. Which then led to another round.

That time, we took it slower, with more passion and love. I fell asleep in his arms, feeling like I was finally home.

I always thought home was a physical place, a permanent roof over our heads. Turns out, that wasn't it at all. Home was a feeling. And right here, in Antonio's arms, the place I was the safest and loved the most, that was my home. That was where I belonged.

Chapter 26

Antonio

M y needs were far from done being met, but I could tell just how tired she was. When was the last time she had a good night's sleep?

I knew mine had been lacking since Miguel first told me the FBI had taken her, but my body wasn't also baking a kid.

My kid.

My hijo, or hija, was growing in her stomach.

And now something else was growing... again. I had a feeling this was going to be happening a lot for a while. I laughed quietly. Not that it didn't before.

I would need to remember to tell John to have our room soundproofed. I read how sensitive women could get during pregnancy, in a good way. I looked down at her beautiful face, grateful for Sam's words that wouldn't let me sleep.

I wondered if Sam had figured out who we were. Was that why she gave me that crypted message?

Huh. I would have to ask her at breakfast... if we left the room. I knew both Francisco and Miguel would be banging on my door in a few hours, eager to search the town. So, we would have to leave, even though I really didn't want to.

I should probably try to get some sleep, but part of me was afraid I would wake up and she would be gone again. And now there was no way I was going to be able to sleep until I took care of one not so little problem.

I could sneak into the bathroom and take care of it myself, but why?

Hmm, how should I do this? Wake her slowly? Try not to wake her at all?

Or just take what I wanted?

I had never been a patient man. She already knew that. I was also very possessive, and I just got her back. It wasn't like she ever complained before.

I slowly moved my arm out from under her head, her adorable little pout made me smile. I carefully moved to hover over her, balancing my weight.

With one hand, I gently separated her legs, until they were wide enough, giving me one of the most beautiful views.

Honestly, I could finish right here, just by staring at her.

That wasn't what I wanted though. I wanted her to feel my need for her, to know she was the only one who could satisfy me.

I moved myself lightly against her, watching her face. Her tiny little gasp and moan was all I needed. I started slow, and then slammed in. Her eyes flew open and rolled to the back of her head as her back lifted off the bed.

I leaned down and started licking my favorite cones. Her back fell onto the bed as her fingers pulled my hair, causing me to moan and sink my teeth into her.

I took what I needed, and I wasn't gentle about it. At one point I felt her energy start to wane, so I lifted her right leg just enough and smacked the side of her butt. That did the trick, for both of us.

I fell to the side, taking her with me. She laughed. "I missed you too, mi amor." Her hand gently stroked my cheek.

Awe, dang it. I groaned as that small touch and her words of love shot the fire right back in. She gasped and then started laughing, feeling my reaction. She pushed me onto my back and took control this time. It only took one climax before she nearly gave out on me.

I did what I could to keep her moving until we were both done, then she laid down and passed back out on my chest. She was still on me in every way, and I had no desire to change that.

I fell asleep within minutes of her. The connection between us helped me to feel more secure and confident in the reality of her being with me once again.

Elizabeth proved to be the other half of my soul the next morning. I first began to stir when she slowly separated us, after purposely moving back and forth.

I didn't fully become aware until she connected us in a different way. I knew she didn't care much for it the first time I had her do it, but she quickly learned to enjoy it. Not nearly as much as me though.

I held her hair this time, gripping it in my fist as I naturally rocked my hips against her. She even stayed long enough to raise me again, but then she moved back up to me.

"Good morning, mi querido." She whispered softly against my lips. Leaving behind the taste of me.

"Good morning, mi hermosa." I kissed her again, slowly, and we welcomed the morning together.

I held her naked body close to mine, my forehead against hers, debating if the next round should be in the shower or in the bed again.

I was about to say both when there was a knock at the door.

Her eyes turned scared and a little worried. Fear I hadn't seen in her since Mexico.

I brushed loose hair behind her ear. "It's alright. It's only Miguel and Francisco. They have been with me every minute in the search for you. They have been almost as worried as me."

Her voice shook as it softly came out. "Will they be mad at me?"

I kissed her nose. "No, mi alma. They both understood why you needed to take some space. They've been my voice of reason through all of this." The knock was harder this time. I smiled. "Let's surprise them though. Why don't you go into the bathroom and wait for the right moment to come out? Entiendes?"

She giggled and nodded her head. I groaned as I watched her run to the bathroom naked. I got up and grabbed my boxers before answering the door.

"What?" I growled.

"Sheesh, someone woke up on the wrong side of the..." Miguel trailed off as he noticed the clothes on the floor that were way too small to be mine. He punched my arm. "What the hell man? Please tell me we have not been searching for her all these months and *now* you decide to screw around? She is never going to come home if you are doing that! We want her to come home! Idiota!"

Francisco walked in the door a minute later, having just left his room.

"What's going on? What did he do now?"

Miguel answered by waving a hand towards the clothes.

"Awe, man! For years we tried to get you to loosen up and now is the time you decide to start! We were already going to have to convince the Senora that she was the only one, and now you do this? I can't lie for you man. I respect her too much for that."

I laughed and they watched me warily. I closed the door, blocking out any other unwanted visitors.

"It's not what you think, I promise. I couldn't get Sam's weird message out of my head last night, so I decided to go for a walk. I thought for sure I was seeing things but coming down the street was the most beautiful angel I had ever seen."

I picked up her clothes as I spoke and threw them inside the bathroom. We waited in silence until the door started slowly opening.

I watched their faces carefully as Elizabeth stepped up beside me, chewing on her bottom lip.

"Hola, mi hermanos." Her cute little voice was all it took.

Miguel was the first to pick her up and hold her tight. He set her down and laid a kiss on her cheek. I pretended to not see the small tear that escaped his eye.

Francisco came up slower and then quickly grabbed her and pulled her in.

"Never do that to me again, hermanita." He kissed the top of her head and then let her go. I stepped forward and wrapped my arms around her from behind.

"Los Siento." She softly apologized to the room.

Miguel wiped her tears away. "None of that now. No apologies. None of this was your fault. Entiendes?" She nodded. "Bueno. Now, I don't know about you all but I'm hungry. After those enchiladas last night, I can't wait to see what Sam will make for breakfast!"

We all laughed, the tension being broken by Miguel being his usual ridiculous self,

"Since you are here, Sam will probably stick to the Mexican theme. She has been very persistent about learning how to cook authentic Mexican food." Elizabeth explained.

I picked up my clothes and quickly dressed, not letting her out of my sight. "I take it you're the reason her enchiladas are getting better?"

She nodded. "Yes. Sam and Miss Anne have been very good to me. The whole town has been really. They are all very nice people."

"Miss Anne is the one that brought you here from the airport?" She had told me the story last night, but my mind had difficulty focusing on her actual words, it preferred to focus on other things.

"Si. It was her phone I borrowed to call Francisco. Anne is very sweet but also very nosey, she listened to the whole thing. I've been staying in a small apartment above her diner and working in the diner. Staying busy helped keep my mind busy during the day. Walking at night was the only way I could get any sleep."

I pulled her to my side as we walked toward the door, I kissed her temple, causing her to smile.

"I'm glad you couldn't sleep last night."

She sighed. "Me too. Of course, I still didn't get a lot of sleep last night."

That caused a round of laughs from everyone. I grinned.

"It was two and half months! What did you expect?" I poked her in the side. "I didn't hear any complaining, or any actual words really." Elizabeth blushed and buried her face in my arm as the hermanos laughed again.

We were all still laughing and talking as we entered the dining room. Sheriff Thomas was there again, helping to set up the food. Sam was just walking out carrying a bowl of fruit. She looked up at us then turned to him.

"You owe me twenty bucks, pay up sucker!" He turned around, saw us, and then rolled his eyes. A smile playing on his lips while he pretended to be upset.

"Did you really bet on this? Small town life getting a little boring for you, Sam?" Elizabeth asked in amusement.

Sam laughed back with a wink. "I just like to prove him wrong and make him owe me. He always promises to pay in money but then never does." She eyed him carefully with a small scowl.

He walked up to her and kissed her head. "You never complain either." He smacked her butt on the way back to the kitchen, her laughter following him.

She stepped over to Elizabeth, who met her part way and gave her a hug.

"I had a feeling last night. I'm glad I was right. You will have to tell me the whole story later. First, try the chorizo and tell me how I did. Wait, can you eat the chorizo? Last time the smell got to you."

Elizabeth took a quick sniff, then smiled. "Smells good, but you know how I am. My morning sickness is more like random, driving me bananas, sickness." They both laughed. I frowned.

While the words were spoken innocently, they were still a reminder of all that I had missed. I would rather be the one with her when she didn't feel well, be the one taking care of her.

Sam saw the look I had and gave Elizabeth a light nudge.

Miguel and Francisco were already attacking the buffet. Elizabeth came back to me and wrapped her arms around my neck.

"You haven't missed much, mi amor. I'm rarely ever sick. It comes and goes randomly. But..." She reached into her back pocket and pulled something out. "When I first got here, Sam took me to the town doctor. Since I couldn't tell my babysitters about the baby, I hadn't had a checkup yet. I've only been once, and it's still too early to tell the gender. Would you like to see a picture of our bebe?"

I smiled. Our bebe.

"Hell yes!" I exclaimed as she held the small black and white photo up for me to see.

She had to point out the bean like thing and said that was it.

"See? There is still a long way to go." She picked up my hand and placed it on her small belly bump. "You will be there for all the important stuff, I promise." I laid my head on hers again, then kissed her softly.

After breakfast, we said goodbye to the Sheriff, Sam, and some crazy old lady, and headed down to the diner. I followed Elizabeth inside, while the other two waited in the car.

Francisco was already online making airline reservations, nobody wanted to drive home. Elizabeth froze in the doorway, blocking me from entering.

"Hey, Anne!" She called out.

"Hey sugar, you're down early this morning. You hungry? What are you feeling like? Pancakes or eggs and toast?"

Elizabeth cleared her throat. "I ate over at the Sunrise this morning. Actually, there is someone I want you to meet. I found him wandering the streets last night." She laughed as she stepped all the way in and to the side. I slid up next to her, my arm going around her waist.

The girl I assumed was Anne, started laughing. A man who looked oddly similar to her, popped his head out of the kitchen.

"Antonio, I'm guessing?" Anne asked, still laughing lightly.

I stepped forward and put a hand up. "Si. Thank you for taking care of mi hermosa." I told her sincerely.

She accepted my hand and looked me up and down. "Ooo, maybe I do need to leave my little town more often." I only gave her half a smile and then moved back to Elizabeth.

Anne pointed at me and then said. "See? What did I tell you from day one? I just met him, and I can already tell that girl was full of crap!" I chuckled and tightened my grip on Elizabeth's waist. Anne sighed before continuing. "You're leaving then, huh?"

"Yes, thank you for everything." Elizabeth leaned in and gave her a hug.

Anne sniffed. "Gah, go pack up. You're gonna make me mess up my makeup. I knew I should have worn waterproof this morning." She then turned towards the kitchen and yelled "Daniel! Make up a plate of fries and fruit." She turned back to me. "She may not get cravings yet, but it's a long drive to the airport and that seems to settle her stomach."

Before I could properly thank her, Elizabeth was pulling me down a hall and up a hidden staircase. Inside the door was the tiniest apartment I had ever seen. Not that I got much of a look before she literally jumped on me. It was a good thing I had fast reflexes.

She pulled her lips away from mine as she ripped her shirt over her head. "I couldn't wait any longer."

I chuckled happily. "I'm not complaining."

I carried her to the small bed while she worked on removing the barriers between our most important parts. I set her down on the small bed and didn't even wait for our pants to be removed all the way.

My sweet innocent, million-dollar angel was not so innocent anymore, and I was perfectly fine with that.

Half an hour later, we loaded up the car again, after promises to stay in touch. I sat in the back with her, holding her close the entire time. The drive to the airport was long enough that she fell asleep on my shoulder. I moved her, so her head was on my lap.

Miguel took one look in the rearview mirror while he drove, then smirked.

"Just don't forget we are in the car too. Unless you want to be like our padre."

I shivered at the thought, causing them both to laugh quietly. The tension we traveled with for two and half months was gone, now we were all at peace.

Our La Jefa was coming home.

Francisco sent out the word to all of our friends and contacts. The search was over. His phone was vibrating nearly nonstop the whole way, as they responded with their congratulations. He promised Levi I would call him tomorrow with the story. Levi and Freddie were already becoming good friends to me.

I could see a bright future for our two familias working together. Levi's cookers could work magic with our product. Somewhere in the future, we could make an arrangement between our children. We could blend the families, strengthen the ties. But that was all for another day.

I knew why Francisco purposely did not book the flight with Delta. Running into Angela would not be good. Miguel had packed a fake ID for Elizabeth when our search first started. As far as the government was concerned, she was still in the wind.

They probably already knew she had returned to me. But there was nothing they could do about it.

I took pleasure in pulling mi alma into the tiny bathrooms on the plane and both of us joined the mile high club. It was a tight fit, but we made it work.

I might have been able to make it through the entire flight if Elizabeth had not proved just how far from innocent she was now.

She asked for a couple of blankets when we first boarded, then spread them over us. It appeared as though mi alma found a new way to control her anxiety about flying. If that was the case, we'd be flying more often. I liked flying like this. Her hands were very greedy on that flight.

Hence the need for the mile high club as soon as the captain turned off the seatbelt sign.

Thankfully, Francisco had the foresight to have the house cleared out before we got home. The staff and my other men would come back tomorrow to celebrate Elizabeth coming home. I took her straight upstairs to our room and locked the door. She was unbuckling her pants and dropping them before it clicked.

"In a hurry, mi amor?" I asked in amusement.

"Ya huh. Now shut up and get over here."

I laughed, shook my head, and walked slowly towards her as she climbed up on the bed. She sat on the edge curling her finger in and biting her lip.

"I think you have started the best part of being pregnant, the rise in the fun hormones."

She groaned at me and tried to grab my pants, but I took a step back laughing.

"Maybe, or maybe I have been dying without your touch and no way to relieve myself. It was pure torture, Antonio." She said my name in a whine as she laid back on the bed.

I moaned in approval and undressed without unbuttoning anything first. She looked up at me and smiled, knowing she was getting her way. But I was still in control. She had to do what I wanted first. And I have had one thing on my mind since she took my hand on that plane.

"Did you take care of that need while I was gone?" I growled. She shook her head no. "Say it. Tell me you waited for me. Tell me you followed my rules."

"I followed your rules, mi amor. Now, please, come put me out of this misery. I need you."

Her pleas turned me on more. "Tell me no one else has touched you." I leaned forward, placing a knee on the bed.

"No one else has ever touched me. I am purely yours El Jefe. Please!"

We slept on and off all night, waking each other up to satisfy our need to keep the other close. We both needed the reminder that the other was still there, and we weren't going anywhere.

If this was what her pregnancy was going to be like, I was going to be in Heaven for the next six months.

Epilogue
Elizabeth

Making love with Antonio had always been good, but now? Wow. I honestly didn't know if it was the pregnancy hormones or if it was just the fact that we were both feeling insecure from being separated.

The day after we got back, we had a welcome home party for everyone. I wasn't the only one who was finally home.

The big surprise was when Oscar and the mothers showed up that afternoon. Bigger than that was when Oscar picked me up into a hug, then rubbed my baby bump. Antonio had told me how concerned his father was about my disappearance, I guess I just couldn't believe it until I saw it. Of course, I was also carrying his first grandchild. Which probably carried more weight for him than I did personally.

Knowing they were in the house somewhere should have put a damper on things, but it didn't. We just made sure they weren't in a room right next to us.

Antonio and I were married within the week. We called a preacher over and he performed the ceremony right there in the living room. We spent a week in the honeymoon suite at the Marriott. There was no point in us traveling anywhere, we knew we would never leave the room.

Which we didn't. Room service was a wonderful tool.

That first night with Antonio, all those months ago, had been scary. I didn't know what was expected of me. I had been thrown into this whole new world, and not by choice. I thought I would live my life as just his mistress, forever fighting with Elena.

I always figured at some point they would stop hating each other. Even if he had to think of me while doing it, eventually she would need to bear him a child.

Now, she was gone, permanently from what I heard, and I was the one bearing his children.

If he had to go out of town on business, I went with him. He learned the benefits of this pretty quick, and not just for safety reasons. The first time I roamed around the room and did different things. The second time he had a different idea.

The brat tied both my legs to the bed in my sleep. All he left me was a flimsy nightgown to wear. I untied myself while he was gone, a girl's gotta pee sometime. I just made sure to tie it again as soon as I was done.

I didn't even have time to say hello before he attacked me.

The holidays were the best I had ever experienced. I was always alone in previous years. The foster homes I was in kept it small and cheap. We usually got a small toy and a new outfit.

With my new family, mi familia, it was a true celebration.

Antonio carried mistletoe around in his pocket. He had it hanging at first, until he realized Miguel kept trying to kiss my cheek under it. Just to mess with Antonio of course.

All these men made me feel loved and wanted. Something I had never really had before.

At the end of April, everyone was feeling anxious. The mothers came out to stay for a few weeks, Oscar with them. He was excited to have his first grandbaby. Miguel commented on him being more excited for this then the last three children his mistresses had given him.

Antonio Jr was born in the middle of the night on April 28th. He came out screaming and ready to feed.

As long as he got what he wanted, when he wanted it, he was happy. He earned his name well. I especially loved when he would cry when his papa tried to kiss me while I was feeding him.

Jr also seemed to have a sixth sense for when his papa was getting too close to his food source. Not that that stopped his papa at all.

For our one-year anniversary we went on a trip back to Mexico. Antonio made good on his promise from the year before. While the mothers watched our son, he drove me around to the different sights and through the market. He even took me on a picnic to one of his favorite hideaways,

We chose to go in the evening and watch the sunset over the beautiful Mexican desert. Antonio had me wrapped in his arms, holding me tight to his chest. And I finally got to do what I didn't get the chance to before.

Be the one to break the news myself, let him be the first to find out.

I slowly pulled up my shirt, out from under his hands, he softly chuckled behind me. He tried to move his hand further, thinking I was going somewhere else with this, but I held his hands firm to my stomach. He growled playfully.

"The night we met your seed claimed me as yours. My body accepted you in every way. From day one, your son refused to wait. My body has barely recovered from him. And yet... your next bebe has already begun being just as impatient."

I waited, letting that sink in. It didn't take long. Nor did his reaction. I squealed in laughter as he swiftly pushed my back to the dirt and laid over me.

"Tell me I heard you right. Tell me you are already carrying another nino for me."

I giggled as he lowered and kissed my belly. I pushed my fingers through his hair as he lifted his eyes to look up at me.

"I'm carrying another nino for you, mi querido." I laughed happily as he kissed my stomach again and then attacked me.

Walking into that club should have been the end of my life. I guess in a way it was. The girl who hid from the world, who had been stomped on by the world, disappeared. Antonio brought me to life.

What I had been doing cannot really be considered living.

I was stuck running into the same brick wall over and over again. Until I tried a new path.

I fell into a pit. But the man who pulled me out didn't just leave me on the ground again. No, he put me on a pedestal and showed me what I was missing in this world.

I was abducted and sold as a mistress. My freedoms taken away from me. But with that, I learned how to fly.

There were still times I thought about those other women, the ones that were not as lucky as me. I wondered what happened to them. I wondered if the federales were ever able to catch up with Andre. I wondered how many of those women were able to be saved.

Oscar had managed to get a message to Andre, but no one has heard from him since. For the sake of women everywhere, I hoped the Feds took him out.

. . . .

Special Agent Stacey Lennings always had a talent for acting. Her parents used to tease her that she was a chameleon, able to take on any persona. Yet, it still took convincing for her to nag her supervisor into letting her be the one to be the bait to catch one of the most notorious human traffickers out there. Andre.

5 Years ago, Ricky's sister disappeared. Maybe if her skin was lighter, and her hair blonder, the cops would have tried harder. As her older brother, it fell to him to find his sister before it was too late. He had to dive deep into the belly of the beast, but he was going to get her back, and no one was going to stop him. Not the beast himself, and certainly not the agent who made the mistake of underestimating the beast.

Read the nail-biting conclusion of the Million Dollar Duet – Pre-order your copy of Million Dollar Screw Up today from your favorite online retailer.

. . . .

The book, Million Dollar Angel, has guest appearances by characters in many of my other books.

The Cooper family stories take place in *The Cooper Family Chronicles*. A 5 book completed series. (Get a sneak peek to book 1 by scrolling/flipping to the next page)

Sam's flee for freedom takes place in *Finding My Sunrise*. Follow her from the moment she wakes up to the nightmare her life had become, to the moment she stood up for herself and what she wanted

In the beginning of this book, Andre mentioned Ryan in New York, he makes his sleeping drug. You can read his story in *Heartbeats*. That story is where the male main character suffers from extreme anxiety. Getting creative with Chemicals, and working out, are his main sources to calm himself. Until he meets Alyssa, or rather, kidnaps her and holds her hostage. Something about her heartbeat has an immediate soothing effect on him.

TJ LEE

Love, Devotion, and trust.... With a side of brownies

Cooper Chronicles book 1
Callie

It was another beautiful Thursday in Seattle, with the rain pouring down. I walked between the chairs, toward the front of my classroom to start class. Homeroom, first class of the day. The class that would set the tone for how the rest of their day would go.

Kids were talking, laughing, and whispering about other kids. Whispering about a fight that had broken out the day before. All typical teenage stuff.

It wasn't a large class, roughly twenty students. Homeroom was generally smaller than my regular English classes.

My room was the size of your typical high school classroom, the main difference, it was sloped like a college lecture hall. I loved it for an English room, drama belonged on the center stage after all.

As I started calling the class to order, getting us on track, there was a knock on the door.

I wasn't surprised, there were always a few last-minute stragglers in the mornings. I can't blame them really. Mornings can be hard to get up and get moving; no matter how old you were.

Then, of course, there were the ones that have to take care of their younger siblings and make sure they get off to school as well. Not everyone has parents or paid childcare providers in the home every minute of the day.

With a nod of approval, Kennedy stood up from her desk to open the door for me, so I could keep talking. How I wish I had been the one to open the door instead of her, a lesson I wasn't soon to forget.

My life, and everybody else's in that room, would be so different. We were all forever changed after that morning, some of us more than others.

Some wouldn't even get the chance to see another day or even another hour.

That would be my first failure of the day.

As soon as Kennedy had the door opened, Scott shoved his way past her, knocking her out of the way. His black hair was wet from the rain and sticking to the side of his head. He was taller than most his age, hard to miss.

He took one look around the room, then paused when he saw Victoria and Todd sitting next to each other.

Todd, who would barely reach Scott's nose if they were to stand next to each other, immediately put a protective arm around her. Scott's face, which was already in a deep and angry scowl when he walked in, somehow got deeper when he saw them together.

I hurriedly walked up the small incline to him to try and calmly have him leave the room. If I could just get him outside, away from the two of them, I could talk to him.

I didn't make it that far, maybe half a dozen small steps, before the gun came swinging out of his jacket pocket.

Chaos swiftly ensued.

Most of the kids ran out of the still open door, mainly only those who he couldn't see.

The ones in his line of sight, knocked their desks over and hid behind the tabletop, too afraid to make the run for it. Fortunately for them, Scott was mainly focused on Victoria and Todd, so quite a few decided they were brave enough to try.

I kept my focus on him, not wanting to bring any attention to anyone else. I wanted him to focus on me and only me. I could handle this better than the kids in this room, that was my hope at least.

"Scott, calm down, let's talk about this. Why don't we sit down, and we can talk?" I softly said to him, with my hands partially raised in front of me.

I tested out a few more baby steps, trying to block his view.

My movement got his attention, and Scott's eye rolled over to me, just as I had wanted. We had always gotten along well. He had come in many times for one-on-one help. Oftentimes he would feel comfortable enough to talk to me about things going on at home.

Oh, how I wish he had felt that he could talk to me about Victoria as well. How much would I have been able to change?

Scott was determined to get a scholarship to Seattle U. He only had this year left, and it was looking good. Mainly due to all the hard work he had put in during those extra study times.

I didn't want him to mess that up now. He was so close to getting out of here and making something of his life. He worked so hard, came so far, and he was about to throw it all away!

"I'm done talking, Miss C. Nobody listens anyway. They only hear and see what they want to." He calmly stated. It was the calm tone that worried me. The tone that says he has made his decision and no longer had any doubts on what needed to be done. A tone of acceptance, the calm tone of resolve.

I shook my head slowly, maintaining that eye contact. "That's not true. You know I always listen to you. I always have, and I always will. So, why don't we sit down and talk about this?" I begged.

While I had his full attention, more kids ran out the door and some ran for better cover. Victoria and Todd ran towards my desk in the front corner. Somewhat behind me.

Scott saw this out of the corner of his eyes, turned his gun, and without another word shots rang out. Immediately followed by screams and the sounds of more desks being knocked over.

Todd fell first and quickly followed by Victoria, falling to the ground. I ran for her, as she was the closest to me, not even thinking.

As I ran, I felt something hot hit my leg, and I fell, landing right next to Victoria.

I heard a few more shots somewhere in the back of my mind as I crawled the rest of the way to her. My focus shifted, now it was only on trying to stop the bleeding in Victoria's gut, ignoring everything else going on in the room.

I pulled my sweater off and held it to her abdomen, trying to talk to her, encouraging her to stay calm, and letting her know that everything was going to be just fine. She looked at me with tears in her eyes, knowing they were just empty, meaningless words.

Then they closed, never to open again.

Never again would she share her opinion on a topic, giving me a new way to think about it.

Never again would she stay late to help clean up after a particularly busy class period.

Never again would she bring me a bag full of cookies from a batch she made over the weekend, letting her six-year-old sister help with the decorating.

Never again would she ask a deep question, yearning to get more than just the basics.

Never again would she hold her new baby nephew and see him learn to walk, hear his first words, or see what he would be when he grew up.

I held her in my arms and cried, the rest of the world no longer existed at that moment. It could have all burned down around me, and I wouldn't have noticed.

That was pretty much how it felt. Like the world stopped turning, stopped moving, it was all just gone. The moment her eyes closed; the world disappeared into a veil of blackness.

How did we get here? How did this happen? Why did this happen?

My mind was grasping at straws, desperately trying to make sense of the mess that my life suddenly became.

This time yesterday, we were all laughing. Victoria and I had both braided our hair and had it laying on our shoulder. It had been a coincidence, something we hadn't planned. So, we ran with it.

I played *Let it go* in the background, and she and I belted it together. All because Todd made a comment about us looking like Elsa. We both have light colored hair, nearly blonde.

The day had been normal. Well, most of it. I would have said the fight was normal, it's high school, kids fight all of the time. I felt my mind wander to that fight and to my complete exhaustion when I got home. When my personal life fell apart. To when the wrong Jenga piece had been removed from the tower of my life, and the walls started caving down around me. Something so small yet ended in catastrophe.

Want to know what happens next? How Callie overcomes this trauma in her life? How her personal life fell apart the night before?

Read Love, Devotion, and Trust...with a side of Brownie, available on all Amazon Platforms and Kindle Unlimited.

Don't forget to leave a rating and/or a review, and let others know what you think of the book.

The Weird World of TJ Lee

MILLION DOLLAR ANGEL

The Cooper Family Chronicles

- Love, Devotion, and Trust...with a side of Brownies (Levi & Callie)
- For Ellie (Emma & Freddie)
- For Emma (Emma & Freddie Cont./Rick & Rachel)
- Forgive & Forget (Tim & Alicia/Zack & Zoey)
- Avenging Angel (Mitch & Charity)

Dark Protectors (frequent crossovers with the Coopers)

- Daughter For Sale (Eli & Vanessa)
- Heartbeats (Alyssa & Ryan)
- Sins of the Mother (Trixie & Ty)

Million Dollar Duet (Crossovers with the Coopers)

- Million Dollar Angel (Elizabeth & Antonio)
- Million Dollar Screw Up (Stacey & Ricky)

Standalone novels (still have crossovers with the others)

- Finding My Sunrise (Samantha/Sarah & Jackson)
- 2 Doors Down (Rose & Ryan)
- Last Christmas (Trish & Noah)

The Yin & Yang Collection (you guessed it, slight crossover here too)

- Oil & Water (Mia & Theo)

The Silver Moon Collection

- Ivory Snow (Snow White - Shifter Style)
- Now Until Forever (Jessica & Jake)

The Cursed Ones

- Revolution
- The Birth of a Queen - Coming Early 2023
- The Witch's Curse - Coming Summer 2023

Follow me on Facebook (@tjleebooks), Instagram (@tjlee2.0), Goodreads (tjlee), TikTok (@tjleebooks) and bookbub (@tjleebooks) for updates on new releases.

ABOUT THE AUTHOR

TJ is an avid reader. Reading was always an escape for her in her crazy messed up world. She's always had a vivid imagination. It wasn't until she was locked in her house for a year and a half, with only her two young kids, and two dogs to talk to, that she finally started writing. She found an even better escape.

TJ is a High School English teacher and a single mom. She holds a bachelor's degree in Cultural Anthropology and Master's in Cultural Responsive Education. Her life motto, one she says with her students regularly, is to "fly your weird flag high!" She wants everyone to learn to be true to who they are. Accept yourself the way you are. Love yourself the way you are.

Lightning Source UK Ltd.
Milton Keynes UK
UKHW012010231222
414383UK00004B/321